3

PUBLIC LIBRARY

NOV 1 4 2011

ORILLIA, ON

D1490525

F GUTTE

Gutteridge, D.
Vital secrets.

PRICE: $12.19 (21742/af/af

OTHER MARC EDWARDS MYSTERIES BY DON GUTTERIDGE

Turncoat

Solemn Vows

VITAL
SECRETS

A Marc Edwards Mystery

DON GUTTERIDGE

A Touchstone Book
Published by Simon & Schuster
New York   London   Toronto   Sydney

Touchstone
A Division of Simon & Schuster, Inc.
1230 Avenue of the Americas
New York, NY 10020

This book is a work of fiction. Names, characters, places, and incidents either are products of the author's imagination or are used fictitiously. Any resemblance to actual events or locales or persons, living or dead, is entirely coincidental.

Copyright © 2007, 2011 by Don Gutteridge

Originally published in 2007 in Canada by Trinity Enterprise Inc.

All rights reserved, including the right to reproduce this book or portions thereof in any form whatsoever. For information address Touchstone Subsidiary Rights Department, 1230 Avenue of the Americas, New York, NY 10020.

This Touchstone export edition July 2011

TOUCHSTONE and colophon are registered trademarks of Simon & Schuster, Inc.

For information about special discounts for bulk purchases, please contact Simon & Schuster Special Sales at 1-800-268-3216 or customerservice@simonandschuster.ca.

Designed by Akasha Archer

Manufactured in the United States of America

10 9 8 7 6 5 4 3 2 1

ISBN 978-1-4391-6371-9
ISBN 978-1-4391-7268-1 (ebook)

For George Martell, with thanks

ACKNOWLEDGEMENTS

I would like to thank my agent, Beverley Slopen, for her constant support and wise counsel. Thanks, too, to my editor for this edition, Jan Walter. I also owe a debt of gratitude to Alison Clarke and Kevin Hanson of Simon & Schuster for their unflagging confidence in the Marc Edwards mysteries.

AUTHOR'S NOTE

Vital Secrets is wholly a work of fiction, but I have endeavoured to convey in it the spirit of the period and the political tensions that led to the Rebellion of 1837. Actions and characterizations attributed to actual historical personages, like Sir Francis Bond Head and William Lyon Mackenzie, are fictitious. All other characters are the invention of the author, and any resemblance to persons living or dead is coincidental.

There were theatres, amateur acting groups, and touring companies from New York and elsewhere in Upper Canada during the late 1820s and throughout the 1830s. While details are sketchy, the first permanent playhouse is reputed to have been the Theatre Royale, located on the upper floor of Frank's Hotel in Toronto. The Regency Theatre described herein is a much more elaborate one than actually existed—though establishments like it were flourishing by the 1840s—and my Mr. Frank is fictitious. For details see Murray D. Edwards, *A Stage in Our Past*. Information on the theatres in New York City during the period may be found in Mary C. Henderson's *The*

City and the Theatre: New York Playhouses from Bowling Green to Times Square.

Finally, by 1835 the new city of Toronto boasted the first municipal police force in North America, a five-man constabulary headed by a chief constable and modelled on the London "peelers."

PROLOGUE

It is March 1837, and Upper Canada is as restive as ever. There had been high hopes when Lieutenant-Governor Sir Francis Bond Head engineered victory for the Tories in the election of June 1836. It was expected that a period of stability would be ushered in, and that the many grievances of the farmers and their representatives in the Reform Party would soon be addressed. It was not to be. Head proceeded to enact repressive legislation and thwart the efforts of the Reformers in the Legislature. Drought had gripped the province, and the banks, safe in the hands of the Family Compact, refused to grant credit. Moreover, the clergy-reserves question still rankled. One-seventh of all the usable land was set aside for the established Anglican Church and was being held uncleared until land prices improved. More grating was the deadlock in the provincial parliament, where the unelected legislative councillors vetoed legislation put forward by the elected Reformers that might favour the suffering population.

As a result of Head's machinations, unrest had become increasingly widespread. A more radical wing of the Reform Party evolved under the strident direction of newspaper editor and politician William Lyon Mackenzie, who had lost his parliamentary seat in the 1836 election. Secret meetings and rallies took place throughout the countryside, and rumours of impending civil strife and the smuggling of arms from the United States were rampant. In a few months a new queen, Victoria, would be crowned, but she would bring no peace to the troubled colony.

PART ONE

MARCH 1837

ONE

For the second time since his arrival in the New World, Lieutenant Marc Edwards was setting out on a winter expedition to Cobourg and, this time, to places eastward to Kingston. On this occasion he was not alone, for at his side, cantering contentedly on a sleek, bay gelding and puffing coils of pipe-smoke into the air along with his frozen breath, was Major Owen Jenkin, quartermaster of His Majesty's 24th Regiment of Foot. The newly risen sun floated above the horizon-line of the forest ahead of them like a disk of burnished brass, as the duo swung up the long curve of King Street towards Scaddings Bridge and the Kingston Road. Behind them, the capital city of the province lay rumpled and quiescent in its coverlet of snow.

"By Christ, but it's good to be on the road again, eh, Marc?" Jenkin said without taking his teeth off the stem of his pipe.

And it was. Ever since he had resigned his post at Government House—on a matter of principle—and returned to the spartan barracks at Fort York after his second investigation, Marc had suffered the boredom of peacetime military routine. He didn't regret his decision, but he had jumped at the chance to go foraging with Owen Jenkin.

"It was kind of you to invite me along, sir. I'm sure you could have managed quite well without me."

Jenkin emitted a rumbling sort of laugh, one that began in his substantial belly and rose up through the smoky realms of his throat till it met the clamped jaws and had to wheeze its way past. The older man had the face of a fallen cherub, with rubicund cheeks so bulging they pinched against his thick eyebrows and made the dancing orbs of his eyes all the more prominent for having to operate in such a confined sphere. The lips, had they been visible beneath the flourishing and unfashionably grizzled beard, would have shown themselves fleshy and sensuous. Evidently the quartermaster was a man who had feasted upon the fruits of life and found them satisfactory.

"Since you've had the impertinence to question why I brought you along, lad, I'll tell you. I'm told that when you came this way last winter on special assignment for the former governor, you passed yourself off as an agent for the quartermaster searching out reliable suppliers of pork and grain."

"There are few secrets in a garrison, I see," Marc said.

"I'm told also that your eye for quality and your nose for the bogus were as keen as a horse-trader's."

"You forget, sir, that I was part of that large foraging party you led two summers ago into the western region," Marc said.

"I do not forget that at all. I was quite aware of you watching me and taking note of every detail of the operation. I also know you were raised on a country estate in Kent, where matters agricultural were close to hand and as natural as breathing air uncontaminated by London soot."

"You know a great deal about me indeed," Marc said in what he hoped was a respectful tone.

"Don't look so worried, lad! I haven't been spying on you. With a mug like mine, espionage would be a hazardous occupation, to say the least."

Marc wondered how much, if anything, the major knew about what had happened last June when Marc had tried, and failed, to win the hand of Beth Smallman. Surely he couldn't know that Beth had left her millinery shop in Toronto last January to return to Crawford's Corners, near Cobourg, to nurse her ailing brother Aaron.

"To tell the truth, I've admired you and your deportment since the day you arrived here. Your exploits and actions are well remarked among the officers of the regiment."

"I'm flattered, sir, but—"

"You're too quick with a 'but,' lad," Jenkin chortled. "The chief reason I rescued you from a death by boredom was entirely selfish: I can't ride a mile unless I have someone to laugh at my witticisms."

Any further talk was forestalled as they clattered across the planking of Scaddings Bridge, which spanned the frozen curve of the Don River. To their right they could see on the flats below the snow-softened outline of Enoch Turner's brewery and Gooderham's distillery with its giant Dutch windmill, whose broad appendages were utterly still in the windless winter air. Beyond these familiar signposts of civilization, the great lake sprawled frozen and silent to a far horizon. A few rods past the bridge, they entered the bush, through which meandered the only highroad linking Kingston and Toronto.

To his surprise, Marc found himself relaxing as the forest drew them into its infinite precincts. The irregular twenty-foot span of the road itself was now the only indication of a human presence. Invariably Marc had entered the bush—winter or summer—with nothing except a shudder and a prayer. But today the sun was shining as if it mattered. The rolling drifts and powdered mantle on bough and branch glistened and beckoned. It might have been England, except that here in the New World, he had begun to realize, bush and stream, insect and beast, lake and ice were the primary datum. All else was secondary. Once you accepted this irreversible fact, Marc thought, you could begin to feel the power and awful beauty of the wilderness.

The Kingston Road, for example, was a fanciful name attached to what was a wagon-track winding through the pine, fir, birch, and maple of the great boreal forest. It provided easy going for the pair of soldiers, as the rutted mélange of mud and corduroy was still frozen stiff, and the recent flurries had been packed down by constant coach- and foot-traffic. And where the odd tree had been downed and blown across the right-of-way, diligent farmers had hauled it aside and cleared away any accumulated drifts. With no wind and not a cloud anywhere in the blue vault above, they expected to travel the sixty miles or so to Cobourg easily. There they could seek out a welcoming hearth and a feather bed. And should their horses flag, they could stop for luncheon and a rest at the hamlet of Perry's Corners. As Marc well knew, much land had been cleared in Northumberland County around Cobourg, and the quartermaster would be planning to visit the many farms there to make arrangements for the purchase of hogs and grain. The actual deliveries would be made later in the fall when the harvest was in and the sucklings fattened.

They rode a little ways along the track before they rounded a bend and the road behind them vanished. The quartermaster took the pipe out of his mouth and picked up the conversation. "I knew your uncle Frederick, as it happens. I've known him for most of my adult life."

Frederick Edwards was the brother of Marc's adoptive father, Jabez Edwards.

"Ah, I see," Marc said with a rush of feeling he could not

quite control. "You and Uncle Frederick fought together, then?"

"We did indeed," Jenkin said, knocking the ashes out of his pipe against the pommel of his saddle. He sat back, loosened his grip on the reins, and let the bay find its own trotting pace.

"Where did you meet?"

"At Sandhurst. We were both striplings, really, not yet twenty, but puffed up with the arrogance of youth and spoiling for a chance to unseat General Bonaparte."

"You didn't have to wait long," Marc said with a meaningful sigh. "Those were momentous days for an army officer."

"Don't get me started on *that* story. Once I get going in that direction, only a cannonball can stop me."

After an hour's stop at the inn of Perry's Corners to feed, water, and rest the horses and to refresh themselves with what the quartermaster called a "traveller's toddy," the duo set out again. For a long while neither spoke. Jenkin returned to the pleasures of his pipe, and Marc let the vast silence of woods and sky settle serenely where it wished.

"Lieutenant Fred Edwards, your uncle Frederick, and I fought side by side for eight years in Spain," Jenkin said, as if their earlier exchange had not been interrupted. "We crossed the Pyrenees and walked all the way across France to the gates of Paris. We helped bring the Corsican bastard to his knees."

"It was Uncle Frederick's stories that encouraged me to

withdraw from the Inns of Court, give up the law, and join the army," Marc said. "It never occurred to me then that Britain might not have any more wars to fight or tyrants to depose."

"There will always be wars somewhere, lad. Of that you can be sure. And I'm not certain one should wish too hard to have them visit us again. Your uncle Fred may have left a few of the less glorious particulars out of his fireside tales."

"It's true, I must admit, sir, that I did wish for some modest insurrection to break out when I first arrived here, with just enough skirmishing for me to prove myself to myself and to my country."

"From what I hear at the garrison, you've gone some ways in that direction already."

Marc made no reply to the compliment. After a while he asked, "Did you know Uncle Jabez?"

"We met, yes. He spoke of you as his son."

Marc smiled. "I call him uncle, to everyone's confusion, because that is the term of endearment I used for him before he adopted me when I was five."

"I know. I met your real parents once. Fine people they were."

"Thank you, sir. I myself have only the vaguest recollection of them, a few memories of my father as he took me about the estate, and of course my mother knitting in front of a huge stone hearth. But the feeling of once having been loved and cared for has never left me."

"You were the only child that Thomas and Margaret Evans ever had." It was a statement, not a question.

"Cholera is a terrible form of the plague," Marc said, alluding to the disease that had felled his parents within days during the summer of 1815. But he was thinking now of young Aaron McCrae, Beth's brother, struck down by typhoid fever, yet another of the recurring pestilences sent by God, it was said, to keep His people humble and in their proper place.

"Did you meet *me,* then?" Marc asked, that odd possibility having just occurred to him.

Jenkin laughed and said, "My word, no. You were not yet born. I came down to the estate with your uncle Fred sometime before ought-six, it must have been, because it was in September of that year that we were ordered to Devon to defend our sovereign soil against invasion by the French. From that day until we reached Paris in 1814, we were soldiers and little else."

"You didn't fight at Waterloo with Uncle Frederick?"

"No. That was the only battle we didn't stand side by side. I was wounded near Paris, nothing serious—until gangrene threatened to set in. The surgeons cut out half of my left buttock, and I was ordered home, standing at attention all the way!"

"But you remained in the army?"

"By then it was the only life I knew. I was thirty-some years old and looked fifty. But I took up a less hazardous line of duty, thanks to Sir John Colborne, as quartermaster of the 24th, a post I've occupied with some satisfaction now for over twenty years, at home and abroad." And here he rubbed a gloved hand across his ample paunch.

"I think it was about ought-five when Uncle Jabez gave up his law practice in London and returned to manage the estate his father had left him."

"And you were not yet a gleam in your father's eye."

"So it was likely that summer that you came down to Kent with Uncle Frederick."

"Most likely. What I do remember clearly is that we were treated like royalty by Jabez. I think he missed the bachelor parties and goings-on in London, and we were gay company, as I recall. Your neighbour, Sir Haughty Trelawney, condescended to invite us to a county fête where Fred and I got regally pissed and made inappropriate advances towards a pair of ageing debutantes."

"I've always suspected Uncle Frederick liked the ladies."

"They weren't all ladies," Jenkin roared. Then, in a more serious tone, he added, "But don't get me wrong, lad. Once Captain Edwards met Delores that year in Paris, he never looked twice at another woman."

"Which is why he's stayed in France all these years."

"Indeed."

"He came over for wonderful extended visits about every second year. But I've never met my cousins, nor my aunt Delores."

"Nor your other aunt, of course," Jenkin said casually, then stopped abruptly.

Marc's horse, an all-purpose mare borrowed from the garrison stables, stumbled on a rut and lurched against the quartermaster's gelding before righting herself. Marc reached out and put a hand momentarily on Jenkin's pack. "It's all right, sir. I know about Uncle Jabez's younger sister."

Marc was relieved to see the smile return to Jenkin's face, where it was a near-permanent feature. Whatever horrors lay locked behind it—and there must have been many during his service in the long, mad Peninsular War—they did nothing to diminish its affable glow.

"I met dear, sweet Mary that same summer," Jenkin said, more warmly than sadly. "She couldn't have been much more than fifteen. A regular sprite, she was, a lively woodland nymph, racing over the hills between your place and the great Trelawney estate like a leggy colt just out of the chute. All blond tresses and freckles." Jenkin squeezed his eyes shut with a slight wince of both cheeks. "I can see her limber and wholesome, as if she were here before me at this very moment."

Marc did not interrupt the major's reverie for several minutes. Then he said, "She died before I was born, or so I was led to believe. Uncle Jabez would never tell me much about her, even when I grew old enough to be more than curious about a young woman who might well have been a surrogate mother to me, as Jabez was my father. All I've ever known for certain is that she went up to school in London and died there suddenly and tragically."

"Would you like to know more, lad?"

"You know what really happened?"

Jenkin nodded.

Marc said, "Please. Tell me about Aunt Mary."

"Well, lad, I got the story in bits and pieces from Fred over the years we served together. Mary grew up on the estate under the easy but kindly care of her father, while her brother Jabez sought his fortune in the law courts of London and, a little later, Frederick went off to Sandhurst and glory. When old man Edwards, many years a widower, died, Mary was alone there and, as I understand it, lived with the Trelawneys next door for a while, until Jabez finally decided to sell his share in the London firm and occupy the Edwards farm, modest as it was. While Fred was too discreet to say so openly, I gathered that Mary had become—how shall I say it delicately?—a free spirit."

"Somewhat wild, you mean?" Marc said. "She seems to have had little adult supervision or discipline."

"Spoken like a genuine trooper." Jenkin chuckled. "But true, nonetheless, and alas. However, Jabez soon took her under his wing and—of this I am certain—formed a powerful filial bond with the sister he hadn't really seen much of in recent years."

"That is what I've always assumed to be the reason behind his inability to speak of her to me or anyone. Even the inadvertent mention of her name could stun him into silence and, occasionally, tears."

15

"So when she was seventeen," Jenkin continued, "he persuaded her to go up to London to Madame Rénaud's finishing school. She was an exceptionally bright girl, and he felt that three years of music, French, and the domestic arts would make a lady out of her. There were, I believe, even hopes that she might prove a suitable match for one of the Trelawney tribe next door."

Marc shuddered: his teenage affair with the young ward of Sir Joseph Trelawney had ended disastrously, and was an emotional wound not yet completely healed. "How did Aunt Mary take to the business of being 'finished'?" he asked.

"Like an unbroken yearling to the bit and bridle," Jenkin said, with evident approval. "But she stuck it out for almost two years, according to Fred, though by this time—it had to have been about 1809 or '10—we were both in Portugal and dancing a jig or two with the Iron Duke."

"Until . . ."

Jenkin sighed, a heaving belly of a sigh. "Until word came to Jabez from Madame Rénaud herself that, just days before the end of the winter term, Mary Edwards had fallen gravely ill with a fever and the bloody flux."

"Yes: Uncle Jabez told me that much, once. He said he'd had no warning, and when he rushed up to London by express coach the next morning, she was already dead."

"Well, if it's any consolation, Frederick insists that she was still breathing when Jabez arrived. She died within the hour, in his arms."

"It's no wonder he doesn't want to remember. But surely he had words with Madame Rénaud; he was a lawyer after all," Marc said.

"I'm sure he did, lad. Fred says that Jabez was torn between anger and remorse. Your uncle Frederick had many letters from him during the subsequent year. They moved him so deeply he could barely bring himself to open them. He burned each of them immediately afterwards."

"I'm glad I wasn't alive to see Uncle Jabez in such a state. By the time I was old enough to be aware of him and who he was, I found him the gentlest soul on the face of this earth."

"I'm sure he came to accept her death eventually. Apparently he did try to sue the school, but his heart wasn't in it after the initial rage had subsided and simple grief had taken over. The old lady must have known the seriousness of Mary's illness long before she wrote to Jabez. But what could he do, really?"

"Just bring her home for burial," Marc replied.

Jenkin sighed again. "The poor man was not able to make even that small gesture. There was suspicion she'd died of typhus, and the authorities apparently compelled him to have her interred in that great stinking maw of a graveyard in central London."

"But, sir, I saw her grave-marker in our garden every time I headed up into the west woods." And even now he could picture that slim, white tablet with the tersest possible inscription: "Mary Ann Edwards, 1789–1810"—as if Uncle Jabez could not bear to add one syllable more.

"Aye, lad. The marker is hers all right. But she's not under it."

As they rode into the clearing that presaged the hamlet of Port Hope, Marc said, "Thank you for telling me all this, sir. It fills in a lot of the gaps in the story of my adoptive family. In a strange sort of way, I now feel as if I actually had an aunt. Perhaps someday soon I can persuade Uncle Frederick to give me more details. After all, he was closer in age to his sister than Uncle Jabez, and they must have played together often as children."

"But you won't tell Jabez about . . . what I've just told you?"

Marc smiled. "No, sir, I shan't. The last thing in this world I want to do is bring pain to my uncle."

They rode in silence for a while, and Marc reflected on the strange and surprising story he had just been told. He wished he could have known Aunt Mary, wished Uncle Jabez had been more forthcoming. That he was related to such a determined and unfettered spirit both alarmed and intrigued him.

BY THE TIME THEY DREW NEAR to Crawford's Corners, a winter moon hung like a silver saucer above the tree line in the southeast and cast a swath of shimmering light across the roadway ahead. The cold black sky around it was studded with stars as bright as a newborn's eyes. Neither had spoken for the past hour and now, in the mysterious calm of evening, it seemed almost profane to do so.

Fourteen months before, en route to his first investigation, Marc had travelled this very road in the dark of a winter night. Memories of that time flooded in. As they approached the crossroads that marked the centre of Crawford's Corners, Marc could feel the presence of the houses and cabins he knew were camouflaged by the bush and the darkness.

"That must be the light from Durfee's Inn," Marc said quietly.

It was a warm, orange glow on the right, no more than twenty yards away.

"We'll be made most welcome there," Marc said. "James and Emma Durfee are good people, salt of the earth."

"They'll be surprised to see you back here," Jenkin said. Then, without warning, he brought his mount to a halt in the middle of the intersection. "And that light over there," he said, "must be from Erastus Hatch's place. I can see the outline of the mill just behind the house."

Hatch had helped Marc with his first investigation, and had become a friend. Just to the north of the miller's land lay the farm of Beth Smallman, leased now to Thomas Goodall and his wife, the former Miss Winnifred Hatch. Beth's house, which Marc knew well, could not be seen from this vantage-point, but he knew Beth was there, nursing her brother Aaron.

Marc urged his mount straight ahead. The quartermaster's

hand on his elbow stopped him. "I will go on into Durfee's," he said gently to Marc. "You are to turn left and make your way up Miller Sideroad."

"I don't understand," Marc said.

"I will carry on to Kingston, and then work my way slowly back westward, doing business with the farmers en route, as I normally do. I should be back in Cobourg in about a week. If you find yourself at leisure here, feel free to make any arrangements with the locals as you see fit, and I'll endorse them when I get here. But should you find more pressing and pleasant things to do, I will cover this region on my return."

"But I assumed you brought me along so we might work as a team," Marc said, genuinely puzzled, though a bizarre and not unsettling notion was now suggesting itself to him. "I still have things to learn from you."

"I will do nicely on my own, lad."

"Sir, I must protest—"

"Marc, my boy, you have unfinished business here in Crawford's Corners, not a hundred yards from where we are presently stalled."

My God, Marc thought, was there anyone left in Toronto who did *not* know about his on-again, off-again romance with Beth Smallman?

"If the lady's answer is no," Jenkin continued, "you can always catch me up."

"Is that an order, sir?"

"It's the true reason I asked you along. Now go."

With that curt command, the major wheeled his horse to the right and trotted off towards Durfee's Inn, leaving Marc alone in the intersection.

Very slowly he made his way north along Miller Sideroad.

TWO

Marc realized that he dare not arrive unannounced at Beth Smallman's door at seven o'clock in the evening, when the entire household would be present: Beth and her brother Aaron, Winnifred, and Thomas Goodall, her tenants, and probably a servant girl. He found himself quite relieved at the thought. Although he had been mulling over in his mind how he might arrange matters so that a brief encounter with Beth would be both possible and plausible (to Major Jenkin), the quartermaster had preempted him most unexpectedly and, incredible as it seemed, with a generosity of spirit that now left Marc feeling almost ashamed. The major had given him a week, free of any commitment or duty, to put his personal affairs in order, to "woo the lady" as the amateur thespians among his fellow officers might have put it.

But he was no Galahad and Beth was certainly no fawning princess. She and her late husband had hacked a farm out of this unforgiving bush, working side by side in the fields and in the barn. She had suffered the violent deaths of two men she adored: husband and father-in-law. She had taken an active part in local politics as a staunch Reformer, and after her husband's death had become more radical and more vocal, risking her status as a "respectable" woman and widow in a society where men were likely to see her more as a threat than as a suffering soul in need of understanding and sympathy.

Unable to run the farm on her own, and with an inheritance from her father-in-law, she had pulled up stakes and moved to Toronto to start a new life as proprietress of a millinery shop on King Street. She had been joined in that venture by her aunt Catherine from the United States. In fact, ever since Beth's rejection of him last June, Aunt Catherine had been his ally, lobbying on his behalf and sending him encouraging notes from time to time during the fall.

Marc dismounted and led the mare up the lane to the miller's house, planning to put the horse in Erastus Hatch's barn and settle her down for the night before approaching the back door. But that door suddenly swung open, and Erastus himself emerged, coatless and excited.

"By the Lord, it *is* you!" he cried, striding through the drifts in his slippers. "I saw you turn into the lane, and when I recognized the uniform, I said to Mary, 'There's only one soldier I know who's six feet tall and walks like a duke!'"

Marc reached out and grasped the hand of his friend, who had been so helpful in the Cobourg investigation and had put in more than one good word for him with Beth Smallman. "Yes, it is me, sir, and I've come to stay for a few days, if you've got room for me."

"You shan't get past the doorway, Marc, unless you quit calling me 'sir.' I'm Rastus to my friends, and I number you among them."

"Rastus it is, then."

"What's brought you all the way out here?" Hatch said, clutching his loose sweater more tightly about him. It was a straightforward question with no hint of suspicion or concern, but that was typical of the man.

"I'll explain the whole thing as soon as I've bedded down the mare here for the night. And if you don't get back inside, you'll catch your death."

"Well, son, you know your way about in the barn, eh? There's enough moonlight to work by if you use one of the stalls on the south wall. Meantime, I'll go tell Mary to put the kettle on and rouse Susie and the little one."

"I'll be as quick as I can."

"By the Christ, but it's good to see you!" Hatch cried, then began to brush the snow off his slippers, gave up with a chuckle, and turned back towards the house. "And I'm not the only one who'll think so!"

The miller glanced to the north, towards the log house of Beth Smallman.

MARC AND ERASTUS HATCH SAT IN the two padded chairs before the fieldstone fireplace and a blaze whose roaring had just begun to die down to a steady, amiable murmur. Two tendrils of pipe-smoke rose drowsily and intermittently into the warm ambience of the miller's parlour. It was nearly ten o'clock. Mary Hatch—who, as Mary Huggan, had served the miller as cook and housekeeper long before she married him—had cobbled together a supper for their guest of cold beef, bacon, eggs, and fried potatoes. Her sister Susie, a carbon copy of her older sibling (red hair, translucent Irish skin, freckles, a wisp of a figure), then brought tiny Eustace Hatch out of the nursery to be admired and cooed at. Marc, of course, said all the appropriate things, but inside he felt an uncharacteristic pang of envy and a sudden intimation of the inexorable passing of time. Then, with the babe returned to its slumber and Mary excusing herself, the two men settled into their port and pipes.

Although considered by the local farmers he served to be a "merchant," Hatch still helped his hired hands with every aspect of the mill's functioning and the working of the land surrounding it. His large, peasant fingers were callused, his face had the red, raw look of the active yeoman, and his modest paunch was well muscled. For a while they traded harmless bits of gossip about their different locales, reminisced about Marc's investigation here fourteen months earlier, then lapsed into a silence that was not uncomfortable.

"So you've given up being a supernumerary constable," Marc said.

"That was not a hard decision in the least. After what happened here last winter, I kind of soured on the law. I try now to mind my own business, do an honest day's work, and treat my customers fairly. Of course, with Mary and the little one, all that's been made much easier."

"You look like a man blessed."

"That I am, though I'd be hard-pressed to say why the Lord's chosen me," Hatch said solemnly, then added quickly, "But I'm not fool enough to keep on asking Him why!"

"Wisely said."

"But I'll tell you truthfully, Marc, I'm one of the few souls in this county who *is* happy."

"It's been a grim year everywhere in the province," Marc said. "Bad weather, lean crops, falling prices, paper money losing value by the month, the banks reeling. Made all the worse, I suspect, because so much was expected after the Tory victory in the election last spring and the governor's promise to bring about real change."

"I've given up on that, too." Hatch turned and looked directly at Marc.

"Being a Tory?"

"Not quite as blunt as that, but something close to it." He leaned back again and spoke between hefty puffs on the pipe.

"I've given up on politics, at least for the time being, and I used to make all the right noises whenever asked to, as you know."

"Noises in favor of the governor, you mean?"

"Exactly. I believed in the rule of law and I still do. But what has happened around here since last June is downright frightening."

"How so?"

"The ordinary folk—who are suffering the most, as they always have since the beginning of things—have begun to give up on the political process, too. Myself, I've decided to do what I can in my own bailiwick. I've extended credit where I shouldn't, ground grain for free when there was no other remedy, and doled out my own flour so some of the kids in the township won't starve. But many of the others, with no resources to fall back on, are growing desperate. And to make matters worse, many of my Tory acquaintances, who wouldn't ordinarily tip their hat to an Orangeman, are starting to spout their fanatic heresies. Both sides have hardened their positions since the election. It's almost impossible to stand anywhere in the middle, or be nonpartisan or even a simple, caring Christian."

"Sir Francis has much to answer for, I'm afraid. Instead of using his majority in the assembly to redress the complaints of the farmers and work towards reconciliation, he has ruthlessly pursued his own agenda."

"You were wise to get as far away from him as possible." Hatch looked at Marc, put his pipe down, and added, "Nobody hereabouts was surprised to learn about your resignation as his aide-de-camp. We knew what kind of man you were."

Marc tried not to look affected by this kind remark. "Then why don't the conservatives repudiate the governor?"

Hatch laughed. "Believe it or not, they blame the actions of Willie Mackenzie's radicals for making Governor Head the way he now is: erratic and spiteful."

"And have there been *actions*?"

Hatch paused, drew noisily on his dead pipe, glanced at it balefully, and said, "I'm afraid there have. People aren't just ranting and raving anymore: they're organizing and holding secret meetings. There's been talk—right here in Hamilton township—of arms about to be smuggled across the border, of trunkloads of American dollars and coinage on their way—to be used for God knows what dastardly purpose."

"But we heard that sort of fear-mongering gossip last year, remember?"

"That is so. But this is not talk. Just last Thursday a gang of Orange thugs discovered a meeting of Mackenzie's followers in progress about a mile east of Cobourg, and decided to break it up. But it was no Reform rally they were disrupting. The conspirators were armed with pitchforks, sickles, axe-handles, and, they say, a dozen or more pistols. There was a regular donnybrook. Dozens were injured on both sides. And by the time the constables arrived, the worst of it was over, and everyone fled who could still walk. Of course, the wounded suddenly contracted lockjaw. Nobody would lay a charge. What I'm saying, and what I fear every time I look into little Eustace's eyes, is that these desperate men are planning an insurrection or show of force sometime soon."

"But they'll be slaughtered, don't they know that? They can't fight the British army with hoes and pistols."

"That may be the only thing holding them back."

Marc heaved a huge sigh. "You mean soldiers like me?"

"Yes, at least until they get guns and training. And they'll need the Yankees for that." Hatch tried to light his pipe with a flaming stick from the fire, without success. "If I were you, I wouldn't wander around the back concessions of Northumberland County with that uniform winking in the noonday sun."

"But surely an offer to buy their grain or hogs at a price well above the current market will have to be welcomed. The army is not their enemy."

Hatch smiled. "They'll certainly let you in the front door, but don't expect a cup of tea. I think the poor buggers are desperate enough to sell their produce to anyone." Hatch chuckled ruefully.

Marc yawned but, fatigued as he was, he did not want to fall asleep here in the cozy security of the Hatch parlour. Instead, he reached down between the two chairs, picked up the decanter, and poured himself a tumbler of port. Erastus declined Marc's offer of more.

The fire, ebbing rapidly, snapped and crackled intermittently.

"Well, lad, there's one subject we seem to have been avoiding, eh?"

Marc turned to face his friend. "Tell me everything I should know about what's happened next door."

"I thought you'd never ask. Let me start with the good news. My daughter and her husband are quite happily married, even though they are very different people. Certainly, I was as surprised as anyone when Winnifred announced she had selected Thomas Goodall, my hired man, as her husband. Thomas is a fine farmer and a good Christian, but he hasn't said more than a dozen words a week since birth—less than that if you deduct the Lord's Prayer every Sunday. Winnifred—well, you know her—she has two opinions on every subject and ain't shy about conveying them to anyone within earshot. When she lived here she was more or less lady of the manor, but now that she and Thomas have their own farm, she's pitched in and done more than her share of the outdoor labour." He paused and lowered his voice. "And she's in the family way."

"That's wonderful news," Marc said sincerely, for he liked and admired this proud, intelligent woman, and wished her well.

"And just in time," Hatch said cryptically. To Marc's puzzled look, he said, "Well, believe it or not, Winnifred's been getting involved in politics this winter, too. Radical politics." This last remark was whispered, as if the walls might have ears.

"But she's an independent thinker and a conservative like her father, surely."

"Indeed she was. But the bad news is that the farm has not prospered. With last summer's drought and the available water being tied up on the clergy-reserve land next to them, they had a poor harvest, despite their effort and the expense of hiring extra help. And what they did take off the fields was sold at prices that didn't cover their costs. They're desperate to get enough cash to pay the leasehold."

Marc was astonished. "But surely Beth wouldn't demand payment or turn them out? After all, they're looking after Aaron for her. And she's got plenty of money."

"All true. She refused to take any payment on the lease. She's offered to pay for any hired help to do Aaron's share of the work until he's fully recovered."

"I'm told by Beth's aunt that the boy has made remarkable progress."

"Yes, he has, and we thank the Lord daily for that."

"But?"

"But Winnifred is . . . well, proud, too proud I'm inclined to think. But she says—and Thomas agrees, according to her—that they ought to be able to make a decent living out of their farm or else abandon it. And when she found that most of the farmers in the county were in the same boat, in spite of the backbreaking work and heartbreaking effort, well, she began to blame the government—and quite publicly. When Beth came down to nurse Aaron in January, she soon discovered that Winnifred was slipping off to gatherings of Mackenzie's malcontents, spouting their slogans, and behaving strangely. Eventually Beth told me."

"Did you succeed in stopping her?"

Hatch sighed. "No," he said with a wry smile that conveyed both regret and acceptance. "My attempts to dissuade her simply encouraged her to become even more committed. When I heard about talk of violence and outright sedition at these rallies, I became worried. I did manage to persuade Thomas to go with her to protect her, and him without a political bone in his body. This she readily agreed to, to my surprise."

"And now that she is expecting?"

"She's stopped going. On her own account, we assume, unless Thomas found enough words to assert himself in the privacy of the boudoir." Hatch smiled at the notion.

"But she hasn't changed her mind about the lease or the success of the farm? Surely, with a child on the way—"

Hatch looked suddenly grim, the customary laugh lines of his face collapsing around his eyes. "She says they'll give it one more year. The babe is due in September. If the fall harvest fails, they'll wait out the winter here, then—my God, I can barely say it, Marc—she, Thomas, and the child will sell everything they have, go down to Buffalo, buy a Conestoga wagon, and head west across the Mississippi to the Iowa Territory."

Marc took this in, then said evenly, "I don't think that will happen, Rastus. There's every chance the governor will be recalled and a new one will follow the British government's policy of conciliation. There are moderate, decent men on both the left and the right: their voices will be heard."

Hatch tried to smile his gratitude. "And you count yourself among the moderates," he said.

"I do," Marc said with some conviction. "It's taken me a while, and I'm still learning, but I've come a long way, I think, in less than two years."

"And we all know it."

Marc was well aware whom the "all" was meant to include.

"But Winnifred's luck hasn't changed," Hatch continued glumly. "Last Friday, Thomas was chopping wood out behind the house and damn near sliced off his left hand. Dr. Barnaby had to stitch it together like a rip in a glove. He's got it wrapped in a great bloody bandage, with a splint on his wrist to keep him from using the hand for anything. He can't even pick up a spoon to stir his tea with it."

This was more serious than Winnifred's political leanings, Marc thought.

"The man has chopped a thousand cords of wood in his lifetime. But he's exhausted and worried to death," said Hatch. "Fatigue will lead to such accidents."

"Thank God for Barnaby," Marc said. Charles Barnaby was a semi-retired army surgeon who lived across from the Durfee Inn but kept a surgery in Cobourg several days a week or whenever it was needed in emergencies.

"He's a splendid gentleman. They don't come any better

than Barnaby. In fact, you won't get to see him tomorrow because he's been in and out of his surgery since the fracas last Thursday night—setting bones and lecturing the participants on their foolishness. I lent him my cutter and Percherons on Saturday so he could transfer some of the wounded home, if necessary."

"I wondered why I didn't see them in the barn."

"That pair can haul a sled through anything. And we've had a bundle of snow this winter. The drifts are six or seven feet in the bush."

Hatch yawned. There was little time left. Marc cleared his throat to ask what had to be asked.

"Beth is fine," Hatch said suddenly. "She nursed Aaron night and day all through January, and for a while there we were very concerned for her own health—"

"But she's—"

"Fine now, as I said. As soon as Aaron began to regain his strength, she did, too. And since Thomas became helpless last week, Aaron's been strong enough to chop firewood and help Winnifred and Beth with the chores in the barn."

"Has she—"

"Ever mentioned you? Not by name. But you've come up in the general conversation several times this winter, and Beth's been an avid listener. I'm sure she knows how much you've changed and that you still love her. But—"

"There's always a 'but,' isn't there?"

"But she's just been too busy with Aaron and with the problems of the farm to turn her attention to her own future. You know how faithful she can be to a task she feels is important, and how selfless she is when it comes to helping those who need it."

Marc nodded.

"Even if she *is* a Congregationalist." Hatch smiled. "What I'm trying to say is, I think you've come at the right time to make your pitch."

"Let's hope she feels the same way," Marc said.

But how far could he hope? How far did he deserve to?

MARC WAS AWAKENED SLOWLY AND LUXURIOUSLY by the mid-morning sun slanting across the counterpane. By the time he had completed the most rudimentary toilet and donned the scarlet, green, and gold of an officer of the 24th Regiment of Foot, the Hatches' dining-room was well warmed by the fire in the wood-stove and suffused with breakfast aromas: bacon, frying eggs and potatoes, and fresh-baked biscuits. The chores had been completed: cows milked, fed, and watered; stalls mucked out; hens relieved of their night's labour; kindling chopped; and the day's supply of firewood lugged indoors. Marc tried not to look abashed when he was greeted by the household as if he were the prodigal son being treated to the fatted calf.

"Sit down, lad, and dig in," Hatch said as he settled into his captain's chair, then took Mary by the hand to stop her fussing with Marc's plate and utensils, and eased her down to her own place next to him. Susie arrived promptly with a steaming platter of food.

"I apologize for sleeping so late," Marc said.

"Nonsense," Hatch said. "You've got a difficult day ahead of you, eh?"

Marc acknowledged the reference to the task at hand with a tight smile.

"How is the babe this morning?" Marc asked Mary.

"He's as healthy as his papa," Mary said.

Suddenly Marc felt his heart lurch. Seeing Erastus Hatch, so long a widower and so lonely just a year ago, happy and at ease here in his home made Marc realize how badly he wanted to change his own life, and how much depended on what might happen or not happen in the next few hours. He decided that he would need to take a long walk and consider carefully what he might possibly say to Beth that would make a difference. He knew also that he needed an hour or so to regain the courage he had imagined for himself when he had played out the reconciliation scene with Beth at least a hundred times since last summer.

Hatch was halfway through his request for more bacon when he was interrupted by the sound of the back door opening and closing. Susie Huggan set down a plate and hurried to answer the door. Seconds later she reappeared with a big grin on her face.

"It's our neighbour," she cried, "and she's brung us a basket of duck's eggs!" Susie stepped aside to reveal both the visitor and her gift.

It was Beth Smallman. She glanced at the figures seated around the table, and stopped when she came to Marc.

The basket fell to the floor, and the duck eggs with it.

THREE

"So, you're in our neighbourhood again—scoutin' hogs and whatnot?" Beth said with that touch of colloquial teasing in her voice that Marc found irresistible. She was alluding to his visit the year before and to his rather inept attempt to pass himself off as an assistant quartermaster. The "whatnot" suggested that she knew full well the true purpose of his abrupt arrival this time.

"And duck's eggs," Marc said, "when they're not broken."

"Things've changed a lot here since last June."

"Little Eustace, you mean, and Winnifred and Thomas?"

"I think you know what I mean," Beth said.

They were walking slowly northward along the snow-packed

path that linked the miller's house with the Smallmans'. It meandered its way more or less beside the frozen creek on their left and the cleared ground on their right. The snow was so deep that no stubble showed through from the fall's meagre harvest. Only uprooted, charred stumps marked the crude outlines of pasture and wheat field.

"Fewer pigs and more radicals?" Marc said, struggling to keep the tone of the conversation light. It felt so good just hearing Beth's voice once again that he found himself torn between wanting the dialogue to continue at any cost and the fear that one wrong turn in its progress would kill it outright. And her physical presence here beside him—their footsteps in lazy unison, the breeze crisp and clean in their faces, the sound of their voices the only sound anywhere, the delicate frost of her breathing mingled with his own—left him so intoxicated that he was sure to blurt out some foolishness or other. He was tempted to reach over and take her elbow, as a proper gentleman should, but he dared not.

"Winn an' Thomas had to keep what grain they took off last fall to feed the oxen, the three cows, and our pigs."

"Erastus told me about their troubles."

"They haven't had it worse than any others in the township." Marc caught the edge in her voice, but when he glanced over, she was staring resolutely ahead.

"Rastus also told me how well you've nursed Aaron through his illness."

The low morning sun blazed through the fringe of Beth's

hair below the tuque and transformed it into a russet halo. It took all of Marc's willpower to resist pulling the tuque away.

"I'd have even prayed to the Anglican God if I'd thought He could help," Beth said.

"Ah, but you know perfectly well He's always been a Congregationalist."

Beth laughed, and for the first time glanced sideways at Marc. The force of her gaze, the infinite blue intelligence of her eyes, struck him like a blow. He felt numb and then, strangely, invigorated. His blood hummed.

"Whichever gods intervened," Beth said, guiding him briefly around a submerged stump, "Aaron's made a wonderful recovery. In a minute you'll hear him chopping wood out behind the summer kitchen."

"Chopping wood? But—"

"Oh, I see that he naps every afternoon. But I figured he needed to get outdoors as soon as he could. He lives for the animals and his chores around the barn."

"And he'll be needed more than ever now that Thomas has a battered hand."

"Seems we just get through one trial when a new one comes on."

"Who'll help with the spring ploughing and planting?" Marc said, trying his best to make the question sound disinterested.

Beth slowed her pace, for which Marc was grateful, as it suggested she was not overeager to arrive at the cabin. In the distance he could now hear the staccato *chunk* of an axe on wood.

"Well, Winn won't take money, from me or her father, so it'll have to be mainly me and Aaron and Winn. Winn and me have done some sewing this winter, so we'll have a few goods to trade for a bit of hired help. And we can work the ox-team together if we have to."

Of that Marc had little doubt, even though, under the bulky mackintosh and cloth trousers, Beth was tiny and trim and not much more than a hundred pounds.

"But that means you might be stuck down here until June or later?"

"It's not a matter of choice. We often get 'stuck' where we ought most to be."

Marc winced at the reproof. And he realized with a sinking heart just how difficult and possibly hopeless a task lay before him. How could he plead a lover's cause in the face of such competing exigencies, of such overriding moral claims? There seemed for him, equally, to be no choice: he, too, was where he "ought most to be." So he plunged recklessly ahead: "But surely your aunt Catherine will be needing you at the shop? Spring and summer are your busiest seasons."

"I hadn't realized you were so well acquainted with the millinery business."

Ah, that teasing tone again, but he persevered. "Your aunt did pull up stakes in New England, as I recall, to join you in Toronto. Surely you can't—"

"Your 'recall' is as keen as it's always been. But I can do without your 'surelys.'"

"I'm sorry."

"No, you're not. But it doesn't matter because I've taken care of Aunt Catherine and the business."

"You haven't sold it?"

Beth laughed for a second time. "No, we haven't. When I left in January to come here to nurse Aaron, we hired a young girl from the town to help Aunt Catherine with the seamstressing side of the business. And next month a distant cousin from her husband's side of the family is coming up to Toronto from Rochester to stay with her."

"Can she sew? And help run the business?"

"He certainly can't sew—"

"He?"

"A great-nephew. About your age, I think."

"And what help could he possibly be in a millinery shop?" Besides being a male presence, and possibly a handsome one to boot.

"Since you're so curious, he's really interested in starting a business of his own. Things've been bad in the States since the dollar went crazy down there, and he wants to start a new life. He'll live in and keep his aunt company, help with any heavy work, and learn how to operate a shop. Any further questions, counsellor?"

For Beth's benefit, Marc managed a smile at this reference to his aborted law career. They walked a few paces in silence,

43

but neither seemed in any hurry to speed up. Something remained to be said.

"How long will it be before Thomas is able to work again?"

"Well, it was his left hand he cut, thank God, so he's still able to do quite a bit with the right. Dr. Barnaby says it should be completely healed in a month, six weeks for sure, if he doesn't tear it open or let it get infected."

"Barnaby should know if anyone does. He's repaired a thousand sword cuts in his time. But what about Winnifred?"

"I see the good news is out."

"Due in late September, Rastus tells me."

"She's as strong as an ox. You'll see quite a change in her."

"Her father was extremely worried about her."

Beth stopped. The axe-blows were much sharper. Along the northwestern horizon a bank of black clouds curdled the otherwise pristine blue of the winter sky.

"You know about her going to the meetings?"

"Not much. But enough to realize how much her thinking must have changed since I last saw her. Moving from church bazaars and social teas to smoky barns and questionable associates is quite a shift for anyone, and incredible for a—"

"Woman? I think we've had this conversation before, haven't we?"

"Surely she won't take such risks now."

They were still face-to-face: assessing, gauging, probing.

"Surely not," Beth said.

"Well, then, I'm glad she's being sensible. And Thomas, too."

Beth put a mittened hand on Marc's arm. She smiled wanly, and he noticed now the dark shadow under each eye and the vexed wrinkling at the corners of the mouth he wanted to press against his own and breathe into comfort. "I haven't been to any of the meetings," she said. "I've been too busy with Aaron."

Marc's relief was palpable.

"I listen to what Winn and Thomas are saying, which isn't a lot—at least not outside their bedroom. But I say nothing."

"It's hard to believe you've given up," Marc said, turning with her and walking, slowly again, towards the ring of Aaron's axe.

"Oh, I haven't given up. But after we lost the election last June, after all our effort and after all the promises made and not kept by the governor, I couldn't summon up the energy to protest—even though I was raging underneath my numbness. Auntie and I worked hard at the business all summer, and hard it was—dispensing bonnets and frippery to the very people that engineered us out of the Assembly. Then, when the bad harvest hit and the Yankee dollar collapsed and Sir High and Mighty reneged on his solemn word, just when my blood was starting to boil like it did when Jesse was alive and we were up to our necks in Reform Party politics, I discovered that everything had changed."

"In what way?"

"The open talk of violence. And I don't mean the vicious talk we've all got used to."

"Talk of revolt, you mean?" Marc could have bitten his tongue, but it was too late.

Beth stopped and looked searchingly at the man who had done so much for her last winter and who had more than once declared his love for her.

"Damn it, Beth, I'm not here as a spy!"

She stared at her boots. "I'd not be honest if I didn't admit that when I dropped those eggs at the sudden sight of you, that was my first thought." She peered up. "But I haven't thought it since. Nor will I again."

"But I'm still in this uniform?"

"Yes, you are, aren't you?" She started walking again, as if afraid to hold his gaze any longer for fear of what she might detect in it and preferred not to see.

"I think we've had *this* conversation before," he said.

They had turned onto the path that wound between the barn and outbuildings towards the back-shed of the split-log cabin ahead. Marc stopped and quickly placed one hand on each of Beth's shoulders. He held her gaze for several long seconds. She made no attempt to look away. He saw what it was he had to know: her feeling for him had not diminished, in spite of everything that had happened over the past fourteen months.

"We've spoken about everything except the thing we really

need to speak about," Beth said softly, her eyes misting over. "I haven't been avoiding it. After lunch, when it settles down inside, we'll sit by the south window like we did last year and have a long cup of tea."

He leaned over and brushed his lips across her cool forehead.

She pulled back, reluctantly he thought, and said, "Now, let's go and say hello to Aaron."

Marc remembered Aaron McCrae with vivid painfulness: a tall, gangling sixteen-year-old with one lame leg that he dragged behind him and slurred, stammering speech. But he was no simpleton to be patronized or mocked by his fellows, though Marc had little doubt they had done so more than once. He had his sister's blue eyes that, like hers, saw much more than they conveyed. In fact, it had been Aaron's observation and reliable memory that had helped solve the mysterious death of Joshua Smallman last winter. But Marc wondered what might have been wrought upon that misaligned frame by typhoid fever and eight weeks of agonizingly slow recuperation.

Aaron spotted Beth and the uniformed gentleman at her side, and put down his axe. A quarter-cord of hardwood lay scattered about him. A big grin spread across his face as he recognized Marc.

"H-h-h-ello, Mr. Edwards."

"Hello, Aaron. I'm so happy to see you are recovered, and

back helping run the farm." Marc made a point of admiring the lad's handiwork.

"Lieutenant Edwards has come for a visit," Beth said. "He's going to stay for dinner."

"G-g-good."

Marc, too, was pleased to hear this, then remembered that "dinner" was sometimes the local term for luncheon, to which meal he had already been invited.

"Just finish up that log, Aaron, and then come inside. We don't want you overdoing it, do we?"

Aaron frowned, then smiled his agreement. Marc was astonished to see that Aaron had grown another two or three inches, bringing him close to Marc's six feet. Moreover, he had "filled out," as they said here in the colony, putting on muscle around bones that had thickened and toughened. His pale face and a telltale hollowness around the eyes hinted at the earlier ravages of the fever, and underneath the loose sweater and denim work pants that new bulk would likely be a bit flaccid and toneless, but the big-knuckled, bare hands and masculine jut of the chin intimated that he was soon to be a full-fledged, powerful man.

"I'll see you inside, then," Marc said.

Aaron grinned again, and gave his sister a curious look before turning back to his work.

At the shed door, Marc stopped for a moment to watch the operation at hand. Aaron gripped the axe with both hands, raised it over his shoulder, braced himself as best he could on the lame leg, then drove the axe downward, using his strong leg for leverage and balance. For a second it appeared as if he must topple, given the angle at which his body was tilted laterally, but at the point of impact everything straightened itself—axe and axeman—so that the plane of the blow ended flush with the propped log. The wood split with a ruptured cry, followed instantly by the lad's grunt of triumph.

"He's learned to adapt," Beth said as she opened the back door. "Now let's go in to lunch."

Like so many of those around him, Marc thought.

THE MID-DAY MEAL WAS OF THE pioneer farm variety—roast venison, potatoes, turnip, fresh bread, slices of cold ham, and several pots of hot tea—cooked by Winnifred and Beth, and served by young Charlene, yet another of the innumerable Huggan clan, before she herself joined them. Quaintly referred to as the "hired girl," Charlene received no pay. ("But I'm keeping track of wages owed," Beth had said, "and I'll settle up with her some day when she may really need the money.")

Arriving late to the table, Thomas Goodall seemed startled to see Marc, then greeted him abruptly. Marc noticed the large leather mitt on his left hand and offered commiserations. Thomas merely nodded in acknowledgement and carefully removed the mitt to reveal a hand bandaged from fingertips to wrist and immobilized by a pair of splints.

"So they've made you quartermaster again," Winnifred said

to Marc with a smile, deflecting his gaze as she passed him the bowl of steaming mashed potatoes.

"To be honest, ma'am, I was asked along by Major Jenkin more or less to keep him company between the capital and Cobourg."

"And he lost track of you somewhere near Crawford's Corners?"

"He suggested that I had some business to transact in this vicinity."

"Whatever those transactions might be, I'm sure we wish you every success." And here she glanced across at Beth in time to catch the full bloom of her blush.

Beth recovered quickly enough to say, "The lieutenant has come to reconnoitre hogs for hungry soldiers, I believe."

Marc laughed, as he was meant to. He was delighted with the banter and quite pleased to be the butt of it. He had been afraid that the travails of the past months and Winnifred's flirtation with Mackenzie's cohorts might have soured her quick wit and frank appraisal of the world—qualities he had both admired and been wary of on his visit here last year. But there *had* been changes. Marriage and impending motherhood had apparently softened the edges of her cynicism and, if her father's account were accurate, had cooled her anger at the injustices meted out to her and her kind.

"I *am* authorized to issue contracts for grain and hogs on behalf of the quartermaster," Marc said in a more serious vein.

"It occurred to me that I might be able to help you out in that regard."

"We decided last fall that it was better to hang on to what we have rather than sell it at a loss. Since then the price of grain's gone lower and paper money of any colour is shrinking."

"The army is offering a price well above market value—with the blessing of the lieutenant-governor."

That remark brought a moment of meditative silence, during which the only sounds were the click of forks and scraping of knives.

"P-p-please, pass the—"

Thomas Goodall, anticipating Aaron's request, slid the bowl of turnips over to the lad with his good hand. The other he kept out of sight below the table. Aaron nodded a mute thank-you, but in spooning out a second helping, he tipped the bowl over. Beside him, Thomas instinctively reached out to right the bowl with the nearest hand—the swaddled one—then jerked it back in pain.

"Are you all right?" Winnifred asked anxiously. The danger of sepsis was ever present in such circumstances, and Thomas's reflexive wince was cause for alarm.

Thomas nodded and tried to smile. But smiling was no more natural to his craggy, ploughman's face than talking was. He looked up at Winnifred with an expression she alone read as reassuring. "Won't be shootin' no more deer fer a while."

Winnifred beamed. "This one'll last us till spring," she said to Marc. "Thomas bagged it in January."

"I'm not so sure you should be trying to work at all until Dr. Barnaby is ready to remove the stitches," Beth said. "Outside of splitting wood for the stoves, there's really not much in the barn that can't wait awhile or be done by Winn and me."

"So stupid . . . so stupid of me," Thomas muttered while keeping his eyes on his food and tucking the injured left hand into the safety of his lap.

"If you need cash, then," Marc said disingenuously, "perhaps you could spare a portion of the grain you've stored, provided it is in good condition."

"I'm a miller's daughter," Winnifred said. "I do know how to store grain." She turned towards Thomas. "What do you think, love, can we afford to sell some of what we've saved for feed and seed?"

Thomas put down his fork and peered ahead in thought. There was definitely a smile in the dark recesses of the eyes. "I figure about half," he said, and brought the fork back up to his mouth.

"That's what I thought as well."

"We can do business, then?" Marc said, but his glance was more towards Beth than Winnifred.

"If the price is right," Winnifred said lightly, but her relief at the prospect of generating some cash out of their failed harvest was clearly evident. "Thomas and I will take you out to the granary later this afternoon, and we'll talk turkey. We'll be expecting you back here for supper. I'll send Charlene over to Papa's place to invite them to join us as well."

"Are you not worried about having a uniformed officer as your house-guest?" Marc said with a broad smile around the table, then realized, too late, the clumsiness of the quip.

Winnifred was the first to break the awkward silence. "You mustn't believe all the rumours buzzing up and down the back concessions," she said. "You're welcome to stay with us as long as you wish to." Then, glancing at Beth, she added, "Or need to."

Sitting here in the welcoming warmth of this Upper Canadian farmhouse among people who had without doubt suffered both hardship and injustice, Marc could not bring himself to believe that these farmers would resort to armed resistance or open rebellion against the Crown. Their capacity and willingness to adapt to circumstance, with imagination and perseverance, was everywhere to be observed and marvelled at by newcomers like himself.

Under his present misgivings, then, a deep calm prevailed. He even felt ready to face Beth, alone and unprotected by sword or uniform.

FOUR

Marc and Beth were together in the sitting-room. The pot-bellied stove glowed cordially in the corner, a pale winter light ebbed through the window in the south wall, and the two cushioned chairs faced one another at an amiable angle. A little while earlier Beth had led Aaron to her own bedroom for his requisite afternoon nap. There, Marc noted once again the small library of political and religious books left to her by her clergyman father, one of them open on her pillow. Thomas had gone out to work in the barn and Winnifred had accompanied him, Marc suspected, to make certain he kept the makeshift mitten on and had any help he might require to otherwise preserve his dignity. Charlene Huggan had been dispatched to the mill to invite the Hatches for supper and to fuss over her sister's baby.

For a long while Marc and Beth sat quietly and sipped their tea, content for the moment to enjoy the presence of the other in the exact place where their eyes had first made contact, and where they had discovered the wordless covenant that quickens love and sweeps it beyond the reach of reason.

Beth put down her empty teacup with a resolute gesture, then leaned forward in her rocker and placed both hands on Marc's knees. "I want to talk, and I'd like it very much if you'd just listen. I need to explain what's in my heart, to you and to myself, and I won't know whether I can find the right words till I hear myself saying them. Do you understand?"

Marc nodded, and gave her his full attention. She averted her gaze, however, as if looking directly at him might cause her to falter. Instead, she stared at the window and the drift of snowflakes now whispering there.

"One thing I know for sure, and so we don't ever have to doubt it, is our love for each other. I used to think that was the hardest part. I was barely eighteen when Jesse came courtin' the minister's daughter. For the longest time I thought he was a nuisance I could do without—go ahead, you're allowed to smile."

Marc did.

"I didn't know I was supposed to feel flattered or have my stomach go queasy whenever he came into a room. Then after a while we got to know one another a bit, and began to talk some, and I started to like him very much. But it was only when he turned up one day in the back pew of the Congregational church that I knew he loved me. He seemed to be saying he was willing to switch gods for me."

The Lord of the Anglicans had lost more than Jesse Smallman lately, Marc thought.

"We went for a long walk, and I was held by a man for the first time, and we never looked back. I'm telling you all this, I think, because I want you to understand that I know what love is and what it asks us to do. You have the same look in your eye—you had it the first day you came here—that Jesse did, and I feel about you just like I did when Jess and I went for that Sunday stroll along the river flats. No, please don't say anything, not yet."

She stared longingly at the wisps of snow against the windowpane. Marc waited.

"First of all, let me say that I know what you did last June during the election, I know why you left the governor, and I know what you did for me and what it cost you not to betray a trust."

Marc started to protest but Beth raised her hand. "I got it from the horse's mouth." She smiled wryly. "Your policeman friend liked his cup of tea and a good gossip with Aunt Catherine."

"Constable Cobb."

"He was your staunch defender and ally, and convinced Auntie to take up your cause—daily. She argued, and I came to believe, that you'd become as weary of politics and hypocrisy and broken promises as I had."

"Then, if I'd come to you before—"

"Before January and Aaron's illness? Maybe. At least I'd have had the chance to look into your eyes myself. But you'd have come, as you have now, wearing that uniform—*please*, let me finish or I'll lose my nerve."

No battle-nerves could be as agonizing as this, Marc thought.

"You know, I hope, it isn't the uniform itself. I believe passionately in law and order and justice and equality. I've read bits of Paine and Rousseau and Locke and Burke. Jess and I worked for the Reform Party because we believed we could change things, get justice for the ordinary folk through politics and lawmaking. So, I wanted you to find the men responsible for my father-in-law's death last January and bring them before the law. To me, a soldier is an arm of the law or ought to be, and so should be nothing to fear. But when the governor himself corrupts the parliament and bends the law to suit him and his rich friends and ignores direct orders from London—then the law becomes something to be feared, and so do those sworn to uphold it."

Even though Marc was keenly aware of where this argument might lead and could feel a chill slowly seizing him, he could not help but marvel at the eloquence and clearheadedness of this tiny, beautiful woman. Little wonder, then, that she had been such a disruptive force in last spring's election.

Nor was the irony of the present situation lost on him: the very qualities he loved most might ultimately drive them apart.

"There's lawlessness on both sides now. The secret meetings are no secret. I don't know for sure but it's a good guess that some of the treasonous talk is already more than that. You can't imagine the terror I felt this winter, the endless nights as I sat beside Aaron coaxing him to breathe, praying like a sinner to any god who'd listen, and worrying myself sick that Winnifred—proud, loyal, law-abiding, churchgoing Winnifred—was miles away in some snowbound barn, cheering and clapping at some sermon of rage and desperation, and all them torches waving away no more than two feet from the nearest bale of hay."

Marc could think of nothing to say.

"These gatherings are still going on, and sooner or later it'll be the troops who'll have to put a stop to them." She glanced across at Marc's tunic, and he was grateful that he had not worn his sword. "Do you know what my recurring nightmare has been?"

"I think I can guess," Marc murmured, and looked away.

For a minute Marc thought she was not going to answer her own question, but finally she said in a hollow voice, "Winnifred and Thomas are running through the woods, being pursued by a dark shadow. Exhausted, Thomas turns around, steps in front of Winn, and faces his pursuer. It is you. You raise your musket, call out 'I'm sorry!' and fire. The noise wakes me up."

Marc shifted his chair so that it was directly facing Beth's.

"Then I'll rip this uniform off my back! I'll buy out my commission—"

With the tenderest of gestures, she reached over and placed a finger against his lips. "Oh, you dear, dear man. I knew you would say that, I knew you'd promise to fetch me the moon if I asked you to. You're still a romantic, and it's hard—oh, so hard—not to love that part of you. But think what you're saying. You're only twenty-seven years old, and already you've tried the law to please your uncle and quit it, and then chose the army—your boyhood dream—and here you are offering to throw that away to marry me. Then what? Help me sell ladies' hats? Live off my inheritance like an English gentleman? Return to the law and hope you don't hate it too much?"

She paused to swallow the lump in her throat. "No, if we're going to come together as man and wife, it's got to be on equal terms: the burden of our love's got to be parcelled out fairly. Surely you see that?"

Marc summoned up all his courage and said as calmly as he could, "So, *I* can't quit the army and *you* can't marry an officer: you're telling me, then, there is no hope for us."

Beth's face brightened, filled suddenly with the gentle mockery Marc loved so much. "Not at all! Let me finish. I did have doubts, but now I believe there's *every* hope. For a start, neither of us has any intention of un-loving the other, despite all that might divide us. And more recently, Aaron almost dying and Thomas's horrible accident have taught me a lesson. Any of us could be carried away at any time. We should not deny ourselves love or happiness—not for politics or religion or want of the perfect moment. The madness that's going on now can't last much longer, and you have your duty and I have mine, but in the meantime . . ."

"In the meantime, what?" Marc scarcely dared ask.

"If you ask me to marry you," Beth said with a slight tremor, "I'll say yes."

Marc took a moment to find his voice, then a wide grin spread over his face. "Can I believe what I've just heard?"

"Is that a proposal?" Beth countered, her blue eyes dancing.

"It certainly is."

"Then yes, you can believe it, and yes, I accept."

Marc held her tightly while his mind raced.

"Say when," he demanded eagerly.

"You must go back to your garrison—there is no question about that. And I must stay here for some time."

"With Aaron, of course."

"And with Winnifred. I promised that I would be with her through her confinement and see the babe safely into this world."

Marc stepped back, calculating. "That means September or October at the earliest."

"I know. But I think she needs watching over."

Marc did not need to ask why. "Then we'll get married to-morrow and just live apart for a few months."

Beth thought about that for a bit. "I'd like it done proper," she said, though he saw the indecision in her face and wished he were ruthless enough to take advantage of it. "I need to prepare Aaron. And I promised Aunt Catherine that, should I marry again, she would be my matron of honour." So, marriage had not been a taboo topic at the King Street shop, Marc thought.

She looked at him with a sudden, solemn intensity that brought him up short. "What's important is that we declare our love openly and publicly. We are engaged, and you can shout it to the world if you like. You can even have the banns read by the archdeacon in that stodgy old church of yours. Our wedding *will* happen, if God chooses to let us live till October. Nothing else can prevent it."

Marc leaned over and gave her a kiss on the lips. "You shame me," he said. "And I love you the better for it."

PART TWO

OCTOBER 1837

FIVE

"I'm in love, Marc."

Marc put down his copy of the *Constitution* long enough to glance across at Ensign Roderick Hilliard, who was sitting on the edge of his cot in the spartan officers' quarters they had shared now for seven months. Hilliard had served under Marc at Government House during the hectic days of the election a year ago last June. "Not again!" Marc exclaimed in mock surprise.

"This is the real thing," Hilliard said, leaning forward intently, as if to forestall Marc's return to William Mackenzie's seditious weekly "rag" in favour of matters of greater importance. "I know you have every reason to be skeptical, given my past history, but I have found the sweetest, most beautiful, most *ethereal* creature God ever created."

Last year Hilliard had made a play for Receiver-General Maxwell's daughter, but when the minister discovered their affair, he threatened to emasculate the young ensign, then shipped his daughter off to Kingston to be properly married.

"It's hearing you use such language that keeps me skeptical," Marc replied. "Do I not recall similar epithets employed to describe the goddesslike charms of one Chastity Maxwell?"

Hilliard looked as if he had been skewered by an épée in a friendly duel. "That was uncalled for. You know I loved Chastity and made her an honourable offer of marriage."

But not before you had hopped into her bed, Marc thought uncharitably before relenting. "You're right, Rick. I do apologize. And I have to admit she was well married and away before you decided to work your way through the debutante rosters of Toronto and the County of York." Marc smiled broadly to let Rick know he was teasing.

"Well, my stock went down considerably among respectable society when Sir Francis cashiered me." He grinned the boyish grin he so often used to set a young woman's bosom aflutter. "But I did try, nevertheless."

Marc had once thought Rick Hilliard to be too brash and overly ambitious to be a friend, until he realized that under the handsome exterior and sometimes impertinent manner lay a keen intelligence and a good heart. And since he, too, had been told that he was forward and ambitious, he could hardly hold these character flaws, if flaws they were, against Rick. When Hilliard followed Marc out of the governor's retinue to the purgatory of the Fort York barracks, Marc had taken pity on him. Rick had actually hoped that he, and not a lackey like Barclay Spooner, would take over Marc's position as aide-de-camp to Sir Francis. The two agreed to share quarters and so far Marc had not regretted it. Although not interested in politics or economic affairs (his father being a very rich mine owner in Yorkshire), Hilliard was a lively and witty conversationalist and a born raconteur. Most significantly, Marc sensed that Hilliard would be a valuable officer on the field of battle, for there was mettle under that mantle of charm and bonhomie.

"And who's the lucky woman this time?"

"Tessa Guildersleeve," Hilliard announced. When Marc did not immediately respond, he added with a sudden burst, "Isn't that just the most mellifluous-sounding name you've ever heard?"

"Sounds Dutch to me."

Hilliard frowned briefly, uncertain as to how he ought to take this riposte. "Her father was a Knickerbocker from New York, but her mother was English," he said, as if that explained all.

"How did she get here?" Marc said helpfully, knowing that, since there was no way he could prevent the whole story from being told, he might as well hurry it along.

"She's with that acting troupe that came to town last Friday."

"Three days ago?"

"I know what you're thinking, but I've spent every spare moment for the past two days in her presence."

"Well, then, two entire days is certainly time enough, and here I thought you were ice-fishing off the island or supervising the road detail."

"There's no need to be sarcastic."

"There's every need. You're telling me that you're deeply, irrevocably in love with an actress from the United States who, if I've correctly read the handbills littering this garrison, is in town for precisely five more days?"

"I thought you would understand," Hilliard groused, crestfallen. "After all, you are a man very much in love yourself, and one who has suffered greatly for it."

"Perhaps it is because I *do* have some notion of what love is about that I ask such impertinent questions, Rick. But at the same time I would be a hypocrite to imply that one cannot fall in love at first sight."

Hilliard brightened at this admission. "I know what respectable people think of actresses, but they would be horribly mistaken in Tessa's case."

"Well, then, you must tell me all about such an exceptional soul."

Hilliard's expression went suddenly dreamy. "The Bowery Theatre Touring Company arrived here last Friday from Buffalo. Their engagement down there was cut short for some reason and the lady who runs the operation decided to come up here a few days early. They don't open until tomorrow night at Frank's Hotel, but Ogden Frank adores the theatre, and he's put them up in the best rooms above his playhouse for the whole week. In return, they've agreed to assist some of the amateur players in town by letting them watch the professionals rehearse and get up fresh scenes and do proper elocution, and so on. Mrs. Annemarie Thedford is the company's proprietor, a very famous actress from New York City and every inch a lady, and so generous with her time and advice."

"And Tessa is a member of this illustrious troupe?"

"Oh, yes. There's six of them in all, seven if you count the black fellow who does the heavy lifting. Tessa plays all the ingenue roles, like Ophelia and Miranda."

"And *is* she an ingenue?" Marc asked, knowing what Rick's answer would be.

"Yes, she's brilliant. I watched her do Ophelia's mad scene from *Hamlet* last Saturday afternoon. There wasn't a dry eye in the audience. Even the old farts from the Shakespeare Club blubbered shamelessly. Afterwards she was very gracious, and we spent above an hour talking. She seemed very impressed that I had done amateur theatricals since I was a youngster. We hit it off immediately."

"So I gather. And of what age might this extraordinary ingenue be?"

Hilliard seemed momentarily puzzled by the question, but said quite proudly, "Eighteen."

Marc sighed but said nothing.

"What does age matter? I'm only twenty-five, and she's a

beautiful woman. And you wouldn't believe the tragic story of her life."

"Oh?"

"She was orphaned at fifteen when both her parents died of the cholera and she learned that all her father left her was debts. She was an only child, without relatives in America. But her parents had always loved the theatre, and she had been taken to plays and musicals since she was six."

"You found out a lot in a little more than an hour."

"Ah, but our own York Thespians were invited by Mrs. Thedford to put on scenes from our spring production of *The Way of the World* on Saturday evening just for her company. Imagine the pleasure we had in performing before true professionals! And how they did laugh. But best of all, Tessa was thoroughly taken with my Mirabell, and invited me up to her room for a nightcap, the most exquisite sherry I've ever tasted."

"And you returned for a further engagement yesterday?"

"We couldn't really do anything on the Sabbath, but with everybody else in the troupe off to see the sights of the city and take up dinner invitations from several of the more distinguished members of the York Thespians, Tessa and I were able to spend the entire day together. The only unpleasant bit was the dressing-down Tessa was given by Mrs. Thedford for not showing up at the Grange for tea, which, I'm embarrassed to say, I was the cause of. But I turned on the charm, and before I left all was once again sweetness and light."

"Thank God for charm."

"But to get back to Tessa's life: as I said, she was alone and destitute—"

"And loved the theatre."

"—and out of the blue Mrs. Thedford arrives at her house just as the bailiffs do, and spirits Tessa away to her Bowery Theatre, of which she is part owner. It turns out that Mrs. Thedford had been a friend of the Guildersleeves, and so more or less adopted Tessa on their behalf—then and there."

"Sounds suspiciously like those three-decker romance novels you find so enthralling."

"There's more, of course. It soon becomes apparent that Tess has a knack for acting, and is gradually worked into plays requiring the ingenue role."

"What else?"

"By the age of seventeen, she's the talk of New York, and being pursued by every cad and roué in that nefarious town."

"So she and the company run off to—"

"I know this all sounds incredibly romantic, Marc, but it happens to be fact. The reason the troupe is on the road is that the Bowery Playhouse burned down last spring, and as the new one won't be ready until this coming January, Mrs. Thedford formed a touring company for this fall. They've been to Rochester and Buffalo, and from here they're going on to Detroit and Chicago."

"And when they do?"

Hilliard stared at the floor. "I haven't been able to think about that," he said gloomily.

"The good news is you've got five more days to find out just how deep your love really goes. And believe me, Rick, that will prove to be a necessary part of the process."

A grateful smile lit up Hilliard's face. "That's true. And the reason I wanted to tell you all this is that we've been invited again to watch a rehearsal of some scenes from Shakespeare—things they've done before but not for some time. It's a chance to see how they whip an act into top shape."

"I'm sure you'll find it interesting, but—"

"I want you to come with me. I want you to meet Tessa."

Marc was surprised, then touched, by Hilliard's request. Of course, Rick did not know that Marc, too, had been briefly intoxicated by the acting scene in London five years ago. He merely wanted to show off his girl to—what?—his best friend.

Thinking that Marc was about to demur, Hilliard said quickly, "Owen Jenkin is coming along, too. He's been in musical hall revues in his youth, and I think he's got the itch again. We'll be the only three there, according to Tessa."

Marc and Major Jenkin had developed a firm friendship ever since their foraging trip last March, with the latter enjoying the role of confidant and avuncular guide. Since then, his fund of stories about the Peninsular War, the Duke of Wellington, and Uncle Frederick had kept Marc entertained through the long, difficult months following his separation from Beth, who was still in Crawford's Corners. Beth wrote to him faithfully every week—rambling, newsy letters about everything that was happening on the Goodall farm and in the township around them. Winnifred's baby was overdue, but no one was worrying. Thomas's hand had healed, though he was left with a dreadful scar.

Some of the news was as alarming as it was tantalizingly vague. Organized gatherings of political resistance were undoubtedly being held, though, thank God, Beth had kept a close watch on the malcontents in her own household. Moreover, the situation in Lower Canada was deteriorating rapidly. Nonetheless, the wedding date had been set, as planned, for Sunday, October 22, now just thirteen days away. Aunt Catherine, who had expanded the millinery shop to include dressmaking, had had one of her new seamstresses make a bridal gown, which had been duly shipped to Cobourg, tried on, and declared perfect. Marc, Hilliard, Jenkin, and three other officers, including Colonel Margison, were planning to ride in state, as it were, to Cobourg two days before the ceremony, where they would provide colour, pomp, and revelry before, and most likely well after, the service at Beth's father's former church. And Aaron would be standing tall beside the other guests, his contribution to the reviving fortunes of the farm well appreciated.

"I'd be honoured to join you and Major Jenkin this afternoon," Marc said. "Maybe I'll get the itch myself."

NORMALLY WHEN THEY WENT TO TOWN, officers and soldiers made the thirty-minute trek on foot. Just as often, after a hectic round of taverns and less savoury attractions, the more affluent would hire a trap or buggy to drive them back to the fort in comfort. But today Quartermaster Jenkin had arranged for horses to be provided, and he, Marc, and Hilliard rode in leisurely fashion eastward along Front Street in the cool sunshine of an early October day. They arrived at Frank's Hotel, on the corner of West Market and Colborne, just after two o'clock.

The Regency Theatre, constructed the previous June by Ogden Frank, was merely an unprepossessing extension of the hotel itself. From the south wall of the original two-storey inn, which faced east onto West Market Street, he had erected an unadorned brick rectangle so that it fronted onto Colborne Street, where a false balcony and a sign in Gothic letters provided the only visual enticement to would-be playgoers. The theatre itself was located in the lower storey of the new structure, and entered via two wide, oaken doors. On the floor above the theatre, and separate from the main hotel rooms, were situated several spacious chambers that served as additional space for hotel patrons or, when visiting troupes arrived, as comfortable quarters for the players. Frank and his wife, Madge, lived in four rooms attached to the rear of the tavern but otherwise discrete and private.

"We're here by special invitation this afternoon," Rick reminded them when they had delivered the horses to the ostler and were about to enter the theatre through the main entrance.

He did not need to reiterate who in the company had interceded on their behalf. "They haven't done their 'Selections from the Bard' show since last winter, so we're going to be privy to a truly professional rehearsal."

Marc endeavoured to look impressed.

"Well, it'll all be new to me," Jenkin said affably. "I did a bit of song-and-dance stuff in my salad days, but nobody dared call it *thee-ay-ter*."

The oak doors swung open at the first touch, briefly flooding the dark, cavernous room inside with sudden light.

"Get the hell out and shut the bloody door!"

The voice came from a raised platform about forty feet away at the far end of the cavern, where the flickering glow from a dozen candles and a single, overhead chandelier exposed five or six individuals. All had apparently been fixated on a tall male figure, downstage centre, but had decided that the novelty of an open door and sunshine was more worthy of their attention.

A very blond wisp of a girl padded quickly over to the imposing male and whispered something up into his ear. He appeared to smile as he turned towards the intruders and said in a stentorian but not unfriendly tone: "Welcome, good sirs. I mistook you for those ragamuffins who've been harassing us all morning. Please, take a seat in one of the far boxes. And be kind enough to keep your lips buttoned. We are engaged here in a serious undertaking."

"You shan't see or hear us, Mr. Merriwether," Rick called

out to him, and then nudged his companions towards a set of crude steps at the top of which was perched a plain wooden box with the front open, like a sort of elevated kiosk.

"Ah," Jenkin whispered, "seats for the mighty."

They ascended, carefully, found three hard-backed chairs in the semi-dark, propped their elbows on the railing in front of them, and prepared to observe the serious proceedings on the stage, now a foot or two below them and about twenty-five feet away. When their eyes adjusted to the interior light, they found that they could see and hear everything before them.

The stage itself was rudimentary: two wooden pilasters and a faded velvet curtain that might have once been crimson composed the proscenium arch, in front of which the playing area extended another five or six feet. Canvas "wings" of a mucus-green hue were set back in receding fashion at each side to effect a sense of perspective. Two small chandeliers on long cables could now be seen beside the large one that was presently lit, and arrayed along the curved edge of the thrust-stage were half a dozen Argand lamps, which, when fired up, would provide ample foot-lighting. Along the side walls, that were about fifteen feet high, iron candelabra were inset in the brick to illuminate the pit below, the six boxes, and the gallery teetering across the back wall. A single door, locked and barred, along the wall to the left opened onto the alley outside and a nearby pair of privies. Two small windows, high up, offered the only natural light and ventilation. No wonder theatres burnt down at regular intervals, Marc thought as he turned his attention to the action onstage.

"We'll start with the death of Lear. I'd like the scene to run right through. I want everybody watching—you're the critical audience, remember. But when we've finished the scene, I don't want to hear a peep from the cheap seats, understood? If I wish to avail myself of your comments—after I've made my own—I'll ask for them."

"Jason Merriwether, the director," Rick whispered.

Merriwether appeared to be very tall, almost Marc's height at six feet, and perhaps in his mid-forties if the graying sideburns were not the result of makeup. But there was no middle-aged paunch or slackening of the skin around the mouth or under the jutting chin. His bearing was imperial, a man of parts who commanded any stage he chose to grace with his presence. His hair was a tawny shade, his chin and upper lip bare, and his nose of ordinary length, but the eyes were coal-black and penetrating, even at a distance of twenty-five feet.

"Annemarie, *ma chère,* would you please give the king your shawl. It may help Mr. Armstrong get in role." The latter half of this remark was spoken with spitting sarcasm and directed at a bent, gnarled man who hobbled forward at the mention of his name. While he could not have been sixty—the dark swatch of unkempt hair was merely speckled with gray—he looked Lear's age without need of makeup or costume. For he had once been a big man, perhaps five foot seven, large-boned and full-fleshed, but the skin on his face, neck, and wrists now drooped as if the flesh had been sucked out from under it without warning. The eyes were murky dots in smudged sockets, and the lips hung loosely in what seemed to be either a permanent sneer or a perpetual whimper. He looked to Marc like a man who wished to hide from himself.

"I don't need your advice to tackle a scene I've played on two continents," he muttered at Merriwether, but did not look his way.

"I think the shawl may help, Dawson," said a tall woman who stepped under the candlelight and gently laid her knitted shawl over the hunched actor.

"Annemarie Thedford, the boss," Rick whispered again.

"It's a bit drafty in here, and you know how easily you catch cold and lose your voice."

"All right, then," Armstrong said sullenly, but he did glance up at Mrs. Thedford like a dog both surprised and grateful that he had not been kicked.

Mrs. Thedford, the owner-manager of the Bowery Touring Company, was also exceptionally tall, near five foot seven or eight, which left her looking down at almost every woman and three-quarters of the men in the colony. Her thick, honey-coloured hair was neatly coiffed, and though her fair complexion would require makeup to project her expression across the footlights, the face itself was the picture of elegance and inborn grace. Her walk could only be described as regal, the consequence of an upright posture and confident carriage. Here was a woman of the world, unbowed by its travails, whose lean and handsomely proportioned figure commanded your attention first, then drew you on to the gaze that held and appraised and fascinated. Marc could not take his eyes off her.

"Where in Sam Hill did Thea get to?" Merriwether roared, making Lear recoil and drop his cloak.

"She was here just a second ago," piped a male voice from the upstage shadow.

"I think she went to puke again," said a sweet and timid female voice.

"That's my girl," her suitor mouthed in Marc's ear.

"I'd better see to her," Mrs. Thedford said with evident concern, then strode quickly across the back of the stage to the right and disappeared.

"Well, she can't very well lie dead in Lear's arms and then start puking at the audience," Merriwether growled after her, but she was already too far away to hear.

Lear himself at that moment began to cough, an uncontrollable hacking that continued for a full minute. When it finally stopped, there was an awesome silence.

"You've been at it again, haven't you? I can smell your stinking breath from here!" Merriwether said with withering contempt.

Armstrong's jaw quivered as if it were expecting a word to emerge, but at that moment Mrs. Thedford swept back in, and Merriwether looked to her expectantly.

"Thea will be here in a few minutes. I've asked Mrs. Frank

to prepare her a tisane," she said, as if she were remarking on the pleasantness of the weather.

"But I wish to do the Lear first, *ma chère*. It needs the most work, obviously."

"*I'm* ready to go," Armstrong said with a pathetic sweep of the cloak about his stooped shoulders.

"He's been drinking again."

"That's a lie!"

"Smell his breath."

"I had one mouthful, for my rheumatism."

Mrs. Thedford took Armstrong's hand in hers and pulled him up to face her. "When we're finished here, old friend—and I expect you to stay till the last word is uttered—I want you to accompany me to your room and give me the bottle. God knows where you managed to hide it."

"I'm sorry, love. It won't happen again. I promise."

"For the love of Christ, can we get on with this farce?"

"I think we're doing that tonight," Mrs. Thedford said dryly, and drew a giggle and a chortle from the back of the stage.

"Am I the director here or not?" Merriwether said somewhere between complaint and petition.

"You are, Mr. Merriwether, and a damn good one."

Merriwether looked mollified. Then with a sly grin he stepped under the candlelight and into the shadows upstage. "Then I am making a casting decision that should have been made weeks ago." Into the spotlight he drew by one tiny white hand a young woman, barely beyond girlhood, but nonetheless stunning for all that.

"Tessa," Marc murmured before Rick could.

Tessa Guildersleeve had the white blond hair of an albino, and it fell where it wished in flowing coils over her bare shoulders, its native lustre merely enhanced by the meagre light above it. Her Dutch skin was unblemished and uniformly alabaster from the brow to the rim of her bosom that winked enticingly from the low-cut, frothy shift she wore—which resembled either a priest's frock or a courtesan's nightie, depending on the angle of observation. Her diminutive feet were caressed by ballet slippers, and she moved her slim, pale arms with the impetus and delicacy of a prima ballerina's grand entrance. She was all elfin innocence in movement, but out of the translucence of her blue eyes shone pure desire.

"Tessa, my pretty, you have understudied the role long enough. Tomorrow night you shall step onto this stage as Cordelia."

"You're not going to wait for Thea, then?" Mrs. Thedford said evenly, but there was an edge behind the remark.

"Thea's getting too old and fat for the ingenue, *ma chère*. She'll be laughed off the stage like she was in Buffalo. We don't want that to happen again, do we?"

"What about Juliet, then?"

"Well, I thought Tessa did splendidly at short notice during the entr'acte in Rochester, didn't you, Clarence?"

At this, a young man in his mid-twenties stepped into the

circle of light that now illumined five of the six acting members of the troupe. He was handsome in a feminine sort of way that contrasted sharply with the aggressive masculinity of Merriwether. He had curly red hair, pale freckles, and a pallor to match, and languid blue eyes that most directors would have instantly labelled a poet's. He peered towards Mrs. Thedford, but she was staring intently at Merriwether. "Tessa always gives her best," he said guardedly.

"Thea will play Juliet tomorrow night, if she's well enough," Mrs. Thedford said.

"You *could* let her take the role of Beatrice," Merriwether said, staring straight back at her with his intimidating, black gaze.

Mrs. Thedford smiled cryptically. "Meaning that I myself am somewhat too advanced in years to play the part?"

"Not at all, my dear. You'll be acting Beatrice and Cleopatra when you're eighty, should you wish to. What I'm suggesting is that, outside of the farce, there are not, in the makeup of our current program, any roles now suited to the peculiar talents of our Miss Clarkson. That is all."

"I would be more than happy to let Thea play Beatrice, Jason, but then it would be incumbent upon us to find a Benedick young enough to be credible."

"I wouldn't think of it—" Clarence Beasley said, looking abashed at both the director and the proprietor.

"But I'm ready to play Juliet! I *am*!" There was no sweetness in the ingenue's statement of fact, only the petulance of a child approaching tantrum. Tessa's pretty features were suddenly contorted, and flushed with an unbecoming rush of crimson pique.

"If you carry on like that, missy, we'll have to put you in the Punch-and-Judy show with a slapstick." Mrs. Thedford spoke in the way a mother might in gently reproving a much-doted-on daughter. "Be content with Cordelia, for the time being."

Rick Hilliard stirred beside Marc, who put a restraining hand upon his friend's arm and one finger to his lips. It was obvious that the actors, in the intensity of this interplay, had forgotten they were being observed, and Marc was thoroughly enjoying his invisibility.

Tessa's face lit up instantly, and all traces of tantrum vanished in the unrepressed joy of her response. "Oh, Annie, you are such a dear! I could hug you to death!"

When she threatened to do so, Mrs. Thedford held up a hand and said, "Save that ardour for Cordelia and Miranda tomorrow night." She turned to Merriwether. "Get on with the scene, then, Jason dear. I'll just go and see how Thea's getting on. We'll need her for the farce tonight."

"We'll need *everybody*," Merriwether said, glaring at Dawson Armstrong, who had taken advantage of the diversion to squat on his haunches and drift into a doze.

Mrs. Thedford left, and the director clapped his hands for attention, as if he were orchestrating a cast of hundreds. "All right, Dawson, you know the routine. Tessa, my sweet, while you have no lines for this particular scene—we'll rehearse your other scene later—it is vitally important that you lie absolutely limp in the old man's arms. I suggest that you let the arm facing the audience droop—like this—and your head should be tilted back so your beautiful, long tresses hang down to almost touch the floor, and you can let one slipper dangle from your toes, and contrive to let it fall just as Lear moves from his 'howls' to his speech."

"Must I wear Thea's costume?"

"I think not. We'll try something gauzier that will let your figure show through—in a modest way, of course. Thea's figure, alas, has to be disguised wherever possible: that was the point about her age I was attempting to make."

"I do hope Thea won't be too upset. She's a very nice woman."

"Dawson! Wake up and take your place!"

Armstrong glared at Merriwether's knees, got up, and strode manfully back into the shadows upstage. Tessa padded after him. Clarence Beasley came and stood as close to Merriwether as he dared, anticipating the action to come. A moment later, Lear began his escalating sequence of howls.

Marc felt a chill down his spine. Lear's cri de coeur was heart-wrenching: a deep animal howl bred in the flesh and bone of love and loss. Armstrong might be old, but he was not past his prime as a tragedian. Slowly the howls came nearer and the ruined old king staggered forward with the hanged Cordelia in his arms and floating, it appeared, on the cloak. Tessa looked lifeless, one arm adroop, the body arched but limp, the hair lifting and falling with the cadence of Lear's step, as if something of her was yet living and not ready to die. Marc was moved deeply, and braced himself for the speech he knew by heart.

It was at this critical point, and just as Cordelia's slipper struck the floor like a severed appendage, that Dawson Armstrong staggered, careened, and toppled sideways. Then, in a pathetic effort to maintain his balance, he dropped Cordelia upon the boards with an ugly thump.

"What the fuck are you doing, you goddamn moron, you drunken pig, you stinking excuse for an actor!"

Marc leaned forward in alarm, as did Rick and Jenkin.

But having spewed this venom at the toppled Lear, who lay semi-comatose where he had fallen, Merriwether dashed to Tessa's side, almost colliding with Clarence Beasley.

"I'm fine, I'm fine," Tessa said, whipping her dress down over her prettily exposed knees and scrambling to her feet. "I fell on my derriere." She giggled, and gave that part of her anatomy a reconnoitring rub. "An' there's nothin' much to hurt down there!"

Beasley insisted on taking her hand, as if she were still on the floor, and giving it a gentlemanly tug.

Tessa rewarded the effort with a dazzling smile. "What'll we do now?" she asked Merriwether.

"First, I'll drag this intoxicated sot into the wings, where he can sleep it off. Then you and I will do this scene properly."

"I'll see to Dawson," Beasley said. He went over to the old

man, spoke softly into his ear, then helped him over to the wings on the left, where he collapsed peacefully.

"We better wait for Annie," Tessa said nervously.

"I'm the director, love."

Just then Mrs. Thedford returned. "Well, Jason, you were right. He's found a bottle somewhere and downed it. I've searched his room, but when he sleeps this off, we'll have to watch him every minute until the show opens at eight-thirty."

"He'll never make it," Merriwether said.

"Now, you know he's an old pro. If he's awake and no more than half drunk, he can outact any of us."

"Jason says he's going to play Lear tomorrow night," Tessa said with just a hint of little-girl mischief in her voice.

"We'll cross that bridge when we come to it. Right now I'm more concerned with Dorothea's health. She's taken a tisane to help her sleep. She insists she'll be ready for the farce tonight. And I believe her. She made no objection when I told her Tess was going to play Cordelia—to lessen the load on her till she's feeling herself again."

"Oh, thank you, Annie. Thank you!"

"So, whether Dawson does Lear tomorrow night or you, Jason, Tess needs a couple of run-throughs right now. Clarence and I will observe."

"Just remember what I told you a few minutes ago and you'll be fine, sweetie," Merriwether said to Tessa as they walked back into the shadows, Merriwether looking very Promethean beside the slight, five-foot figure of the girl-woman.

"They've edited out the other parts, so there's just Lear and Cordelia," Hilliard whispered. But Marc's attention was riveted on the stage.

There was a collective intake of breath in expectation of the five howls. Out of Jason Merriwether's mouth they came, but this time they were more bellowed than uttered, more impressing than impressive. From the upstage shadows emerged this other octogenarian with the rag doll of his daughter draped across his outstretched arms. Merriwether was nothing if not the consummate actor, for, despite his height and imperial bearing, he looked now the bowed and broken monarch, his every wearied step a defeated trudge. Moreover, his hunched bulk rendered the slender, unbreathing Cordelia that much more vulnerable and pitiable. And when he laid her down and began his great speech of self-insight and contrition, there was no anomalous thump, only the cadence of the bard's pentameter. But, scarcely noticed except by the quickest eye, the old king's left hand, as it slipped Cordelia's lower half stageward, lingered a split second more than necessary on the curved clef of her buttocks and, just possibly, gave them an impertinent squeeze. The girl herself gave no sign, not even a blink.

Marc heard the rasp of Rick's breath and felt him rising from his chair. With well-coordinated movements, Marc pressed him back down with one hand and placed the other over his mouth in time to throttle the cry of outrage there.

"They're only acting," he hissed, and Rick reluctantly sank back.

Someone else had noticed the king's incestuous touch, for Marc saw Mrs. Thedford's eyes widen in disbelief, then fix upon the girl while Merriwether completed his series of lamentations over her prostrate form, and made a fine, rhetorical demise. Beasley began applauding, but Tessa turned her newly opened eyes upon Mrs. Thedford and smiled—knowingly, Marc thought. Owen Jenkin began to clap as well, and when Tessa rose to take her bow beside Merriwether, Rick joined him lustily. Marc felt obliged to clap politely, but Annemarie Thedford did not.

Well, well, Marc thought, the acting business hasn't changed much since I dipped my toes into its roiling waters five years ago.

THE NEXT HOUR AND A HALF unfolded less contentiously. The company showed a predilection for death scenes, with the demise of Antony, Cleopatra, Romeo, and Juliet being added to that of Lear. All of this gloom was leavened only by the razor-keen repartee of Annemarie and Jason as Beatrice and Benedick from *Much Ado About Nothing*. As far as Rick Hilliard was concerned, and he made his concern quite vocal, Tessa as Juliet (standing in, for today only, in place of Thea Clarkson) was the show-stopper, despite a less-than-satisfactory Romeo (Clarence Beasley), whose Yankee twang nearly ruined the balcony scene and certainly depreciated the glowing iambics of the beloved above him. And while all of the actors essayed some sort of approximate English stage-accent, Marc detected a trace of genuine English dialect in Mrs. Thedford's speech, even when she wasn't in character. Her performances as Gertrude and Lady Macbeth, opposite Merriwether's Claudius and Macbeth, were the highlights of the afternoon.

The various bits and pieces usually taken by Armstrong or Thea Clarkson were merely read by one of the other players, and Mrs. Thedford agreed with the director's suggestion that the scenes from *The Tempest* be dropped from the bill due to the comatose condition of Prospero. Rick groaned at the patent unfairness of a decision that would deprive him of seeing Tessa play Miranda, the quintessential ingenue. Miranda herself seemed blithely unconcerned.

Just as they were finishing, Thea Clarkson made a dramatic entrance, pale and fevered, and insisted on taking her part as Juliet, even though this set had already been run through twice with clear success.

"How nice of you to make an appearance, love," Merriwether said acidly. "You look more like Lady Capulet or the Nurse than a fifteen-year-old virgin."

Thea seemed about to burst into tears. Illness or not, she no longer gave the illusion of a woman in first bloom, for though she had a pretty, moon-pale face and striking almond eyes, she had put on weight that did not sit on her bones attractively. Moreover, her expression was that of one whose confidence has been shaken by the discovery of some knowledge still too daunting to admit.

"There's no need for gratuitous cruelty," Mrs. Thedford said to Merriwether. "Thea, dear, you and Clarence can rehearse the *Romeo and Juliet* scenes tomorrow afternoon. You need to rest now so you'll be fresh for the farce tonight. After all, it is *you* who must carry the piece."

Thea beamed her a bright smile, then began to weep quietly.

At this point in the proceedings, Dawson Armstrong woke up. "Where in hell did my Cordelia go?"

"Don't you just love theatre people?" Rick exclaimed.

SIX

"Tessa has offered to give us a tour of the facility," Rick called down to Marc and Jenkin, who were standing by the pot-bellied stove warming their hands. "And Mrs. Thedford has invited us to stay for the supper the Franks are laying on for the company in the hotel dining-room."

"We'll take the tour," Marc said, "but this is my night to have supper with Aunt Catherine at the shop."

"Speak for yourself, young fellow." Jenkin laughed. He winked at Marc: "That Thedford woman's a fine specimen of her sex."

Rick hopped down, and they followed him through a curtained doorway to the left of the stage and into the gloomy space beside it, where the actors could rest between entrances.

Tessa was waiting for them, her blond hair shimmering in the near-dark. She led them down a long, narrow hallway, on either side of which were several cubicles that Tessa, still leading the parade, referred to as dressing-chambers. Rick insisted on exploring the one assigned to Tessa and Thea Clarkson, professing his amazement at the drawerful of makeup paints and glues, the wig-stand, and the bedraggled mannequin with the evening's costume in place upon it. Marc peered into Merriwether's carrel, where several playbills caught his attention. One of them, an advertisement for *Hamlet* at the Park Theatre in New York, featured a sketch of a younger Merriwether as Claudius, with a wig of curly black hair, bushy brows, and a trim Vandyke of similar hue—looking very much the smiling villain of the piece. Having exhausted the wonders of the airless, windowless dressing-rooms, they retreated as they had come in, and Tessa pointed up the steps to the stage itself, indicating that they were to cross to the other side.

"Where does that door go?" Rick asked, glancing to his left.

"Oh, that takes you into Mr. Frank's quarters," Tessa burbled, reaching down for Rick's hand. "The Franks've got the most beautiful furniture you've ever seen. It's just like a doll's house!"

They crossed the stage—the chandelier was now extinguished—and, through the wings on the right, down into another unlit space. There was a door to their left and a set of steep stairs straight ahead. The door appeared to be the only link between theatre and tavern. Tessa eased it open. They could see the bar just ahead and beyond it a room full of boisterous patrons, not of the drama but the bottle. Tessa eased it closed again.

"Show us *your* rooms," Rick suggested slyly.

"Oh, wait till you see them! We had nothin' like this in Buffalo!" Tessa testified, and skipped up the stairs with Rick on her heels. The party paused on a landing, and then continued up again to the second floor directly above the theatre.

"Is this the only way in here?" Marc asked anxiously. The upper storey of Frank's addition appeared to be self-contained and separate from the original building.

"That's right," Tessa said. "Unless you want to go through that window at the far end of this hall and jump off the balcony onto the street."

"I could call for you like Romeo from underneath the balcony out there," Rick teased.

"What if there's a fire?" Marc asked.

"My, would you look at this!" Rick cried, ignoring Marc's question. He pointed through the partly opened door to the first room on their right.

Tessa blushed, giving the effect of a white carnation magically transformed into a red one. "That's our bathroom. You ain't supposed to peek in there!"

But peek they must.

An elephantine copper tub squatted ostentatiously in the centre of the room, around which, on clothes-horses, were arrayed a dozen bath towels of varying pastel tints. In a far corner a Chinese folding-screen offered privacy to the diffident bather. On top of a pot-bellied stove, spitting and aglow, sat a kettle big enough to swim in.

"The Franks have a maid who readies the bath whenever we wish," Tessa said.

"Looks like that tub could hold more than one person," Rick said, and was rewarded with another full-petalled blush.

A guttural cry directly across the hall from the bathroom interrupted this bit of by-play, as if someone had muttered a curse while stumbling over a coal-scuttle or bag of nails.

"What on earth was that?" Jenkin asked.

"Oh, that's just Jeremiah's babble-talk," Tessa said. "Don't pay him no mind."

At this, the three men turned to the open doorway of a storeroom, where a huge black man was staring at them with white-eyed, menacing curiosity.

Tessa made what appeared at first to be several flirtatious gestures with her hands and fingers across the top of her bosom. Jeremiah, if that's who he was, relaxed immediately, and greeted the newcomers with a gleaming smile that consumed most of his large, round face and bald head.

"He doesn't speak English?" Rick wondered.

Tessa laughed, a bubbling little-girl laugh. "He don't speak at all."

"He's mute, then?" Jenkin said.

"Aaargh," Jeremiah said forcefully, with a painful contortion of both lips.

"He's deaf and dumb," Tessa said matter-of-factly. "But he can read and write and read lips a little—can't ya, Jeremiah?" Here she flashed him a sign, and he nodded vigorously.

"He does the haulin' and settin' up of the flats. Annie—Mrs. Thedford—picked him up off the street and gave him a place to sleep. I told her he was probably a runaway slave but she don't bother listenin' to anyone, especially when it comes to pickin' up strays."

Like you, Marc thought, and raised his opinion of the imperial Mrs. Thedford another notch.

"What's that?" Jenkin asked, indicating a slate that hung by a rope from the man's neck.

Jeremiah smiled, and Marc could discern the intelligence in that face, whose age might have been twenty-five or forty. He realized that the overly demonstrative facial gestures and hand movements were an attempt to communicate almost physically, but might easily lead people to assume he was a simpleton. Marc thought of Beth's brother Aaron and winced inwardly.

Jeremiah drew a piece of chalk from a big pocket in his smock and wrote something on the slate: "My name is Jeremiah Jefferson." Then he held the slate out to Major Jenkin, who erased what was there with the sleeve of his tunic, and wrote: "I am Owen Jenkin."

"Jeremiah, get back to your work!" Tessa ordered suddenly,

and accompanied her command with several intimidating hand-signs. "You got props to get ready for the farce tonight."

Jeremiah did not seem to take offense at this rude outburst. He merely bowed his head and backed into the storeroom, but what lay behind the mask of his eyes and his practised public demeanour could only be guessed at. In the room behind him, they saw a straw pallet surrounded by half a dozen steamer-trunks.

"You brought all this with you?" Rick said with enough interest to have Tessa pause and lean against his nearest shoulder.

"Those are trunks with the props and costumes we're gonna need in Detroit next week but not here. There's one or two more downstairs somewheres that Mr. Merriwether's plannin' to send back to New York—stuff we used in Buffalo but don't need no more."

"But how on earth do you haul all of this stuff?" Jenkin asked, his quartermaster's curiosity piqued. "Not over our roads?"

Tessa gave him an indulgent smile, glanced at Rick, and said, "Our stuff comes down the Erie Canal on a barge and then up from Buffalo by boat on the Welland Canal. That's what we got Jeremiah for—to ride with it. And, of course, to protect us from dangerous strangers." She batted her near-invisible lashes at Rick.

"But he's deaf," Rick said with real concern.

"He sleeps right there at the top of them stairs with the door open all night. The teensiest vibration will wake him up straightaway."

Jeremiah was busy opening one of the trunks as they turned to move farther along the carpeted hallway.

"We each got a trunk in our rooms. We're responsible for our own costumes once they get here, though we do help each other dress." She checked out Rick's response to this double entendre, and was not disappointed.

"Who does the repair work?" Jenkin asked, ever interested in the care and deployment of uniforms. He stumbled for a second over a decorative spittoon near one of the doors, righted himself, and continued: "You must have a lot of it with all the costume changes."

"Thea does the little bits of stitchin' an' patchin'. She's real handy with a needle. But if we're stayin' put for a week or so, like here, Mr. Merriwether finds us a local seamstress." They were moving down the hall now, where doors on either side indicated the sleeping chambers of the cast. Tessa revelled in her role as tour-guide, with Rick at her elbow endeavouring to bump against her at every opportunity. "This here's Clarence's room and that one's Mr. Armstrong's," she said, pointing to the next two rooms on the right, and then putting a forefinger against her pretty lips. "They like to have a snooze after the afternoon rehearsal."

"And where is *your* room?"

"Here at the end," Tessa said, "across from Mr. Merri-wether's."

As Tessa opened the door on the left, Marc glanced out the dusty window onto Colborne Street, and noted that the balcony which adorned the front of the Regency Theatre was indeed a false one, making it a dubious escape mechanism for those fleeing a sudden fire and a precarious perch for would-be Juliets.

"The maiden's bower!" Tessa gushed as they followed her inside.

Marc had to admit that the room was nicely decorated, with lavender wallpaper aflutter with sprites and fairies, a thick carpet in some neutral shade, a commode-and-vanity with tilting oval-mirror, a quaint Swiss clock, a settee embroidered with daisies, and a four-poster bed swathed in pink. On a nighttable, a decanter of sherry winked at the interlopers.

"Mrs. Thedford insisted I take this room. Usually I have to share with Thea."

"Where does Thea sleep?" Rick asked. "With Mrs. Thedford?"

"Lordy, no. Annie always stays by herself. Thea's sleepin' on her own in a little room in the Franks' place. Annie's afraid the rest of us might catch whatever she's got."

"You've a fondness for sherry," Jenkin said with a smile.

"Oh, that. It's somethin' Mrs. Thedford taught me—to have one or two small glasses after a performance to help me sleep." Giving Rick a sidelong glance, she added, "'Course I do *share* it once in a while."

"Well, that leaves us with all but Mrs. Thedford accounted for," Jenkin said in what he intended to be a disinterested tone.

"We've gone past her rooms," Tessa said.

"Rooms?" Jenkin asked, intrigued.

Tessa led them back into the hall and pointed to the door next to her own room. "I'll just give a tap an' see if she's still up."

"Oh, please don't disturb her," Rick said.

But Tessa, who apparently liked to have her own way whenever it could be arranged, had already rapped, and a moment later the door opened.

"Oh, do come in, gentlemen," Mrs. Thedford said. She stood tall and elegant in the doorway, clad only in a satin kimono, her coiffed hair almost touching the lintel above her. "I heard you in the hall and was about to step out and invite you in."

Jenkin demurred. "We don't wish to disturb you at your . . ."

"Toilette?" She laughed, giving the word its French pronunciation. "Don't worry, sir, you're not invading milady's boudoir."

As they followed her in, they realized that the owner-operator of the Bowery Touring Company had a suite of rooms befitting her status. After introductions were made and requisite courtesies completed, Mrs. Thedford offered them sherry, sat them on her comfortable chairs and settee, and regaled them with witty tales of theatre life in New York. Marc noticed two things: Owen Jenkin was quite taken with the woman, and she herself appeared as regal, confident, and genuine as the image she had projected from the stage. Nor did she seem to be playing a role, of which she was perfectly capable. And if she were, it was one she believed in.

At one lull in the conversation, she looked at Marc and said, "Edwards . . . my, what a fine English name."

"I can't take credit for having applied it to myself," Marc said, and it was plain from her approving expression that Mrs. Thedford—who slept alone in the adjoining bedroom and was, according to her story, long a widow—appreciated the witticism and the lineaments of the man who'd made it. Good Lord, Marc thought, surely I'm too young for her attentions. Besides, it was Major Jenkin who was paying court to her with all the Welsh charm he could muster.

"I noticed the lovely lilt of your accent," the major said gallantly. "Do I detect a shadow of English in it?"

Mrs. Thedford gave him a smile worthy of Cleopatra.

"The merest shadow, Mr. Jenkin. My father was English, but he brought me to Philadelphia when I was still a toddler. I have, alas, no memory of my birth-country, only a few of the unconscious traces of its glorious speech."

"Which is no drawback in the theatre," the major replied.

"Those pieces on your commode there look very English," Marc remarked, admiring a pair of silver candlesticks. "I remember seeing something of that design in London."

"You are very observant, Lieutenant. In fact, the hairbrushes, hand-mirror, and the candlesticks were especially made for my parents as a wedding gift, a matched set. Or so my father told me when I was old enough to understand. They are all that I have left of them—or England—and I bring them with me everywhere."

"Aren't you afraid they'll be stolen?" Rick asked.

"Not with Jeremiah nearby, I'm not. And as he's been complaining of a toothache all day, I expect he'll be more vigilant than usual at his post tonight."

"And we've got policemen patrolling our streets," Rick said, as if he himself were native-born and a major contributor to local improvements.

As they were getting up to leave, Mrs. Thedford said, "I hope you all plan to come to the farce tonight, as guests of the company. And, of course, you're welcome to join us in the hotel for supper."

"Thank you. I wouldn't miss either for the world," Jenkin said with a brief bow.

"I'll be here every night this week," Rick said with an artful glance at Tessa, who had sat through the polite chatter without saying a word, though she and Mrs. Thedford had exchanged cryptic looks, and the latter had given Rick what could only be described as critical scrutiny.

Tessa beamed him a conspiratorial smile, then turned to determine its effect upon Mrs. Thedford. But that lady's gaze rested on Marc.

"And how about you, Mr. Edwards?"

"I must decline, ma'am. I am engaged to dine with my fiancée's aunt this evening."

"Ah, I understand." Mrs. Thedford's eyebrows rose in

interest. "But you'll come later in the week, to the Shakespeare, perhaps?"

"Yes, I will," he said, and realized with a start that he meant it.

Rick accompanied Marc back through the gloomy theatre to the front doors. "Isn't Tessa just the most darling thing you've ever set eyes upon?" he asked imploringly.

"You've got quite a girl there, Rick," Marc replied, and left it at that.

CATHERINE ROBERTS WAS BETH'S AUNT, HER mother's sister, who had grown up with the McCrae family in Pennsylvania. After Beth's mother died, her grieving father had taken his children to a new Congregational ministry in Cobourg. Aunt Catherine married and went to live in New England, where her affection for things English had taken root. So much so that when she herself was widowed just two years ago, she had readily accepted Beth's offer to come to this British colony and invest jointly in their millinery shop on fashionable King Street. Ever since his engagement to Beth had been announced ("proclaimed" would be a more accurate description), Marc had arranged to have supper with Aunt Catherine on the second Monday of each month.

"Right on time, Marc." She smiled as she led him through the shop towards the stairs that would take them to her apartment above. "It must be the military in you."

"Or the lawyer," Marc said. He loved to watch the soft gray eyes light up in their bemused way behind the gold-rimmed spectacles. Like Beth, she was a diminutive woman with an Irish complexion and sunny disposition. Without ostentation, she always dressed and carried herself with a spare dignity that impressed her wealthy customers and helped to account for the success of the enterprise—that, plus her Yankee business acumen.

"What's going on in the back room?" Marc asked at the sound of strange voices.

"I've had to hire a pair of extra girls," she said, "to handle the dress-making side of the shop. It's doing very well for us, and the girls do like to talk while they're sewing."

"That's not a girl's voice."

"Oh, that's George. He's just come in the back door. He's been away every time you've come for supper—not deliberately, you understand."

"I find you incapable of subterfuge."

"George, stop teasing my girls and come in here for a minute!"

As the giggling died down behind him, there emerged from the door to the workroom a man of twenty-five or so, of medium build, with a baby-faced handsomeness that would appeal to a certain breed of undiscriminating young woman. His dark eyes were still dancing with the charm he had just loosed on the seamstresses. But when he spied Marc, he stopped in his tracks, and glowered at him with undisguised disdain.

"George Revere, wipe that frown off your face and shake hands with Lieutenant Marc Edwards." There was an edge of authority in Aunt Catherine's voice that Marc had not heard before.

George Revere glanced at his aunt—slyly? fearfully?—and dredged up a smile. "Pleased ta meet ya," he said with a noticeable New York accent. His handshake was limp.

"George, as you know, has come up from the States to help me here until Beth comes back. After which he hopes to be in business for himself."

"Sorry, Auntie, but I gotta meet someone in a few minutes."

Aunt Catherine gave him a knowing nod, then added, "But not before you take that costume on up to the Regency Theatre and pick up the others we've promised to mend."

George Revere muttered something rebellious under his breath, wheeled, and ran out the back way.

"Thank God he's not a blood nephew," his aunt said.

By six-thirty they had finished supper, and while one of the girls from the shop came upstairs to clear away the dishes, Marc and Aunt Catherine repaired to the sitting-room, where a low fire was keeping the early-evening chill at bay. Usually, they sat comfortably here for several hours, conversing when they felt like it, sipping a sherry or not, reading or reading aloud, whatever the mood of one or the other dictated.

"George is a good lad at heart," Aunt Catherine said suddenly. "But I'm afraid he has it in for anybody in a British uniform."

"Oh?"

"His maternal grandparents had their plantation and home burned to the ground by the English army in the War of Independence. And, like a good republican, he's taken up the resentment with the zeal of a convert."

"What's he doing up here, then?"

"Ah—he only hates the English when they're in tunics." She smiled wryly. "And I think he feels that Upper Canadians will soon come to their senses, throw off their shackles, and join the Union."

Aunt Catherine was fiddling with something in the pocket of her apron, and when she caught Marc noticing it, she stopped abruptly. "But he's got a head for business, and if he settles down and proves himself, Beth and I plan to buy into a haberdashery down the street on his behalf."

"What *is* that you're toying with?" Marc asked, more amused than irritated.

Aunt Catherine looked suddenly solemn. "I went to the post office at noon and saw a letter there for you from Beth."

"Well, for heaven's sake, let's open it and read the good news together."

"I—I wasn't sure it would be good news and so, very selfishly, I decided to wait till we'd finished our supper."

Marc smiled assurance, and took the letter from her

trembling hand. He began reading it aloud, editing only those parts obviously intended for his eyes only. As was her custom, Beth wrote her weekly missive in installments as things happened around her or came into her mind. Hence the first two pages were detailed accounts of the harvest (healthy yields, ruinous prices), Aaron's improving health, Winnifred's brave front in respect to the baby's being overdue, Thomas's occasional stints on annual road-duty, the fancies and foibles of the unmarried Huggan girls, and so on. At the top of page three came the news they were both hoping for: Winnifred was delivered of a baby girl, mother and child having come through their mutual ordeal in fine shape.

"Wonderful!" Aunt Catherine cried. "And that means all the plans we made for the wedding are actually going to happen! It's hard to believe."

Marc seconded that.

"Is there more?"

"Yes. The babe's been named Mary, and Beth says, 'When Winn told me that she and Thomas had called the girl Mary, after his late mother, I burst into tears, and quite alarmed Thomas. Then, without thinking, I told them about the story you related to me last March in Cobourg about the Aunt Mary who died before you were born and whose sudden death so upset your uncle Jabez that he could never speak about her in public or private again. I hope you don't mind me telling that bit of family history, for I consider it part of our history now. Anyways, the Ladies Aid of the church are now moving straight ahead on the details of the ceremony a week from next Sunday. I expect you and Auntie will be getting more than one letter a week from now until that wondrous day. All my love, Beth.'"

"Well, such news as this calls for a celebratory drink," Marc said, reaching for the sherry. Included among the "good news" was the fact that Thomas Goodall was too busy with the harvest, road-duty, and a new babe to be involved with Mackenzie's rabble-rousers. "What do you say?"

"Oh my, Marc, I forgot to tell you, but I've been anticipating this letter so much it slipped my mind."

"Not *bad* news?"

"No, no. Quite the opposite. As part payment for mending their costumes, the theatre people have promised me two box seats for tonight's play. It's a French farce of some sort, so it ought to be mildly diverting."

Marc grinned. "It'll take a lot to divert my thoughts tonight, but let's give the theatre folk a chance to try."

SEVEN

Marc took Aunt Catherine's arm and they strolled eastward along King Street in the cool twilight of the Indian summer that the city had enjoyed for several weeks: warm and dry in the day and frosty and dry during the lengthening nights. As a result, streets and roads were amazingly passable, and conditions for the fall harvest were the best in recent memory.

The play was to start at eight-thirty, so they stretched their fifteen-minute walk to Colborne and West Market Streets to half an hour, pausing to enjoy the window displays of the many shops along King. At Church Street they admired the way the white stone of the courthouse and the jail seemed to have absorbed the last of the sun's light and were now radiating it back into the semi-dark. Reluctantly, they turned south to

Colborne, and swung east again towards West Market, a short block away. They were greeted by a scene that was anything but pastoral.

"Well, I didn't expect this!" Aunt Catherine said.

Neither had Marc. Ogden Frank had pulled out all the stops for the four-day run of the Bowery Touring Company, the first professional troupe to grace his Regency Theatre. He had set bright candle-lanterns on stanchions all along the boardwalk in front of the building. Into their pools of light spilled a dozen carriages and their stamping, fretful teams. The rutted but dry streets had tempted the more prosperous citizens to drive to the Regency in style, though the reception was nowhere near as orderly as they might have wished. Frank had evidently hired a number of stable boys to act as grooms, footmen, and greeters—a few even wore some sort of ill-fitting crimson livery—but the lads, eager enough, were occasioning more confusion than courtesy. A team of matched grays and their vehicle was being hauled towards the stable yard with one outraged gentleman still in it, while his bonneted lady stood in befuddlement under the canopy of the false balcony. Another extravagantly attired chatelaine had her brand-new, imported boot stepped on by an anxious greeter, and in jerking away in pain, she managed to put the other boot into a puddle of fresh horse-dung. Farther down at the corner, a lead-horse had taken offense at the strange hand on its bridle and bolted, the vacant carriage clattering behind like a rudderless skiff. The sidewalks on both sides of Colborne were now jammed with couples and parties jostling and otherwise enjoying the drama on the street.

Aunt Catherine laughed out loud. "It's like a dance at the Grange run by the inmates of Bedlam!"

Ogden Frank himself was oblivious to these minor lapses of organization, for he stood proudly in front of the oaken double-doors, accoutred in the military uniform his father had worn at the Battle of Lundy's Lane. He exclaimed his welcomes so effusively that no one except his wife had any idea what he was sputtering at them. Madge Frank stood just behind him and took tickets from those few people she didn't know and tried her best to smile on those she did. The three Frank children were acting as ushers inside, guiding patrons to their boxes or pointing others to the gallery above or the benches in the pit.

Marc boosted Aunt Catherine up the final step and into their box at the back-left of the main room. He held out a chair for her, then sat down beside her. There were two other chairs in the box, but no-one else came to join them.

"*Milady Surprised,*" Aunt Catherine read from the hastily printed program. "*A Farce in Two Acts.* I think we'd better brace ourselves."

Marc was looking at the transformed theatre around him. Candles, which had been lit in candelabra along the walls, threw a wash of pale light over the hundred or so people who were now filling the available seats. The stage area itself was brightly lit from above by three chandeliers and from below by six Argand lamps that served as footlights. Several flats had been erected at the rear of the stage to give the illusion of a windowed interior, and the most prominent feature of the various domestic props within it was a gigantic bed—Jeremiah's handiwork, no doubt.

"I see what you mean," Marc said.

To the left of the stage, near the curtained door, the enterprising Franks had set up a bar, behind which was temptingly displayed a tapped keg of ale. The interval should prove lively, Marc thought, even if the play doesn't.

"Oh, there're your friends, I think," Aunt Catherine said.

In a box on the wall opposite but right next to the stage itself sat Owen Jenkin and Rick Hilliard among several other officers from the garrison. Rick was leaning on the railing, the better to stare into Tessa's eyes during the performance. Jenkin waved at Marc and smiled. In the other two boxes across from him, Marc noticed many familiar faces from among the members of the Family Compact, along with two ardent Reformers, Robert Baldwin and Francis Hincks. Those in the pit and the gallery at the back looked to be a cross-section of tradesmen, small businessmen, and local farmers out on the town.

"My God, I don't believe what I'm seeing!"

"What is it, Marc?"

"Over there, in the front row of the gallery. It's Constable Cobb."

"Why, so it is," Aunt Catherine said cheerfully, and waved

a hanky until she got Cobb's attention. In turn he waved and smiled, as did the woman seated beside him.

"And he's brought Dora. How nice."

"You've met his wife?"

"Oh, yes. Horatio brought her along one day last August, for a new hat. She's a very interesting woman."

Constable Cobb had been a significant and courageous partner in the investigation Marc had led into the death of a privy councillor, during which the policeman had had occasion to visit the millinery shop and, thereafter, to stop in on his patrol regularly for tea and gossip. Since then, Marc had bumped into Cobb on the street from time to time, and always spent a few minutes reminiscing about their joint adventure. But the rough-edged constable's appearance in the audience of a French farce surprised him. Was he here on some sort of official business? Nothing more could be said about the matter, however, because the players had now arrived onstage to an enthusiastic welcome from the drama-starved citizens of Toronto and York County.

Mrs. Thedford had assured them earlier that what they would see this evening would not in any way reflect the fractious goings-on of the afternoon rehearsal. And she was right. These were professionals through and through. Tessa's French maid, in black satin and crocheted cap-and-apron, was sprightly, and her staccato dialogue and double-takes delivered with a speed and confidence that belied her youth and inexperience. Even the Yankee twang and dropped *g*'s had vanished. And, as Mrs. Thedford had insisted, it was Dorothea Clarkson who did have to carry the play as the paramour of the philandering husband in the piece. As such, she was plopped in and under and behind the big, adulterous bed at stage-centre, in addition to being stuffed into a trunk and made immobile behind an arras, all the while emitting a series of aborted shrieks, cries of surprise, and wails of uncorrectable regret set amongst sympathy-gaining appeals to the capricious gods of love. She gave no sign of illness or fatigue and, in fact, her energy seemed to feed on the laughter she drew in raucous waves from every corner of the theatre.

Merriwether played the ageing, and alas married, roué with stolid good humour, while Mrs. Thedford shone as the outraged wife, even though her scenes were few in Act One. Clarence Beasley played the hapless bumpkin from the country in hopeless pursuit of Mistress Thea with much body-wit and mugging of face, qualities that Marc would not have inferred from the young man's somewhat wooden attempts at Shakespeare. Here the dreadful nasalities from south of the border were deliberately deployed to great comic effect. Finally, if Dawson Armstrong had unearthed another bottle of whiskey, it did nothing to diminish his polished performance as the innkeeper who is the ostensible friend and co-conspirator of the cheating spouse but at the same time lusts after his chum's wife when he isn't ogling the maid.

The first act ended with a burst of applause and approbation that was sustained for a full minute. In the midst of which it occurred to Marc that here in this simple chamber was represented a cross-section of Upper Canadian society, including the staunchest members of both the Tory and Reform parties, and they had just joined together, spontaneously, in a kind of communal laughter in which social boundaries and political divisions had been magically dissolved. It was hard to believe that at this moment treasonous rallies might actually be taking place within a mile of where they were sitting.

"You can bring me up a glass of wine if they have any," Aunt Catherine said to Marc as he started down the ladder from their box. "I don't fancy risking those steps again."

Marc nodded and stepped down into the crush below. After he had handed up a glass to Aunt Catherine, Marc nudged his way through the throng and thickening pipe-smoke to where Cobb and Dora were standing at the foot of the ladder to the gallery, munching on apples they had brought with them. They had not spotted him yet, so Marc stopped for a second to have a long look at Cobb and gain some first impressions of his wife.

Cobb looked much the same as he always did, a sinewy troll of a man with a face that could have played Nym or Bardolph on the Regency's stage without makeup, and an incongruous pot-belly that had no forewarning slope to it, top or bottom: it was as abrupt as a butte on a prairie. Tonight, though, it was partially camouflaged by the waistcoat of the suit he was wearing, one that had probably been his wedding attire, with the trousers now let out several inches and lapels that were a good foot from meeting each other. A bowler hat concealed the uprising of his soot-black hair. And while the angular features were softened by shadow, the mellow but flickering candlelight accelerated the glow of his big nose and the wart blinking nearby.

Mrs. Dora Cobb was something else again. Marc thought instantly of Mr. Spratt and his missus, for Dora was as round as she was high (which wasn't more than four foot ten), but her obesity was modulated by the perfect neatness of her dress and person, by the tightly curled black hair, by the Indian-bead necklace placed just so, by the exact meridian of her wide leather belt, by the creaseless fit of her blouse and skirt, and by the trim shoes on surprisingly tiny feet. She so resembled a child's bulbous top that Marc was chary of bumping against her for fear he might set her rolling out of control. Her expression peered out at the world from a penumbra of cheeks and chins that merely accentuated the cheerful kindliness of her whole demeanour, while the eyes alone signalled that here was a woman who, when challenged, would brook no nonsense and give no quarter.

"How nice to see you again, Constable," Marc said heartily.

"Evenin', Major," Cobb said, using his nickname for Marc. "Enjoyin' the carryin's-on?"

"And this must be—"

"Dora Cobb," said Mrs. Cobb in a rich alto voice, amplified no doubt by her diva's lungs and bosom. She darted a critical glance at her husband for his lapse of manners.

Cobb winced, but kept his smile going.

"Pleased to make your acquaintance, ma'am." Marc reached out to take her hand preparatory to bussing it. Before he could accomplish this standard gesture of courtesy, Dora latched onto the offering with both of her ample palms and began levering it up and down, as if she were trying to prime a balky pump.

"Well, it's bloody well time we met," she boomed. "I was beginnin' to suspect Mr. Cobb was deliberately keepin' you to himself. Either that or you had two heads an' three eyes!"

"Now, Missus Cobb, you know that ain't—"

"Truth is, you're as high up an' as handsome as the ladies of the town—if I may defer to them as such—have been tellin' me. You're enough to make a gal's knees buckle."

"Now, Missus Cobb—"

"I'd be pleased, Mr. Cobb, if you'd desist and decease from 'Missus-Cobbing' me like some woodpecker with his peck jammed!"

"Are you enjoying the play?" Marc said quickly.

"A powerful lot of jumpin' in an' outta bed, wasn't there?" Dora said approvingly, "accompanied by a great deal of 'pleasure *inta-ruptured*'!" She shot a teasing glance at Cobb to be sure he had caught her mimic of his habitual play on words.

Cobb was about to protest but thought better of it.

"I am pleased to see so many people come out to the theatre," Marc offered.

"And I see you're a mite surprised to spot the likes of us here?" Dora said with a wry grin.

Marc denied any such thing, while silently remarking that little in the behaviour of those around Dora Cobb would go unnoticed or unappraised.

"In my case, curiosity, more'n anythin' else," Cobb said.

"Nonsense, Mr. Cobb, an' you know it!" She turned to Marc, pivoting her entire person to do so. "Why, old James Cobb was a regular *thesbian* in his day. He'd rather jump on a stump an' recite a bawdy ballad than he would haul it away to make room fer his corn. And at our weddin' in Woodstock, the old rapscallion hopped on a table durin' the toasts an' spieled out every last verse of Mr. Gray's '*Eligible* in a Country Church'!"

"Now, Missus Cobb, do not *eggs-agitate*—"

"An' this crab apple here—warts an' all—didn't fall far from the tree."

Dora began a chuckle somewhere deep within, and while it worked its way out, Cobb said to Marc, "Funny, but we ain't had a *gen-u-wine* murder in town since you an' young Hilliard skedaddled off to the fort last year."

"Then I must be sure to stay put."

"So, when are you gonna come to our place for supper?" Dora said loud enough to turn heads ten feet away. "All I get is feeble excuses from Mr. Cobb, but now I'm lookin' right at the flesh-an'-blood—"

"You're embarrassin' Marc," Cobb said, part plea and part warning. "Ain't she, Major?"

"Not in the least. I'd be pleased to come," Marc said, initially out of politeness and good breeding, but then with a growing sense of enthusiasm. Why shouldn't he have supper with these good people? Who was he, pretending to be a gentleman, when he himself was the offspring of a gamekeeper and his peasant wife, and one who had had the undeserved fortune of being raised up by a lonely bachelor and member of the petty aristocracy?

"How about Wensd'y? Say, six o'clock? I'll hide the chickens an' make the pig stay outside till we're done."

"*Missus* Cobb!" The constable's wart ignited.

Marc laughed. "I'll be there with bells on."

"Long as they don't wake the goat!"

At this point Cobb was spared any further discomfort by the reappearance of the players upon the stage, announced by three blasts of a trumpet from the wings. Jeremiah Jefferson making a wayward, joyful noise, perhaps?

WHEN THE PLAY ENDED AND THE last of six curtain calls was gracefully acknowledged, Marc led Aunt Catherine towards the exit onto Colborne Street. "I'll walk you home, then come back here for my horse," he said.

"Sure you won't come up to Mrs. Thedford's room for a nightcap?" Owen Jenkin called out just behind them. "We've all been invited." He looked imploringly at Marc, who suddenly got the message.

"Both Aunt Catherine and I have had a long day, Owen. And some personal excitement I'll tell you about later."

"Yes," Aunt Catherine said agreeably. "It's past ten-thirty and I've a full work-day tomorrow. We're mending some costumes for the company here."

"Where's Rick, then?" Marc said.

"Probably in the ingenue's boudoir, if I know him."

"I sincerely hope he behaves himself."

"I'll see to it, Marc."

"I'll wait for you outside when I come back from the shop in about half an hour, and we can all ride home together."

"That should work out well for everybody. See you then." And he trundled off to throw himself at the feet of the prima donna from Philadelphia and New York.

Just as Marc and Aunt Catherine started along Colborne, Cobb popped out of the alley leading to the stables. He had his bowler in both hands. "You don't haveta come," he said with acute embarrassment. "Dora gets carried away sometimes."

"I'm coming on Wednesday because I want to, old friend," Marc assured him.

MAJOR JENKIN WAS WAITING AT THE livery stable with two horses in hand.

"Where's Rick?" Marc wondered, a rhetorical question in the circumstances.

Jenkin nodded up towards the theatre. "He swore to me as an officer and a gentleman that he would have one drink with Miss Guildersleeve and leave when she asked him. Mrs.

Thedford was very gracious with me: I was utterly charmed by her. But I'm afraid I may have inadvertently misled her into thinking Rick was going to leave when I did. Tessa is really like an adopted daughter to her, and it's hard enough for actresses to gain respect without having footloose soldiers dallying in their rooms. But I wasn't going to go barging in on the youngsters like an outraged papa."

"I think Rick believes he's truly in love with the girl. The odds are he won't do anything to harm her reputation. But you're right: Rick's a grown man, and I'm sure he realizes that Tessa's guardian is next door. Come on, let's be on our way."

The two men, so recently and unexpectedly friends, rode out together towards the garrison a meandering mile or so west of the city centre under a splendid moon and a backdrop of stars. They fell into easy conversation.

"I thought the days of this old war-horse dreaming about a particular woman were over, Marc. But Annemarie is really something."

"So I gather. I must say she impressed me tremendously. In a motherly way, of course," he added with an appropriate chuckle.

"I asked her about Merriwether, for example, because the man intrigues me. Unlike her, I got the feeling he was acting out a role for himself, perhaps because he wasn't happy with who he really was. Well, she told me the whole story. Seems he was a great star of the Park Theatre for twenty years, before his wife died and he hit the bottle. By the time Annemarie arrived in New York from Philadelphia and established herself, about fifteen years ago, Merriwether was on the way down. She'd met him while she was doing bit roles at the Park and admired his talent. Five years later she had become a star and part owner of the Bowery, and took it upon herself—when everyone else in the theatre world of New York was shunning him—to take a chance on the man, on condition that he give up the drink and attempt to regain his former lustre."

"As Tessa remarked, the woman has a weakness for strays."

"That's an approach I'll have to consider."

"Well, it's obvious she succeeded in rehabilitating him."

"Almost. But she admitted to me, after assuring me they had never been, ah, intimate, that while Merriwether did regain much of his lost talent, he remained a difficult and often unattractive human being."

"I expect she did what she could. And as professionals, they have certainly worked well together, as the mounting of the farce tonight showed. I've seen pieces like that botched many times in Drury Lane itself."

"She seems a very giving person to me. She was kind enough to ask me about my experiences in the war, knowing full well, I trust, that such an opening is in danger of never being closed thereafter. Anyway, I did chatter on about Sandhurst and Portugal and Paris and the exploits of the Iron Duke."

"I envy you that," Marc sighed.

"Please, don't, son. War is tolerable only when you're well away from it."

MARC WAS IN THE MIDDLE OF a dream in which Beth was floating somewhere just above the foot of his bed, beckoning to him as her nightdress sailed away behind her, when a cold finger on his chin brought him reluctantly awake.

"Beth?" he murmured.

"It's Corporal Bregman, sir. Sorry to wake you up at this hour. I've come straight from Colonel Margison."

Marc sat up, shivering in the cold room. It could be no more than 2 a.m. Why would one of Margison's orderlies be rousing him in the middle of the night?

"What is it?"

"Instructions, sir. For you."

"At this hour?"

"I'm afraid so. A fast horse is being saddled for you right now. You are to proceed at once to the Regency Theatre."

"What's happened?"

"One of the actors has been murdered."

Mark glanced quickly at Rick's cot. It was empty.

"Is Hilliard all right?" Marc asked.

"Not quite, sir." Bregman had turned white.

"What do you mean, 'not quite'?"

Bregman gulped hard, and said almost in a whisper, "They're saying he done it."

EIGHT

Marc did his best to shut down his naturally speculative mind as he rode furiously towards the city from the fort, soon leaving behind the young messenger who had brought the disturbing news. But until he knew which actor had been murdered and whether Bregman's comment about Rick Hilliard's being an accused killer was itself speculation or fact, there was no point in fretting unnecessarily. Nonetheless, there was no denying that something terrible must have happened for Colonel Margison to have become involved and issue commands in the wee hours of a Tuesday morning. It was with a genuine sense of dread that Marc pounded up Colborne Street towards Frank's Hotel.

He was about to wheel into the alley that led to the stables when he spotted someone in uniform waving at him from under the false balcony in front of the theatre. It was Ogden Frank, still in his militia outfit. Though the street was silent and utterly deserted, Frank was motioning him to dismount quickly, while glancing left and right as if he expected shutters to be flung open all along the thoroughfare.

In a hoarse, frightened whisper, he said to Marc, "My boy'll see to your horse; just leave it here and come inside right away. Nobody else knows what's happened upstairs, and we'd all like to keep it that way."

All? Who else had arrived ahead of him?

"They're waitin' fer ya inside."

Marc followed Frank through the double-doors, which Frank was careful to secure with a bar, and into the theatre itself, now steeped in gloomy shadow. The proprietor seemed able to navigate without benefit of light, and led the way through the curtained door at the right side of the stage and up the stairs towards the actors' rooms above.

"I don't know what I've done to deserve such a calamity as this," Frank was muttering ahead of him. "If this news gets out, I'll be ruined. I'll have to store hay in the pit."

On the landing—with a candle-lamp in hand, a uniform more dishevelled than usual, and hair rearing up at all angles from a helmetless head—stood Constable Horatio Cobb.

"Thank Christ you're here, Marc. This is the worst bloody mess I've ever seen. It's like an abattoir up there."

"Where's Hilliard?"

"He's in the tavern, through that door at the foot of the stairs, in the charmin' arms of General Spooner."

"Spooner?" Lieutenant Barclay Spooner was the governor's current aide-de-camp, the man who had succeeded Marc in Bond Head's office. "Sir Francis is in on this? What the hell has happened?"

"I'll show you in a minute, though it ain't pretty. Doc Withers is upstairs an' Sarge is in the tavern herdin' all them *hyster-ect-ical* actors an' makin' sure General Spooner don't set off another war with the States." "Sarge" was Cobb's colleague, Chief Constable Wilfrid Sturges.

So that was it, Marc thought: one of the American actors had been murdered and one of ours—a British officer—had been accused of the crime. That would be more than enough to bring the governor wide-awake with his political antennae twitching.

"Go on back to the tavern, Ogden," Cobb said not unkindly to Frank, who was dry-washing his hands in futile frenzy, "an' help Sarge keep a stopper in Spooner's gob, if you can."

Frank nodded, thankful to be doing something other than contemplating his imminent financial ruin.

"Who is the victim?" Marc asked as he and Cobb reached the hallway on the second floor. The name he had been repressing for the last half-hour now forced its way into his consciousness: Tessa Guildersleeve.

"The fella who played the whorin' husband," Cobb said, pointing the way towards the far end of the hall.

"Jason Merriwether?" Marc asked, astonished. How in the world could Hilliard have been involved in murdering Merriwether?

"That's the fella. Stabbed through the chest with Hilliard's sword."

Yes, Marc recalled, Hilliard had strapped on his sabre before leaving earlier in the day in order to impress the girl. "I can't believe that, Cobb."

"Me neither, Major. But they claim he was found with both hands on the haft."

Marc froze in his tracks. Whatever he had been steeling himself for, it was not this.

"In here," Cobb said, easing open the door to Tessa's room. "Brace yerself."

Someone had brought one of the Argand lamps from the stage to illuminate Tessa's room, in addition to several other lit candles. Marc was unprepared for the sudden light that greeted him when he entered. He blinked, then slowly directed his gaze towards the horrors on the carpeted expanse before him.

Jason Merriwether lay flat on his back, as if he had just made the perfect theatrical pratfall and was waiting for a burst of applause before popping up to take a bow. But the famous tragedian and farceur had taken his last curtain call. Like a stake driven through a vampire's heart, Hilliard's battle-sword was sticking straight up out of Merriwether's chest and, in the unsteady candlelight, appeared to be still quivering from the force of the blow. The details surrounding this pièce de résistance Marc took in at a single glance. Blood had geysered out of the wound, splashed indiscriminately over the victim's nightshirt from throat to crotch, trickled down his bare thighs, and was still seeping into the beige carpet. Angus Withers, physician and surgeon to the rich and highborn, the governor's personal doctor, and county coroner, was crouched beside Merriwether's head. With his fingertips he was probing a vicious wound at the base of the cranium. That area of the skull appeared to have been crushed by a blow made either by a heavy, blunt object or something lighter delivered with tremendous force. From his vantage-point several feet away, Marc could see pieces of bone protruding through matted hair and blood. Had the man been attacked twice?

Dr. Withers looked up and flashed Marc a grim smile of recognition and welcome. They had met briefly during Marc's second investigation and taken an instant liking to each other. "Looks like somebody wanted to make sure he went straight to his Maker," Withers said, and picked up from the pool of blood on the far side of the body a large, bronze ashtray. "This could've been used on his skull, but I can't be sure. It was already covered with blood when I found it here."

But Marc could not take his eyes off Hilliard's sabre. There was no doubt that it belonged to Rick: the initials *RH* were visible even through the gore smeared all over it. Had the killer dipped his hands in the victim's blood? Surely the founting of it from the wound could not have reached the haft on its own.

"I'm damned glad you and Cobb are here. That jackass Spooner roused me from a rare erotic dream to inform me that the governor was near apoplexy—again, I must add—over the murder of some prominent American by one of his officers in a den of iniquity. Spooner had orders, duly passed along to me, to keep this mess contained. What he didn't know was that Frank panicked after visiting Government House and beetled on down to the police station and blabbed it all to Chief Constable Sturges, who had fallen asleep in his office."

"An' that's like disruptin' a hibernatin' bear," Cobb said gleefully. "It was me who took the brunt of his temper when he come fer me, though Missus Cobb herself was just comin' home from one of her customers an' managed to keep him from poppin' the buttons off his vest."

"Which blow killed Merriwether, then?" Marc asked, suddenly hoping that there might be some explanation other than the obvious.

Withers gave the question careful thought before answering. "Well, it seems certain the blow to the back of the head stunned him, and he must have tried to stand up before collapsing onto his back right here where you see him. That blow alone would eventually have resulted in his death, but I am compelled to say honestly—and will have to testify so—that the sword to the chest was the immediate cause of death. I can say this with certainty because the heart was still pumping blood when the sword-blade cut the aorta. You can see the consequences for yourself. In fact, the sword is imbedded in the floor under the body."

"But why would anyone crush the man's skull and then savagely drive a sword through him?"

"That's for you to discover, lad," Withers said.

"What do you mean?"

"Looks like the governor may have forgiven you your apostasy. Among the orders he issued to Lieutenant Spooner, who as we know will obey them to the letter no matter how repugnant to him personally, was that you are to lead the investigation. Spooner's charge is to keep things contained until you catch the murderer."

"That explains why my colonel was involved." Marc was trying to take in what he was seeing and being told, while still trying not to think the unthinkable. "But how could all this have been managed in such a short time? Major Jenkin and I left Rick here with Tessa Guildersleeve no later than eleven-thirty or so."

"Whatever provoked this carnage didn't take long to develop because we know the precise time it took place," Withers said. "The actor who found the body—"

"The fella who played the country bumpkin—Beasley," Cobb said.

"Yes, Beasley. He heard the scream and came running in here at twelve-thirty, according to that clock in the corner."

"What scream?" Marc said.

"Tell Marc what we think we know," Withers said, getting

up and moving over to Tessa's bed. As Marc watched him, he noticed several things he had not observed before: droplets and smudges of blood were scattered on the carpet in an irregular trail from the feet of victim to the settee, where more blood was smeared, one patch of which appeared to resemble a handprint. Had the killer wallowed in Merriwether's gore, then gone back and sat on the settee to admire his handiwork?

"I've only had a chance to talk to Beasley, so we've got just his version of what happened," Cobb said. "But I gotta say he's the only one of that whole bunch who ain't gone *bear-serk* on us. The women are squallin' like heifers with their teats tied, an' that fella Armstrong's as drunk as a skunk. The mute seems fine, but he ain't sayin' much, of course."

"Beasley heard Tessa scream at twelve-thirty?"

"Well, you'll need to *interro-grate* 'em yerself, but what he told Sarge an' me when we got here a while ago, was a woman's scream woke him up, an' by the time he got himself awake an' figured out where the scream'd come from, he found Ensign Hilliard standin' over the body with both hands wrapped 'round the handle of the sword."

"But what was Merriwether doing in Tessa's room after midnight?"

Here Cobb glanced beseechingly at Withers, who grimaced and said, "It gets worse, laddie. Hilliard was seen going into the girl's room with her about eleven o'clock, laughing and carrying on like lovebirds."

"That's right," Marc said. "Owen Jenkin left him there

shortly thereafter and we rode home together. But Rick had promised the major he would do nothing dishonourable and, in fact, would stay no more than half an hour for a single glass of sherry."

"And he may well have kept that promise," Withers said solemnly. "We found Tessa comatose on the bed there, and it's possible Hilliard may have dozed off. The room was quite dark when Beasley entered it with a candle in his hand, except for the little swath of moonlight coming through the window and that stub of candle beside the bed. Cobb and I speculate that Merriwether must have come in a bit later expecting Tessa to be alone, probably with evil intentions on his mind."

"That makes sense," Marc said, thinking hard. "We spent yesterday afternoon watching the actors rehearse, and all three of us saw Merriwether make an improper gesture while carrying Tessa in his arms. And, I must admit frankly, she seemed to approve of the assault, though her guardian, Mrs. Thedford, did not."

"And if it was almost dark in here," Cobb added, "he mightn't've spotted Hilliard dozin' on the settee an' . . ."

"And forced his attentions on the young lady," Withers said as delicately as he could.

"And you think Rick heard Tessa scream for help, woke up, grabbed the ashtray—"

"Or the butt of his sword," Withers said. "It's smeared with blood, too, so we can't be sure."

"In either case he smashed the villain on the back of the head to prevent his ravishing the girl," Marc said with a rush.

"Which means he was justified in his actions. Tessa did scream, did she not? That's the critical point."

"Loud enough to wake Beasley up at the other end of the hall," Cobb said.

"But why not any of the others?"

"That's easy," Cobb said. "Armstrong was pissed to the gills in his room. When Frank got up here shortly afterwards, he went in to check on him and the old sot couldn't remember what country he was in."

"But Mrs. Thedford's room is next to this one, a thin wall away."

"That's so," Cobb said, "but she was asleep in that little bedroom on the far side of her . . . whaddycallit—"

"Her suite."

"—with wax plugs in her ears, accordin' to Beasley, who woke her up," Cobb finished.

"And Jeremiah is deaf."

"An' the other woman, the one who played the connivin' mistress, was stayin' downstairs with the Franks."

"So you figure Hilliard bashed Merriwether's brains in, probably because he had been wakened suddenly, was confused, heard and saw a young woman he was desperately in love with being assaulted by a large stranger clad only in a nightshirt—remember, Merriwether was almost six feet tall and powerfully built—and simply reacted as any officer and gentleman would have in the circumstances?"

"I wish that were so," Withers said sadly. "Then there would be some hope for Hilliard. But when Beasley got here, no more than two or three minutes after the girl screamed, Hilliard was stooped over the blackguard about to pull his sword out of Merriwether's chest. And that, in any court in the kingdom, is premeditated murder."

It was simply impossible for Marc to accept this version of events. Hilliard's passion and romantic folly might account for the reflex action of defending his lady's honour by any means within his reach. But then to have drawn his sabre and, looking down into the face of Tessa's disabled assailant, raise it above his head with calm deliberation and drive it through Merriwether's chest—well, that was something he was absolutely certain Rick Hilliard would never do. Not even in the heat of battle. The very thought of such an ignominious act was monstrous.

"I figured at first," Cobb said, "that maybe one person banged on the noggin and another put the sword in. But there wasn't enough time. Beasley come runnin' from the end of the hall where the stairs are, so nobody could've dashed in an' done the stabbin' an' run back out again without Beasley seein' him."

"And the girl couldn't've done it," Withers said. "Even if she was faking being unconscious, she isn't strong enough to have driven that heavy sword into Merriwether, not even in a rage. Besides which, she would've been covered in blood."

"Like the ensign was," Cobb felt obliged to add.

"Well, I'm going to question Clarence Beasley very closely, you can be sure. We've only got his word for all this."

"It seems the mute was on the scene shortly as well," Withers said. "And Hilliard, of course."

"Has Rick said anything about this? Surely he's denied it."

Withers fielded that query with reluctance. "He's said very little. He's fanatically worried about the girl, but I've given her a sleeping draught and put her into Madge Frank's care for the night."

"He hasn't admitted anything?"

"All he says is that he fell asleep while he and the girl were sparking on the settee, and when he woke up he was standing over the corpse in the dark and wondering what had happened—when Beasley came in and found him."

"But surely he couldn't have slept through a woman screaming rape and be uncertain whether he had hit Merriwether on the head, waited till he was flat on his back and then skewered him, while the blood gushed all over him? And, don't forget, he also had time to go back to the settee, sit down for a spell, then get up and go over to retrieve his sword. And all this while sleepwalking? I don't believe it for a minute."

Dr. Withers was standing beside the night-table that held Tessa's little candle, a half-full decanter of sherry, and two empty glasses. He ran the decanter, unstoppered, slowly under his nose, then, very carefully, took a minuscule sip and let the wine roll over his tongue. "He may not have been sleepwalking." He pushed his nostrils into each of the glasses. "Laudanum," he said. "A lot of it. Enough, I'd say, to knock an elephant to its knees."

"But that means that both Tessa and Rick were drugged," Marc cried, his hopes rising. "And there's only one reason I can think of why that would happen. It's obvious, isn't it, that Merriwether slipped in here sometime yesterday—everybody in the troupe knew that Tessa took a glass of sherry before she went to bed after a performance—and put laudanum into the decanter. He couldn't have known that Rick would be up here sharing the sherry with her when he first put the opiate into it. Later on, I'm sure he knew Rick was in Tessa's room, and maybe he was inflamed with jealousy, and came across the hall, peered in, and found both of them comatose. And I'd lay odds that he decided then and there to have his way with the girl, and when she woke later, she would assume Rick had been her assailant. How she might have reacted, we don't know, but Merriwether certainly knew how Mrs. Thedford would have taken the outrage. So the blackguard would be able to enjoy Tessa and have Rick take any consequences. All he had to do was snuff the candles out and set about the dastardly deed."

"Well, that's plausible," Withers said. "But how will we ever know what really happened if Tessa and Hilliard were indeed unconscious? And if they'd had more than a mouthful of this stuff, they would have been. Neither of them can give us rational testimony."

"In the meantime," Cobb said, "we got a witness who swears he saw Hilliard with the murder weapon in his clutches an' with the whole front of his tunic covered in blood. You'll see it for yourself."

"And, alas," Withers said with a sad shake of his head, "with his flies wide open."

"You're not implying that Rick was the girl's attacker? That's preposterous."

When neither Withers nor Cobb responded to that assessment, Marc continued. "There must be blood on Merriwether's privates!"

"There was blood everywhere—on both men."

"Well, if there's a court-martial, I'll argue that Rick was drugged, dazed, provoked to his actions by the noblest of motives, and was therefore not wholly responsible for what he may have done."

"You gonna take out yer *law-yer's* licence again?" Cobb enquired.

"Even so," Withers said, "it's a stretch to claim that a befuddled man with altruistic intent pulled a battle-sword out of its scabbard and drove it unerringly through the centre of Merriwether's chest so forcefully that it stuck in the floor under him."

"Damn it all, that's what I'm saying!" Marc shouted. "Dazed or sober, my friend Rick Hilliard could not have done that. He had already saved the girl he loved from harm. He had maimed the assailant. What could possibly have incited him to such a senseless, despicable act?"

"Maybe it was this," Cobb said, holding his lantern high over Tessa's bed.

There on the white, freshly starched sheet was a bloodstain, no bigger than a virgin's fist.

NINE

Having covered the body with a sheet and snuffed the candles, the three men went out into the hall.

"I don't want the corpse moved or anything else touched in there," Marc said. "I'll need to examine the room in the morning light. And we can't have anyone who might conceivably have been involved going in overnight to tamper with the evidence."

Dr. Withers reached into his medical bag, pulled out a wad of sealing wax, softened it in his fingers, and pushed it into the slim crack between the door and the sash near the floor. "How's that?" he said with a wink. "You'll know if a mouse tries to break and enter."

Cobb was leaning over the sill of the hall window that

overlooked Colborne Street. "Nobody's come in here," he said, dragging a finger through the thick dust. "Least not since the invasion of Muddy York."

"Unless the interloper was part monkey, able to climb vertical brick walls," Withers added, "you'll have to devote your attention to those people who were in this building from eleven o'clock onward."

"And if they'd tried a ladder under the girl's window, it'd've been stickin' out on Colborne Street like a roofer's thumb," Cobb said. "But I'll check the alley an' street fer any signs just the same."

"Someone could have hidden around the stage area and waited for his chance," Marc said, grasping at straws.

"Then how did the bugger get out again?" Cobb said. "Frank swore to the God of all Orangemen that the front doors an' privy-exit were barred from the inside right after Major Jenkin left. And when he lit out fer Government House, he went out through his own quarters with his wife standing watch. Anybody leavin' that way couldn't've barred the door after them from the outside: when Sarge and I got here, those theatre doors were still barred."

Marc sighed.

"An' there's no other way out of the theatre," Cobb continued, "except through the tavern, an' that door was locked with a slidin' bolt by Frank before he went to bed, as usual."

They were now heading down the only stairs towards the stage and the tavern just behind it.

"All right, all right," Marc said testily. "It's a long shot, I confess. Certainly we've got to focus on the actors first, though I'm not going to rule out Ogden Frank or his wife, or even Thea Clarkson: any one of them could have left their quarters, slipped through the barroom, unbolted the door behind the bar on this side of the stage, sneaked up the stairs, and been a party to murder."

"An' sneaked back before Beasley got out into the hall, I suppose," Cobb said. "An' drippin' blood all the way?" They had spotted no bloodstains on the hall carpet, but only a thorough examination in daylight would settle the question.

"They could have been in it together! The lot of them!"

Withers pushed open the door to the tavern. "Might I suggest that we begin by looking at the obvious evidence first, then move on to the fanciful speculation?"

They emerged into a well-lit room and peered over the bar at a most arresting tableau: two rather shortish men of a middle age, each uniformed, were wrestling over possession of a set of leg irons.

"You are *not* gonna put this man in chains unless *I* say so!"

"I bear the authority of the governor, and this man is now my official prisoner! I order you to release these shackles so that I may secure the felon."

Wilfrid Sturges, erstwhile sergeant-major in Wellington's peninsular army and chief constable of the five-man municipal police force, gave a sharp pull on his half of the shackles and almost succeeded in wresting the whole from Barclay Spooner's grip. Without outside intervention, there was no doubt as to which combatant would eventually triumph. Although both men were of slight build, Lieutenant Spooner, aide-de-camp to Sir Francis Bond Head, was a man whose aggressive movements and gestures could only be described as rigidly crisp but otherwise ineffectual, while Chief Constable Sturges was slimly muscular and deceptively quick, a tough little beagle of a man. Behind them, slumped in a captain's chair with his chin in his hands, was Rick Hilliard. He looked like the sole survivor of a sanguinary battle.

"Gentlemen, would you please drop those shackles," Marc barked at the belligerents. "No one is going to put Ensign Hilliard in chains. I'm in charge of this investigation, and I'll determine who's to be labelled a prisoner and a felon."

Marc's outburst distracted Spooner long enough for Sturges to recover the leg irons and stuff them into his overcoat pocket. "Thank you, Lieutenant. I was just attemptin' to persuade Mr. Spooner 'ere on that very point."

"You are interfering with the Queen's business," Spooner spluttered, whether at Marc or Sturges was not clear, as his moustache, ruthlessly trimmed, twitched at one end and then the other.

"Are you suggesting that I am not in charge of this investigation?" Marc demanded.

"Not in the least, sir. You deliberately misapprehend my intentions. I made the not unreasonable assumption that a man brandishing a murder-weapon smeared with the victim's blood—and his roger hanging out—was, in the least, a prime suspect. Further, as the officer designated to contain the political consequences from this catastrophe, I was endeavouring to put this upstart policeman in his place."

"We'll see who's the upstart," Sturges said, his face reddening. "As far as I can see, we have a civilian murdered, possibly by an army officer, in a buildin' clearly under my jurisdiction."

"And this civilian, as you so quaintly put it, just happens to be a foreign national, making this potentially an international incident. In any event, the governor has seen fit to put Lieutenant Edwards and me exclusively in control of matters here. Mr. Frank had no authority to invite you to interfere. Do you wish me to report your insolent insubordination to my superior when I return to Government House?"

Sturges glared at him.

Marc decided to take full control. "I'll be the one to decide who I might require to assist me. Right now I wish to speak to Mr. Hilliard, without further comment from either of you. Where are the others?"

"Mr. Frank's put them over there in the dining-room," Sturges said to Marc. "I 'aven't been able to get a single, sensible sentence from any of 'em," he added with an accusatory glance at Spooner.

Marc walked to the open archway between the taproom and dining area, and peered ahead. Ogden Frank was seated at a large table, around which the remaining members of the Bowery Touring Company were arrayed. An open bottle of port and half a dozen glasses, kindly supplied by Frank, sat untouched. Marc made a quick survey of the actors, one of whom he believed had ruthlessly slaughtered another of his or her fellows. After the initial tears and incredulity, it appeared as if deep shock had taken over. Thea Clarkson, in a pink robe thrown carelessly over her shoulders, looked seriously ill. Her skin was rippled with cold sweat and she was trembling uncontrollably. Annemarie Thedford's reaction was registered in the sudden appearance of lines and wrinkles that one did not notice when she was smiling and in command of her surroundings. Her eyes, bloodshot with weeping, were kindled by more than one kind of pain; after all, she was enduring the knowledge of her ward's violation and the simultaneous loss of a professional partner in her life's work. The financial and personal loss would be both acute and irreparable.

Clarence Beasley was staring straight ahead with a glazed expression that was unreadable, but exhaustion was telegraphed in every aspect of his collapsed posture. Leaning on his shoulder, unremarked, was Dawson Armstrong, who, having sobered up enough to have realized the severity of what had happened, had then promptly fallen asleep. Lastly, Jeremiah Jefferson lay with his head on the table, holding his left cheek and moaning softly. His bloated countenance was not likely due to any remorse or particular sorrow over Merriwether's demise.

Unfortunately, Armstrong seemed to have the most obvious motive for doing away with his rival while having the least capacity for doing the deed. Thea Clarkson appeared too ill to have wielded that bloody sword, even if Marc were able to discover a motive for her. While he could envision Mrs. Thedford defending her ward against attack from any quarter, she would have to have been mad or bent on self-destruction to have plunged a sword through the heart of her own enterprise. His best bet seemed to be Beasley, although if he had smouldering depths, they were ingeniously disguised. The mute was a possibility, but a slim one. Marc wanted to sit them down one by one right then and thrash the necessary truths out of them, but he realized he would get nothing coherent from any of them until morning.

Poor Frank looked worse than any of the actors. His eyes, very far apart in his moon-face, seemed to be searching for each other without much success, and his hand-wringing was pathetic to behold. Though he was a known Orangeman who might conceivably hate Americans, it was not plausible that he had built a theatre worthy of attracting professional troupes from abroad, only to murder the first bona fide star to step onto his stage.

"What do you want us to do now?" Frank asked. "Miss Guildersleeve's asleep in our spare room and my missus is beside herself with worry."

"I'll decide what to do with everybody in a few minutes. Try to keep from despairing, sir." Other than this vacuous advice, Marc could think of nothing to say that might be remotely consoling.

"Lieutenant, it is now nearly three o'clock in the morning. The governor will be frantic—"

"Please leave me alone with Hilliard," Marc said curtly to Spooner.

"I think we should do as the lieutenant suggests," Withers said with a barely suppressed yawn.

"Five minutes, that's all!" Spooner said to Marc with a lop-sided twitch of his moustache, which simultaneously activated a similar twitch of the left eyebrow. "And I'll be standing beside the bar, where I can keep an eye on you."

"Do you want me to help?" Sturges said.

"May I have Constable Cobb to assist me?"

"Well, what do you say, Cobb?" Sturges said to his favourite constable.

Cobb had been standing aside in deference to his superior, but not without periodic, baleful glowerings at Spooner when loyalty demanded such. "Ya mean fer the rest of the time it takes us to finish the job?" he enquired.

"I do," Marc said.

"But you have no authority to deputize anybody!" Spooner bellowed from his post at the bar.

"I believe the governor will back me up," Marc said. "And this way, the local constabulary will have a say in what is at least partly their affair."

"What a fine solution," Sturges said, and moved across to join Spooner at the bar some ten paces away.

Marc took a deep breath and drew a chair up beside Rick, who had not raised his head once since Marc and the others had entered the taproom. It was doubtful if he'd even heard a word of the conversation around him. Cobb placed his generous profile between Rick and the men at the bar.

"Rick, it's me. I'm here to help you."

"Marc?" The voice was shrunken, scarcely recognizable; the eyes remained downcast. Merriwether's blood had begun to dry in ugly brown smears on his scarlet jacket with its green-and-gold trim. His flies were still untied, but the flaps had been closed. There was blood on his pants, on the backs of both hands, and on his head, where his palms had rested in despair or remorse.

"I need to talk to you, man-to-man."

"They won't tell me what happened to her."

"Tessa is resting. She's had a terrible shock, but I don't think she's badly injured."

"They won't let me see her."

"I'll talk to her the second she wakes up in the morning. That's a promise."

Rick's next statement was nearly a sob: "I'm not sure she'll want to see me."

"A lot depends on what you can tell me now, Rick. I realize that it must be horrific to think about what happened up there, but I've been sent by the governor to find the truth, all of it. Don't worry about that trumped-up martinet Spooner; I am in charge. You can trust me." Marc leaned over and whispered into Rick's ear: "And I don't believe for one moment that you drove your sabre through an unconscious man."

Rick Hilliard raised his head slowly, peering up at Marc with round, enquiring, frightened eyes. "What can I tell you?" He looked away with a sigh, but when his gaze fell upon the bib of blood on his tunic, he looked back up at Marc and kept his eyes steadily upon his friend.

"Tell me everything you can remember about tonight, starting with what Tessa and you did when you went into her room shortly before eleven o'clock."

Rick seemed puzzled by the question, or else was just more deeply in shock than Marc realized. But when Marc merely waited, he said at last, "We just laughed and talked . . . about the play . . . and how wonderful she was in it . . . and how much the audience loved it . . . just talk . . . *you* know."

"Yes, I do. But think carefully now. When did you or Tessa take a drink of the sherry?"

"Not for a while. She was bubbling with excitement. Her eyes were like saucers. It must have been about eleven-thirty or after—there was a clock in the corner chiming the quarters, I remember—when I suggested we have a drink. I did promise Owen I would not stay long . . . I wanted to, oh, how I did, but I know that he . . . he saw us go into Tessa's room—"

"Merriwether?"

"Yes, and Mrs. Thedford, too, but she smiled and told us to be careful. I didn't want to let Owen down, or Mrs.

Thedford either, and I didn't want to harm Tessa's reputation . . . but look what I've done. Oh, God, this is awful . . . this is unbearable."

"Get on with it, Edwards! I'm not going to listen to this blackguard blubber and wail all night!"

Cobb looked as if he were about to take five giant strides to the bar, pick Spooner up, plop him over the curve of his belly, and snap his brittle pomposity in two like a tinder-stick. But he stayed put.

"You can't hold me here! I'm an American citizen!" Apparently Dawson Armstrong had risen briefly to the surface.

"Shut up in there!" Sturges yelled.

"So you had your toast to success," Marc prompted. "Just one?"

"Tessa had one, then insisted I have another . . . just one more for the road, she said, and laughed so deliciously my heart melted . . ."

"Then what happened? You must tell me everything."

"We were sitting on the settee. I don't know how she managed it, but suddenly there was only one candle lit in the room, over by the bed, and a shaft of moonlight came in through the window and laid itself over us . . . we were in each other's arms . . ."

"Go on, Rick. How far did things go?"

"Too far. She was so young, but so beautiful there in the moonlight . . . and she wanted me. I started to feel very drowsy. I thought 'How odd,' because I was getting very aroused, you see, even as my eyelids started to feel like lead . . . I swear to God, she opened my flies."

"Was she getting sleepy, too?"

"I don't think so . . . it's hard to remember because everything was starting to get fuzzy in the room, but I did see her get up, like a ghost in her white dress, and sort of drift over to the bed. I couldn't see clearly, though, because of my grogginess and the shadows on the bed. I remember her dress floating to the floor . . . she was in her shift, that gauzy thing she wore in the *Lear* scene. She was sinking back onto the pillows . . . I heard her giggle . . . I started to get up . . . and oh, Christ, I knew what I was going to do, and she was there—I swear it—with her shift raised above her knees . . ."

"And then?" Marc could hardly breathe as he waited for the answer.

"My legs went rubbery and I started falling backwards and the last thing I recall is the settee hitting the backs of my knees, and I sank back onto it. Then the room went away."

"Listen carefully. Both you and Tessa were drugged. If you've remembered these details accurately, you took twice as much drink as Tessa. You're sure Tessa drank her glassful?"

"Oh, yes. We clinked glasses and watched each other drain them. But who would do something like that?"

"I need to know exactly when you came to, and what you saw. Your life may depend on your answer."

Rick paled, checked Marc's face for signs of duplicity, found none, and, struggling for the right words, said, "I heard Tessa cry out. I thought I was dreaming it, but my eyes opened. The room seemed dark except for the strip of moonlight over the settee and a bit of candlelight somewhere. I turned towards the bed, but all I could see—I was still groggy—was the white crumple of something on or under a sheet. I felt a sort of black panic . . . Tessa was hurt or in trouble, was all I could think, then nothing. I've been sitting here for an hour trying to remember what happened during those blank seconds. But I can't."

"But you did come to again?"

"Yes. I was sitting on the settee, something wet and sticky all down my front . . . I knew it was blood, I don't know how, and there in the moonlight I saw my sword sticking up out of the carpet. I walked slowly over to it and that's when I saw the body, Merriwether . . . ghastly. I thought, 'I've stabbed Merriwether.' I was reaching to pull the sword out when I remembered Tessa and I was just about to turn towards the bed when the door swung open, and Beasley, I think, was standing there with a candle in his hand and a horrified look on his face. One of us screamed. I was rooted to the spot, couldn't move a muscle."

Marc waited while Rick struggled to control his emotions and Cobb dared Spooner to disrupt the proceedings.

"I could hear Beasley banging on doors and creating havoc, but it was nothing compared to the havoc in my mind. Then Beasley was back with Mrs. Thedford and Jefferson . . . I heard her shriek and I thought Tessa was dead and my heart stopped, but Mrs. Thedford picked Tessa up off the bed as if she was a doll and ran out of the room with her, Jefferson following. Beasley pulled me aside . . . sometime later the room was full of policemen."

With the aid of Cobb's lantern, Marc carefully examined the bloodstains on Rick's jacket, breeches, and boots. The smear patterns on the jacket appeared to have been caused by Rick rubbing his hands over the splotches there, but there was a curious and unexplainable absence of blood spatters. If Merriwether's ruptured aorta was spouting blood, surely there should have been spots of it where it had sprayed and landed.

Marc knelt down in front of the distraught ensign. "You could only have blanked out the second time for a minute or so at most," he said calmly. "Beasley's told Cobb he heard Tessa's cry, too, and reached the room as soon as he could. It appears, and I say *appears,* that Merriwether was struck and stabbed in the time between Tessa's cry and Beasley's arrival. Now tell me: you say you've concluded that you murdered Merriwether, but you have no actual memory of doing so?"

"I have no memory of killing Merriwether. I had no idea he was even in the room."

"Then, until you do remember it, I am going to assume you are innocent, and look for the killer elsewhere."

Tears of gratitude welled up in Hilliard's eyes. "But I must've done it, Marc. Tessa had to be saved from—"

"Stuff and nonsense!" Spooner cried, prancing across the room with a sequence of stiff manoeuvres found in no training manual. "I've heard enough of this drivel!"

Cobb stepped out in front of him, but Marc drew the constable gently away. "Lieutenant Spooner, I intend to report to Sir Francis in the morning that the case is still unresolved. Ensign Hilliard is a prime suspect, but there was, patently, a rape or attempted rape engineered by the victim with the aid of drugged wine, something I need to know a lot more about before laying any charge of murder."

"You have no evidence for that assumption!" Spooner tipped up on his toes, but the effort merely brought his bristling gaze level with Marc's chest.

"I intend to get it, sir."

"The girl'll be able to tell us more in the mornin'," Cobb added.

A smirk spread across Spooner's narrow face, he jutted out his receding jaw, and his metallic locks shook. "Mrs. Frank says the girl is saying nothing. So how do we know that it wasn't your friend Hilliard who attempted to violate the young lady, was interrupted by Merriwether, who heard her cry from his room just across the hall and came running to the rescue in his nightshirt, only to be butchered by this scoundrel?"

Rick flinched, but said nothing.

Marc was seething inside, but he realized the deceptive plausibility of this version of events. "So Ensign Hilliard drugged himself as well as Tessa in order to facilitate his purpose?" he asked sarcastically.

"Attempts at drugging have gone awry more than once," Spooner sputtered, tipping up on his toes to drive his argument forward like a puff-adder seeking the insertion point. "And if you don't inform the governor of this possibility, I shall take it upon myself to do so."

"The only thing you're gonna take on yerself is my fist!" Cobb hissed.

"Gentlemen!" Dr. Withers chided, coming across the room.

"We all need to put a damper on our tempers," Sturges said with a sharp look at Cobb. "It's the middle of the bloody night an' we're all damn near bushed."

"What in hell're we gonna do with all these people? And a dead body?" Cobb said, back in control.

Without diluting the venom in his smirk, Spooner said, "I'm taking the 'prime suspect,' as you call him, with me to Government House, where he will be placed under twenty-four-hour guard."

"Not in irons, you ain't!" Sturges snapped.

"Then I'd like you to accompany me, sir. I don't want this disgrace to a uniform making a dash for the woods."

"Okay," Sturges said with a resigned sigh.

"What about everybody else?" Cobb said.

"The governor wants this mess contained at any cost. I'm using his executive authority to order this establishment quarantined—"

"You can't do that!" Ogden Frank rolled his rotund body into the room from the dining area. Sweat beaded his hairless dome. "I'll be ruined!"

Spooner ignored him. "I want all these actors placed in their rooms upstairs and a guard posted. Mr. Frank, you will see that they are fed and watered. No-one is to have access to them without permission from me or from Lieutenant Edwards. I want no loose-lipped chambermaids near that upper floor—"

"But who will—"

"Your good woman, Mr. Frank: she already knows what's happened. But no one else must get the slightest inkling of the grotesque events here tonight. No one. Lieutenant Edwards will remain here to question the witnesses in the morning. And I'll be back with fresh instructions from Sir Francis." He gave Marc the courtesy of a final nod.

"I'll prepare sleeping draughts for these people before I leave," Withers said through his fatigue. "They're in pitiable shape. The black fellow's got a wicked toothache, but if he can't get to the barber tomorrow, I'll try and pull it before I leave."

"I'd like a sleeping draught for the wife," Frank said.

"I'll make up two," Withers offered.

Marc took Rick's arm. "You'll have to go with Lieutenant Spooner and the chief constable to Government House. Dr. Withers will come along as soon as he's finished here. I'll see you again before noon tomorrow. Tessa's going to be all right. Try not to worry."

Sturges helped Rick across the barroom, and he was escorted out the front door of the tavern onto West Market Street, more like a man trudging off to the gallows than to the relative comfort of confinement in Government House.

But as badly as he felt for Hilliard, Marc realized that he must bring matters to completion here immediately, and start afresh in the morning. He went over to the entrance to the dining-room. Five pairs of glazed eyes looked up at him as if he were perhaps a kindly executioner come to put them out of their misery. "Dr. Withers will give you each something to help you sleep. Mr. Beasley, take Mr. Armstrong to your room for the night. Mrs. Thedford, would you be good enough to let Miss Clarkson share your room? And would you convey to Mr. Jefferson that he may return to his sleeping-place, where the doctor will attend to his aching tooth."

"Are we under arrest?" Mrs. Thedford said, and the sudden resonance of her deep, authoritative voice seemed to revivify the others, who now turned to stare at her, then at Marc, with something resembling self-interest.

"No, you are not. But I will not be satisfied that Ensign Hilliard is guilty until I have questioned each of you carefully tomorrow morning. Until then, at least, the lieutenant-governor has ordered that all of you are to be held as material witnesses. Food will be brought up to you and maid-service supplied—"

Ogden Frank groaned behind him, wondering how he was to inform his "good woman" of this disquieting news.

"A police guard will be posted at the bottom of the stairs, but largely for your own protection," Marc said unconvincingly. He saw Mrs. Thedford shake her head slightly.

"What about our Tuesday evening performance?" she asked with steely calm.

"Surely you can't be thinking of continuing?"

Mrs. Thedford smiled wanly. "We are a theatre company, Mr. Edwards."

Ogden Frank tugged at Marc's sleeve. "Wouldn't it be best to carry on as if nothing has happened?" he suggested, hope rising improbably for the first time since the mute had pounded on the tavern door and he had crawled out of a warm bed to answer its grim summons. "If the tavern and theatre don't carry on normally, folks'll start to get mighty curious."

"He may be right, Major," Cobb said to Marc.

"We could tell the customers Merriwether took sick." Frank looked to Mrs. Thedford for support.

But Marc said, "We'll make those kinds of decisions after I've interviewed all of you—including you and your wife, Mr. Frank—in the morning. Now please take your sleeping draughts from Dr. Withers."

Withers had set a number of glasses of frothing liquid in a row along the bar. "Come and get it," he called, tapping a spoon against the nearest glass.

When Cobb and Marc were left alone at last, Marc gave his comrade-in-arms a weary but welcoming smile.

"Constable Wilkie'll likely be sent along when he comes on duty at seven," Cobb said. "Who'll watch that lot till then?"

"I'm going to curl up in a blanket at the foot of the stairs through there. You trot on home to Dora now. I'd like you back at ten to sit in on the interviews."

Cobb looked amazed. "But I'm just a 'peeler,'" he said, "not an *interra-grater*."

"You'll come anyway?"

"I'll be here, providin' Missus Cobb rolls me outta bed an' props my eyes open with pipe-stems."

"In the meantime, I've got to give Merriwether's room a thorough going-over. There isn't a scintilla of doubt that he put the laudanum in Tessa's sherry, but if Spooner goes to the governor with that ludicrous story of Rick being a rapist, I've got to have physical proof to counter it. There's bound to be a vial somewhere up there. And if he didn't bring the stuff with him from Buffalo, we may be able to trace it to one of the chemists in town."

"That Spooner!" Cobb snarled. "He's like a banty-rooster in a harem o' hens with its cock in a knot!"

Marc could have hugged him.

WITH EVERY CELL IN HIS BODY crying out for rest, Marc let Cobb out the main tavern door, barred it, and with the aid of Cobb's lantern made his way around the bar and through the door into the dark recesses of the theatre. He heard Frank slip the bolt into place behind him. All was quiet on the upper floor. Jeremiah was asleep on a mat with the storeroom door ajar, a bloody handkerchief tied in a sling for his jaw. He did not stir.

Merriwether's room was very tidy—Marc wasn't sure why he should have been surprised—and with several candles to aid his search, Marc combed through the drawers and cupboard of a high wardrobe, peering under linens, cotton vests, and silk stockings, and rummaging through the pockets of shirts, waistcoats, and frock coats. The man must have rented a barge on the Erie Canal for all this. Marc found no vial or stoppered apothecary bottle. Behind the door sat a large costume trunk, a fine wooden piece with copper straps and fittings and the initials *JDM* stamped on the top for all the world to admire. It was locked, but Marc had already found a key in one of the drawers. It opened the trunk on the first try. Inside, neatly packed in layers separated by swaths of fine paper, were costumes that appeared to belong to the Shakespearean program scheduled for Tuesday evening. Meticulously, Marc searched every pocket and sleeve, without success.

He stood up, frustrated, then stepped back and studied the trunk from a distance. He peered back inside, reached down, and stretched out his fingers till they touched the bottom. He repeated this crude form of measurement on the outside of the trunk. And smiled. It had a false bottom, there being at least a five-inch discrepancy between the depth inside and outside. Excited now, he ran his fingers lightly over the surface of the lid and then the sides. Often there was a hidden trigger to release any latch holding a false bottom or secret drawer in place. But he found none. So he lifted the costumes out of the trunk until it was empty. He ran his fingers around the edges of the false bottom, but they seemed to fit the rectangle of the trunk neatly. Then, on the table that Merriwether used as a writing desk, Marc spotted a thin letter-opener. He slid it between the edge of the false bottom and one side of the trunk, and lifted. The false bottom came up towards him far enough for him to grasp it with three fingers and pull it all the way out. He held the lantern above the trunk and peered down.

There was no secret vial of laudanum, but something far more arresting: two brand-new French Modèle rifles—U.S army issue and the most sophisticated infantry weapon in the world—and a box of ammunition. And tucked under the polished hardwood stock of one of them was a folded note. Marc drew it into the light and read:

We understand that you have the merchandise with you. We have the money you require. Please bring a sample with you after the performance on Wednesday evening. Using the same means of communication, you will be supplied at that time with a map showing you the rendezvous point. In the meantime, we will be watching. Vigilance is the byword. Destroy this note.

Several thoughts raced through Marc's mind. These two guns were a sampler: Where were the others and how many were there? By what clandestine system of communication had this note been delivered? Was Merriwether a lone gunrunner among the Bowery Company? To which group of treasonous dissidents were these weapons destined? With Merriwether dead, what chance would there be of setting a trap for the insurrectionists? And finally, did this discovery have anything to do with Merriwether's murder and the fate of Ensign Hilliard?

Marc found himself incapable of further thought. He closed up the false bottom of the trunk, then pulled two blankets off Merriwether's bed, trudged to the other end of the hall, stretched his six-foot length across the opening to the stairwell, and fell asleep.

TEN

While Ogden Frank supervised breakfast for the "material witnesses," Marc decided to begin his interrogations with Tessa Guildersleeve. He wanted to get as much accomplished in this regard as possible before Spooner returned and was necessarily apprised of what Marc had discovered in Merriwether's room—a discovery that was certain to throw Sir Francis into paroxysms of one kind or another. He rapped discreetly at the door in the tavern that led to the Franks' quarters. Madge Frank opened it a mere crack, grimaced, then opened it wide. She was a lean, angular woman who could have used her elbows, shoulders, or hips as weapons, with chestnut hair indifferently tamed, sallow skin, and dark, mistrusting eyes that seemed forever to be seeking something they didn't want to find.

"Whaddya want?" she said.

"Please take me to Miss Guildersleeve. It is imperative that I speak with her now."

"People in fancy getups are always imperative about somethin' or other," she grumbled, but stepped aside to let him in. "I'll see if the poor creature's awake," she said.

"If not, I'd appreciate it if you'd wake her for me."

She glared at him, then heaved a woman's deep sigh that clearly conveyed a message about the incurable callousness of the male species. "Come with me."

Tessa was sitting up in bed, dipping a piece of dry toast in the mug of tea on her lap. She was wearing one of Madge's flowered bathrobes three sizes too big for her. Her face seemed no paler than usual, but her eyes were puffy and her lips drawn tight with tension. However, there was no sign of lingering shock or the kind of trauma that might have been expected from the ordeal she had suffered. She gave Marc a smile with her eyes, much to the disgust of her nurse.

"Tessa's gone through the most horrible thing that can happen to a young lady," Madge Frank said with a twist of her features to indicate that she was vicariously experiencing the horror of it.

For a moment Marc thought that Tessa might have winked at him, but her general expression was one of intense concern as she gave him her full attention.

"I'd like to speak to the girl alone. You wouldn't mind, would you, Tessa?"

"I ain't leavin' this room," Madge Frank declared through clenched teeth as she set her arms akimbo and took her stand in the doorway.

"Suit yourself, then," Marc said civilly, and sat down on the edge of the bed. Tessa showed no sign of being afraid, but he heard Madge suck in her breath. "I'm here as the governor's appointed investigator into the tragic events that took place in your room last night."

Tessa's expression clouded over, and Marc could see a flutter at her throat where the robe parted. Even in distress she was incredibly beautiful in an innocent, unfinished sort of way. "I'll try to help you if I can," she said bravely, though it was clear she had questions of her own she would like answered.

"First of all, I must inform you that both you and Rick were drugged last night. Someone put laudanum in your sherry decanter."

Tessa seemed about to lose her carefully constructed composure, but whether it was the result of hearing the word *laudanum* or the name *Rick* couldn't be determined.

"Who would do that?" she whispered. "An' why?"

"I intend to get answers to both of those questions. And you can help by telling me what happened after you and Rick went to your room."

Tessa blushed a deep peony red, Madge Frank cleared her throat threateningly, but something in Marc's steady, unjudgemental gaze encouraged the girl to begin her story. As she recited it, she kept her eyes on the tea-mug in her lap most of the time, peeking up only once a minute or so to make sure this handsome, kind-eyed officer was still listening and approving. In her own accented vernacular, Tessa's narrative jibed with Rick's at every essential point.

"So you were both seated on the settee, and you asked Marc to stay for one more drink?"

"Yes, I did. I was feelin' so mellow an' cozy and I didn't want things to end."

"I forbid you to take this improper conversation any further!" Madge Frank had started towards the bed, her eyes black with indignation.

"Mrs. Frank, please stand outside the door and observe if you must, but if you say one more word, I'll remove you and shut the door."

Madge huffed indignantly, but did as she was bidden. Marc hoped that he would not need her as an ally anytime soon. "Please go on, Tessa. I know this is very hard, but every detail you can remember may help Rick."

He could see she wanted to ask him about Rick but dared not—yet. "I started to feel real sleepy and I saw Rick yawn, so I went over to the bed an' laid down on it, and I was so groggy I thought I was about to faint, but, still, I really wanted Rick to stay, so I . . . I started to lift up my shift—"

Madge Frank was heard clattering down the hall.

"And?"

"Nothin'."

"Nothing?"

"I must've passed out."

"But you woke up later?"

"Yes." The memory of that wakening flooded back, whole and hurting. "But I was only half awake. There was a huge weight on top of me and a raspy breathin' in my ear. An' before I could say or see anythin', I felt a sharp jab between my legs and I cried out with the pain of it."

"Did you know who . . . was doing this thing to you?"

"No," she said, barely audible. "I fainted dead away again."

"Part of that was due to the drug, Tessa." Two perfect teardrops had slipped out of her pale blue eyes and now sat, one on each cheek, glistening. "Could it have been Rick on top of you?" Marc asked quietly.

Amazement, then fear, filled her face. "Oh, no, it couldn't've been Rick. He would never do anythin' to hurt me. You can't think Rick did this?"

"No, I don't. But I had to ask."

"Rick saved me from bein' murdered!" she cried with passion and a kind of defiant, childlike pride. "Mrs. Frank's told me about . . . about Jason."

"Did you *see* Rick . . . save you?"

Tessa shook her head and shuddered. "I don't remember anythin' except cryin' out at the pain. Then I was driftin' in the dark, and all kinds of nightmares were scuttlin' through my head, and I saw Rick with a knife stuck in him an' he was all bloody and I screamed so loud I woke myself up—here in Mrs. Frank's bed."

Marc sighed. "So you're telling me that you were unconscious from the moment you first cried out in pain, and thus can tell me nothing of what happened in that room after that point?"

"I only know what Mrs. Frank told me: that Jason was stabbed by Rick because he did that awful thing to me." At this, she began to sob softly, and Marc went to the door and called Madge, who appeared instantly from around a corner. "She needs you, ma'am."

"What's gonna happen to Rick?" Tessa cried out from the bed. "What's gonna happen to the company?"

"I don't know yet," Marc said honestly as Madge bustled by him and took the girl in her arms, stroking her hair and murmuring in her ear.

As Marc left, he heard Tessa say like a lost child, "Get Annie. Oh, please, Madge, I gotta see Annie!"

As Marc emerged from the Franks' quarters into the tavern, Ogden Frank was just unbarring the street-door across the room to let Cobb in.

"I hope nobody spotted you," Frank said fretfully as he slammed the bar back into its slot.

Cobb ignored him, and brushed by towards Marc so abruptly he sent the roly-poly little man a-wobble. Cobb looked as if he had dressed in the dark with one hand: his coat buttons were misaligned, his shirt was inside out, and his helmet sat precariously on one side of his head. But he smiled gamely at Marc, who himself would not have passed muster at parade.

Before Marc could speak, Cobb said, "I've checked the alley: there's no sign of footprints or a ladder bein' underneath the windows."

Marc nodded and said, "I've got news."

"I've never known you not to," Cobb said.

They sat down at a table, and Cobb removed his coat to reveal a portion of Dora's breakfast preparation on his vest.

"Do you want to tell us something?" Marc called out to Frank, who had stopped wobbling and was now loitering near the door to his quarters.

Frank came close enough to say with a certain spiteful glee, "I heard him an' the woman shoutin' at each other yesterday morning."

"Who and what woman?" Marc said.

"That Thea creature an' Merriwether—jawin' away at each other in the dining-room when they thought nobody was listenin'."

"What were they arguing about?"

"I couldn't tell fer sure, but I'd say it was a lovers' quarrel."

"And how did it end?"

"The woman screamed somethin' like 'I ain't gonna take it no more!' an' she come streakin' past me bawlin' her eyes out."

"Thank you, Ogden. I appreciate your assistance. Is everything all right with those upstairs?"

Frank looked pitiably grateful and flashed Marc a fawning smile. "They've had their breakfast, but it's put Madge in a fearful rage. Do you think we'll be able to go ahead with the show tonight?"

"I'll let you know right after noon," Marc promised.

"I gotta open the taproom at one o'clock," he said. "Lucky fer us, nobody's stayin' in the hotel rooms above us except my two housemaids."

"Let's keep it that way, shall we?"

Frank nodded as if he were a co-conspirator, then waddled away to deal with his much-put-upon wife.

Marc proceeded to give Cobb a brief account of what he had found at the bottom of Merriwether's trunk.

Cobb arched an eyebrow, whistled through his teeth, and said, "Couldn't we ever get us a plain an' simple murder? Now we got politics muddled up in it."

Cobb was alluding to last year's investigation, and Marc was reminded of a remark Beth had made then that in Upper Canada everything was politics. "But politics or not, Cobb, we've still got to find evidence to clear Rick of this crime."

"Assumin' he didn't do it."

"I'm assuming that," Marc said, staring at the constable.

Cobb didn't react, but merely said, "Ya had a chance to talk to the girl yet?"

Marc gave him a summary of his interview with Tessa.

When he had finished, Cobb said, "Well, Major, that don't seem to be a lotta help to Hilliard."

"It's worse than that. She's convinced he did it in defense of her honour—such as it is, or was. And he's still besotted with her."

Cobb frowned. "Then we better keep her away from him."

"Right now I'm anxious to interrogate the rest of that bunch, but you can see the immediate problem we have."

Cobb nodded. "Ya gotta tell Sir Francis Bone Head about them guns."

"Yes. And I'm positive that what I saw last night was only the sample referred to in the note from the buyers."

"Where would the rest of them be, then?"

"My best guess is that there are more trunks with false bottoms. The one in Merriwether's room was improvised—hand-made, I'd say."

"Well, Major, I saw this crew come off the boat from Burlington last Friday with enough baggage for a regiment or two."

"They were planning to try out a number of playbills, here and in Detroit and Chicago. Where would they be storing the props and costumes not in use?"

"Frank's got a big shed and ice-house out back."

"Then let's have a peek." Marc rose stiffly out of his chair.

"You look like ya slept on a sack of potatoes," Cobb said.

"THEY'RE ALL LOCKED." MARC SIGHED, SURVEYING the six steamer-trunks they had found in Frank's storage-shed.

"I've never found that a problem," Cobb said. He fished

about in his greatcoat pocket and drew out a ring of keys of varying shapes and sizes. "This one usually does it fer these kinda trunks." He bent over the nearest one, jiggled the chosen key as if his fingers had suddenly developed palsy, muttered what was either a curse or an incantation, and then, with a decisive twist, exclaimed, "Aha!"

The trunk yawned open.

Over the next fifteen minutes, the two men opened each of the trunks in turn, carefully removed the contents, pried up the false bottoms in three of them, and found what they were looking for. There were twelve U.S army rifles in addition to the two in Merriwether's room, and several boxes of ammunition. They replaced the contents with equal care and relocked the trunks.

Back inside, Marc said to Cobb, "It's possible the others know nothing about the rifles. But we can't be sure. God knows what the governor will decide to do. In any case, I want some time to question the actors before Spooner gets here, so I'm going to give you this incriminating note and have you go up to Government House with it. That and the news of the guns out there in the shed should occupy Sir Francis and Spooner for a little while, time enough for me to see what I can do to help Rick."

"You're not worried about the guns?"

"Of course I am. We are probably facing some sort of planned insurrection—high treason for those involved. But

I'm just a soldier now, Cobb, and I'm content to leave these entanglements to the governor and his aides."

Cobb's grunt indicated his skepticism about the latter claim, but he did not comment further. "I'm on my way, Major."

"Would you mind asking Wilkie to bring Jeremiah Jefferson down here to the dining-room before you go?" Constable Wilkie had arrived late at seven-thirty to rouse Marc and place himself on the landing with a stool, a candle, and a copy of this week's *Constitution*.

"The mute? I thought you'd want to see Beasley first. Seems to me he's the one that's got the goods on Hilliard."

"Very true. But Beasley's already outlined his account to you and Spooner. I need to question the others closely to see if I can find the discrepancies in it. If I don't, it's going to go badly for Rick."

"I'll wake up Wilkie an' put him to work, then," Cobb said, pleased with this modest attempt at levity.

JEREMIAH JEFFERSON SAT OPPOSITE MARC WITH the air of man who was concerned with the unpredictable turn of events but innocent of any direct involvement in them. Nonetheless, his past experience with authority had left a residual wariness in an otherwise open and unsuspecting face. Mrs. Thedford had apparently done more than merely shelter him from the slave-catchers, Marc thought: there had been some kind of miraculous rehabilitation.

The interview was conducted by a combination of questions and answers being written on the slate placed between them, and of gestures, lip-reading, and accompanying facial expressions.

Your tooth is better?

Vigorous nod and display of gum-gap.

It kept you awake after the play?

Yes. Couldn't sleep.

Did you see anyone come up the stairs after the others were asleep?

No.

Did anyone come back down the hall and go down the stairs?

No.

Did you see Mr. Beasley come out of his room?

Yes. He scared me.

He looked frightened? Worried?

Yes. Running.

You followed him?

Not right away. He started banging on doors.

What did you do?

Clarence and I banged on Mrs. T's door.

Did she answer?

No. We went into her bedroom.

Was she awake?

No. Earplugs. Shook her.

Then you all went to Tessa's room?

Yes. Terrible.

Marc then took Jeremiah detail by detail through what he saw there: Rick still holding the sword, Tessa unconscious, blood everywhere, Mrs. Thedford running out with Tessa in her arms and Jeremiah following, then being sent to rouse the Franks, helping Madge and Mrs. Thedford get Tessa downstairs and away from the dreadful scene.

Thank you. You've been very helpful.

Say thank you to the doctor for me.

THE INTERVIEW WITH JEREMIAH HAD BEEN helpful, perhaps, but not to Rick Hilliard's case. So far, the various accounts meshed in every important detail. Marc decided to see Dawson Armstrong next, not because he expected the dipsomaniac actor to provide credible evidence about the crime, but because he was the most likely among the members of the troupe to have detailed knowledge of Merriwether's background and behaviour. Despite what he had told Cobb, Marc was eager to discover all he could about the gunrunning operation. In addition to being a loyal subject of the newly crowned Queen Victoria, he had a personal stake in seeing that no citizens' revolt erupted in Upper Canada—with farmer and soldier staring each other down, weapons at the ready.

As he motioned Armstrong to a chair across the table from him, Marc noticed, behind the crumpled features and depleted expression of the veteran actor, Madge Frank walking slowly across the taproom with Tessa on one arm. They shuffled into the theatre, en route to Mrs. Thedford no doubt.

"You were drunk when all the fuss broke out?" Marc asked, hoping to get this part of the interrogation over with quickly.

"You won't believe this after what you saw yesterday afternoon on the stage, but I've been sober most of the time since we left New York last month," Armstrong said wearily, as if he were beyond caring about anything anymore.

"Yet, according to what I heard Mrs. Thedford say, you managed to bring along a contraband supply of booze."

Armstrong's posture stiffened, and the creases in his face did their best to express umbrage at the accusation. "I did nothing of the sort."

"Then how did bottles of whiskey mysteriously appear whenever required?"

Armstrong blinked. "I've begun asking myself that very same question. At first when I found a half-drunk bottle in the bottom of my trunk, I thought it was left over from a trip I took to Philadelphia last fall. But yesterday after lunch, when I began pulling out my Lear and Prospero outfits, I found another part-bottle in one of the pockets, and I've been so upset lately with Merriwether's putdowns and insinuations, well, I just started in on it. And you saw what happened after that. Annemarie was furious."

"Could Merriwether have planted those whiskey bottles deliberately?"

"That bastard would do anything to destroy my career!" Lear's anger flashed in the tragedian's eyes.

"Did you hate him enough to kill him?" Marc asked quietly.

Armstrong was not surprised by the question. "Of course I did. But after the fiasco of the afternoon, I went up to my room and thought mightily about finishing the bottle I'd hidden well. We had a play to put on, and I managed to resist. But after the play, I came straight up here and started in on it. I took it down in three or four swigs and passed out. When I woke up, it was pitch dark. I felt like hell. I puked all over the rug."

Marc knew he had to ask the next question: "Did you hear Tessa cry out?"

Armstrong did not answer right away. He looked down at the table, and when he raised his eyes again to face Marc, they were brimming with tears. "Yes, I did."

"What did you do?"

"I am ashamed to say I did nothing. My door was ajar. So was Tessa's. I heard her shriek, like she'd been stabbed. I knew she was in some sort of danger. But I was sick, I was woozy, my head was pounding, I was filled with self-loathing."

"Did you see Clarence Beasley come running towards Tessa's room?"

"Yes. And I felt a wave of relief."

Marc hated himself for continuing, but he did his duty: "Do you remember how long it was after the cry that you saw Beasley pass your doorway?"

"It wasn't right away, I know that, because I started

crawling towards the hall. Then I heard Beasley's door open and saw him coming to help."

"Isn't it possible that Beasley may have come out of Tessa's room, slipped quietly back to his own room, and then pretended to be the rescuer by running noisily past your door?"

Armstrong was genuinely puzzled by the question. He gave it due consideration before answering. "I see what you're driving at but, no, that's not the way it happened. I heard Tessa scream. My door was open about a foot, and from where I was lying in my puke I could see Tessa's doorway across the hall. Nobody came out after the scream. Then, maybe a minute or two later, I saw Beasley come past."

Marc tried to suppress the discouraging implications of Armstrong's testimony and concentrate on his next task. "While I have you here, Mr. Armstrong, I'd like to learn a bit more about Merriwether. I assume you've known him for some years, as both of you have starred on the New York stage, as rivals and colleagues."

"What do you need to know other than the fact that the man was a monster with an ego the size of Manhattan Island?"

"Was he interested in politics?"

Armstrong snorted derisively. "That would have meant giving some thought to the welfare of others or the future of America, and Merriwether was obsessed with only his own appetites and satisfying them as often as possible."

"He belonged to no political party or organization that you know of?"

"He didn't vote and even bragged about it."

"He was attracted to women?"

"And they to him. But Annemarie kept him in his place. I'll give him his due there: he seemed to sense, like any cunning beast will, that his recovery and his progress in the world were bound up with Mrs. Thedford and her good grace. He was pathetically afraid of her, though he tried not to show it."

"And yet he raped her ward?"

Armstrong winced at the word *raped*. "The son-of-a-bitch stepped over the line, didn't he? And got what he deserved. I hope they hang a medal around young Hilliard's neck."

A noose was more likely, Marc thought.

"How is Tessa doing?" Marc asked Mrs. Thedford, who now sat across from him—fatigued, concerned, but with no loss of poise or inherent authority.

"She is recovering remarkably well. The drug that knocked her out kept her from seeing any of the horrors perpetrated in that room. The loss of her virginity appears to have been a physical trauma only. Nevertheless, I have insisted she rest in my room with Thea until this afternoon's rehearsal."

"The show must go on," Marc said, recalling that phrase from five years ago in his brief flirtation with summer theatre in London.

"If it is allowed to," she said simply, holding his gaze in hers.

"But you've already rehearsed the Shakespeare program."

"Yes, as you observed yesterday. But one of our characters has played his death-scene too well, and cannot be replaced." Despite the natural beauty of her deep blue eyes, lustrous skin, honeyed tresses, and regal carriage, a profound sadness enveloped her. "Jason was a troubled and difficult man. Few people liked him. I made the effort to find the best part of him and have it take possession of the whole person. I thought I was succeeding."

"I hate to be so blunt, but the man betrayed you by ravishing your ward."

"I know," she said angrily, "and I'd've picked up the nearest heavy object and brained him with it if I'd caught him at it—or clawed his eyes out as Cornwall did Gloucester's, and with as little remorse."

"But you didn't?"

"Someone beat me to it."

"You believe Ensign Hilliard did it?"

"All I know is that Clarence and Jeremiah shook me awake and dragged me in my nightdress down to that room, and your ensign was still standing over the body, clutching the sword. Everything else is a blur, because once I saw Tessa lifeless on the bed, I seemed to go blind with panic. Somehow I got her out of there, and I don't know what I was thinking of, but I didn't feel she would be safe till I got her as far away from there as I could. Madge Frank calmed me down, and I was persuaded to leave Tessa in her hands."

"But why would Hilliard drive his sword through a man he had already disabled?"

Mrs. Thedford seemed to find the question disingenuous. "Surely you know the young man was in love?"

"But you loved her, too, in your way. Would you have driven that sword through Merriwether's chest as he lay, in all probability, dying?"

"That's very difficult to answer, Mr. Edwards. Each of us has the capacity to love and hate, and either quality has the potential to incite us to actions we would normally consider beyond us. But you saw what Tessa was up to during her scene with Lear? The girl is young and ambitious and feeling the urgency of her desires. What happened to her was almost inevitable, though I've done everything I could to forestall it. But to answer your question: I think that in the fury of seeing the deed being done, I'd've cracked the villain on the skull. But why would I then, with forethought and in cold blood, kill a man I admired and whose loss to the Bowery Company will likely prove ruinous?"

"Thank you for your candour, ma'am. I'm trying to understand the degree of hatred and moral outrage that must have propelled that sword through a man's torso into the floor underneath it. According to statements already made by Mr. Beasley and Mr. Armstrong, no one entered that room after Tessa's cry at the moment of the . . ."

"Penetration?"

Marc flushed. "Yes. And no one came out who hadn't been in there already."

"Well, I'm relieved to hear that."

"There is one other important matter you can help me with."

"Please, name it."

"Who arranges for the disposition and delivery of your many steamer-trunks?"

"An odd question, but one easily answered. I looked after all the financial aspects of the company, Jason and I shared the artistic responsibilities, and Jason alone handled the travel arrangements for us and the disposition of the baggage. Jeremiah does most of the actual lifting. Why do you ask?" She seemed more amused than anxious by this turn in the conversation.

"You have six trunks in Frank's storage-shed."

"Probably. Only Jason and Jeremiah would know for sure. Have you counted them personally?"

"Humour me for a while longer, please. I take it that the contents of these trunks are not required here in Toronto?"

"Jason told me that he had put all the materials we no longer needed into three trunks and was arranging to have them shipped to New York City."

The three with the rifles in them, Marc thought, and they would have been mysteriously "lost" en route. But exactly where would they have been "lost" if Merriwether had not been prematurely murdered? And who would have "found" them?

"Did anyone other than Mr. Merriwether have keys to those trunks?"

"No. We each have our own trunks, but only Jason had keys for the others." Suddenly she lost her composure for the first time, and with a breaking voice said, "He kept them in a secret pocket inside his King Claudius robe. He thought I didn't know where they were, and I went along with it."

"Please, don't upset yourself over the matter, Mrs. Thedford. I only asked because it might be necessary at some point in the investigation to have access to anything which might have belonged to him."

If she were puzzled by this lame explanation, she had the good manners not to show it.

"Do you know if Mr. Merriwether had any money troubles?"

"Not really," she said, back in control of herself once more. "No actor ever has enough money, but Jason had no one to support but himself, and I was the one risking my meagre capital in the quixotic venture of owning and operating a theatre in New York."

"And you were counting on his return to star status?"

"Yes. That was the main reason we were trying out so many different plays and playbills. I had hoped that Jason would also do some directing at the new Bowery, but now . . ."

"Thank you for your co-operation. I'll let you know after the noon-hour whether you'll be able to carry on this evening."

"Thank you. As I started to say earlier, if we can, we will substitute our musical and recitation program for the Shakespeare. It's something we have done on rare occasions when one of us is too ill to go on: it's a simple series of 'acts' we can mount and adapt with an hour's notice."

"I am amazed at the resilience of actors."

"Would you do *me* a favour?" she said, getting up to leave.

"Of course."

"I promised your friend Mr. Jenkin that I would have luncheon with him today in the dining-room at one o'clock. He's riding in from the fort. I know you want to keep the news from getting out—"

"Yes, but we also need to do nothing out of the ordinary to arouse suspicions. I'm sure you and Mr. Jenkin will find many more pleasant things to talk about."

And, Marc thought, it'll give me a chance to make up a cover story for being in town and for Rick's unexplained disappearance—and have Owen take it back to the garrison.

"Thank you. Whatever we might say in our anger and our grief over the next few hours, please believe me when I say that we appreciate your kindness and courtesy." With that she walked across the taproom and into the theatre.

Marc was about to send Wilkie to fetch Thea Clarkson when he heard the front door to the tavern slam open, and turned to see Lieutenant Spooner strut in and put an end to both kindness and courtesy.

ELEVEN

Lieutenant Spooner marched to the middle of the barroom with epaulets bristling, executed a teetering two-footed halt, and, regaining the perpendicular, whipped his shako-hat down to his thigh with an intimidating strop. Then he swivelled his head like a horned owl with a fixed stare, as if he expected to discover a cache of Yankee rifles under every table. Constable Cobb followed close behind but walked towards Marc.

"I think Mr. Spooner would like a word," he said.

"Ah, there you are, Edwards. Why didn't you reveal your position at once?"

"It seemed to me that I might actually be observable," Marc replied.

"Constable, please leave this room. What I have to say to the lieutenant is strictly confidential."

"I'll stand out here by the bar an' watch the doors," Cobb said with a helpless shrug in Marc's direction.

Spooner waited until he thought Cobb was out of earshot, then sat ramrod straight opposite Marc.

"I gather that Cobb has shown the note to the governor and mentioned our discovery of the contraband weapons?"

"Don't patronize me, Edwards. You could be court-martialled for revealing that note to an illiterate bobby who may be sympathetic to the enemies of Queen Victoria himself. But the milk has been spilt, and Sir Francis is extremely agitated."

"Has his agitation prompted a plan for us to deal with the situation?"

Spooner appeared momentarily flummoxed, both eyebrows in a regular tantrum of indecision. Then he managed to snarl, "The governor does not have enough information to formulate a response, as you know perfectly well."

"Well, then, Lieutenant, let me lay out the situation as I see it—for you and the governor."

"The guns must be secured before anything else is considered."

"They are secure, sir. You have my word as an officer on that score. I'll have Cobb show you their location, if you like, but my advice is to leave them where they sit."

"To what end, sir? Leaving them open to unlawful appropriation by Cobb or one of his cronies?"

"I am assuming that Sir Francis, being an astute gentleman, is more concerned with tracking down the rebels to whom the rifles were heading than he is in impounding the guns themselves."

Spooner's face went as scarlet as his coat.

"Am I right?" Marc asked casually.

"Yes, damn you. He decided not to accept my advice that the weapons be seized and every known radical be rounded up and interrogated until the last dram of truth was squeezed out of him."

"Please inform Sir Francis, then, that my preliminary investigation into Jason Merriwether's untimely death has pretty much excluded assassination by any political fanatic. The killer is almost certainly one of the other actors. Whether more than one was involved or why there was a falling-out, I don't yet know. But I intend to find out."

Spooner was first astonished; then mocking. "Have you gone mad? The assassin is safely locked away at Government House. Sir Francis wants a full written report on the matter from you before noon tomorrow, after which Hilliard will be charged with murder and thrown into military prison to await trial. You are under direct orders from your supreme commander to concentrate all your efforts upon the business of discovering whom these guns are meant for."

Marc took a deep breath. It appeared he had about twenty-four hours to find the real killer and save Rick from the noose. But there was a way in which he might be able to buy more time and simultaneously ingratiate himself with Sir Francis: a plan to flush out the seditionists was forming in his mind.

"Have you gone catatonic, sir?"

"Not yet, Lieutenant. But I want you to take a proposition back to Sir Francis for his approval."

"I'd refuse if I could," Spooner sighed.

"Explain to Sir Francis that if the news of Merriwether's death can be contained within these walls until Wednesday night—and so far you've been successful in doing that—then the final contact for the guns may still be made, and the identity and whereabouts of the traitors disclosed."

"But Merriwether was an actor and—"

"And this is what I have in mind," Marc smiled, and outlined his proposal to a speechless aide-de-camp.

When Spooner had left on his mission to the governor, Marc went over to Cobb. "Did you get all that?"

"Every *silli-babble,* Major."

COBB, WHO MADE NO COMMENT ON the audacity of the proposal, now joined Marc for the interview with Thea Clarkson. Of all those questioned so far, Thea appeared to be the most personally devastated. It could have been the consequence of her recent ill health, but if Ogden Frank had been telling the truth, it was almost certainly due to her relationship with the victim.

She really did appear physically ill: haggard, pale, and

loose-fleshed, her hair unkempt, her eyes swollen from weeping. Could she have killed Merriwether in a fit of jealous rage upon discovering him with Tessa, then regretted it? But how could she have managed it? Marc mulled over these questions as he sought the best and least cruel way to approach her. Last night she had been asleep in the Franks' quarters, where no sound from the floor above the theatre could be heard. Hence, if she had somehow slipped by Jeremiah Jefferson, awake with a toothache, and stumbled upon Merriwether at the very moment of the rape, would she have had the strength to strike him unconscious with the ashtray and the wherewithal to drive Hilliard's sword through him? Moreover, Armstrong now claimed to have seen Beasley answer Tessa's cry several minutes after it pierced the night, but he had not seen Thea. Further, Armstrong had seemed sure that no mad-eyed assassin had come running out of Tessa's room and down the hall to the only exit. Could both Jeremiah and Armstrong be lying? If so, to what end?

At any rate, one glance at Thea's devastated face and fragile composure caused Marc to begin obliquely and gently. "Miss Clarkson, we have been told that you were in love with Jason Merriwether."

She surprised them with a smile, and for a fleeting second they were privy to the beauty and warmth that had made her attractive to playgoers and suitors alike. "Not everyone has been kind enough to put it like that," she said in a low but steady voice. "But yes, Jason and I were lovers."

"For how long?"

"Our liaison began last winter when I joined the Bowery Company after a year away in Boston. We tried to keep it secret—Mrs. Thedford does not approve of affairs among her actors while they're sharing a stage—but I'm sure everybody in the company knew of it. I think Annemarie realized how much Jason and I needed each other."

"Everyone so far has spoken highly of Mrs. Thedford."

"Everyone will—she's the finest human being I've ever met."

Marc cleared his throat. "And yet Mr. Merriwether was found in Miss Guildersleeve's room—in compromising circumstances," Marc said quietly.

"Jason was attracted to young women, *very* young women, probably because they were attracted to him. And I've found most men cannot resist sustained flattery." There was no coyness or the least irony in her remark: it was simply a statement of what was and is.

"But you quarrelled loudly with Mr. Merriwether yesterday morning? Over Tessa, I presume?"

For a moment Marc was certain she was going to deny this, but all she said was "yes."

"When did you learn that something dreadful had happened upstairs?"

"I was awakened by the commotion in our quarters. Mr. Frank ordered me to stay put, but I did hear them bringing Tessa downstairs and placing her in Mrs. Frank's bed next door. Mrs. Frank told me what had happened. Then the police came."

"Thank you for being so candid, Miss Clarkson. If it is any consolation to you, I intend to find Jason Merriwether's killer and bring him to justice."

"Are we going to be allowed to carry on tonight?"

WHILE THEY WERE WAITING FOR WILKIE to bring Clarence Beasley down, Marc said to Cobb, "Miss Clarkson certainly had motive enough to brain him and passion enough—even in her weakened condition—to put a sword through his body. But there's no way she could have got up there and, even if she had, her timely arrival takes coincidence beyond credibility."

"Ya mean it's too good to be true."

"Precisely. Unless, of course, they're all lying and in this thing together."

"Well, Major, we gotta remember these folks are actors."

Marc sighed. "And I can't see Thea Clarkson being a gun-runner or fire-breathing republican."

"But she might've been jealous enough to've helped somebody else do him in."

"Like Beasley, who also had his eye on Tessa, I'm sure."

At this point the latest potential suspect arrived, and the last of the interviews began.

SINCE BEASLEY HAD ALREADY GIVEN COBB, Sturges, and Spooner an account of his actions and reactions last night,

Marc saw his task as having Beasley go over the narrative and flesh it out with details, details that might indicate a lie or an uncertainty. If Beasley's account and corroboration of it by Jeremiah and Armstrong went unchallenged, Rick Hilliard would hang.

Beasley was maddeningly co-operative, forthright, ingenuous almost. He listened to each question with the care he would have offered a director giving notes, paused to take it in, then answered in plain and unambiguous language, keeping eye contact throughout. If this were acting, then Beasley was destined for stardom.

"The number of minutes between Tessa's cry wakening you and your reaching her room are critical to our understanding of what happened," Marc said. "Tell me exactly what you did when you awoke."

"I sat upright. I recognized Tessa's voice, and there was terror in it. That's the first thought I had, and then that I must go to her as quickly as possible."

"And did you?"

"No. My bed is partly under the roof-line and, in my panic, when I went to jump out of bed, I bumped my head against a rafter. I did not black out, for I was aware of falling back onto the bed and then onto the cold floor. But I was dizzy and momentarily confused."

"You heard no further cry or other sounds from Tessa's room?"

"No. And I remember being very worried that I did not.

'Has she been murdered?' was my thought, and I staggered to my feet into the pitch dark, feeling about for my tinderbox and not able to remember where I had left it. I was cursing myself all the time and knocking things over."

"But you found it?"

"Yes, where it was supposed to be: on my night-table. My hands were shaking so badly, it took twenty or thirty seconds for me to get it working and light a candle. By then, my head was throbbing—right here—but I was no longer dizzy."

Cobb put his pipe down, came around, and dutifully inspected the lesion and modest bump on the top of Beasley's head.

"I half ran and half staggered out into the dark hall, but I could see a tiny wedge of light coming out of Tessa's doorway at the far end. I hurried up, and stubbed my toe on that spittoon near Armstrong's door—I think it was ajar, but I can't be sure—righted myself, and crashed into Tessa's room. What I intended to do I do not know. I am not a brave man. I had no weapon except the saucer holding the stub of candle. But its glow and the candle near Tessa's bed were enough light to show me the situation."

"So, if you did not black out when you bumped your head, the time between your hearing Tessa's cry and your arrival could not have been less than, say, a minute, and not more than, say, two minutes?"

"That is my own estimate, yes."

Beasley then repeated the description of the scene that was

now depressingly familiar to Marc: Hilliard standing over the victim with both hands on the haft of the bloodied sword.

"Why didn't you go to Tessa immediately? You ran out of the room like a madman, hollering and banging on doors."

"I did not see Tessa, or if I did, the horror of Jason's body stuck like a pig, and blood everywhere, and this soldier standing over him—all that blotted her out. I ran, like a coward, to get help."

"Leaving Tessa, to whom I believe you are strongly attached, with a vicious killer?"

Beasley coloured. "Yes," he whispered. "I am ashamed to say I did. But I will not lie to you. I stumbled back into the hallway and headed across to Dawson's door. It was already open and I saw him lying inside in a pool of his own vomit, still drunk or hopelessly hungover, and I just carried on to Mrs. Thedford's door, and pounded on it like a child trying to waken its mother. The racket alerted Jeremiah, who joined me, and we went in there together."

And the rest they already knew.

Beasley was about to get up when Marc stopped him with another question: "Do you know any reason why Mr. Merriwether would be in need of money? Desperately in need, perhaps?"

Beasley sat back down and thought about the question, giving no sign that it might have some malign purpose or raise matters that could implicate him personally. "Yes, now that I think back on it, he did."

Cobb removed his pipe and leaned forward.

"Please, go on," Marc said. "Strange as it may seem, your response to the question could be vital to this investigation."

"As you wish. I don't want to speak ill of the dead—even though I did not like Jason or his arrogance, he gave me professional advice and was not unkind in his way—but just before we set out on this tour, I overheard him talking with a theatre manager named Mitchell, a rival if you will, and they were discussing the possibility of opening a new theatre on Canal Street as joint owners. But it was obvious that, at that time anyway, Jason did not have the kind of capital required. Nor would he ever, I thought, if he stuck to acting for his livelihood."

"Was this not a betrayal of Mrs. Thedford, who had given him a second chance when nobody else would?"

Beasley was amazed. "You don't know the theatre world in New York, sir. Mrs. Thedford might have been disappointed in him, but in the end she would have wished him well. When it comes to the crunch, every actor, director, and manager is ambitious for himself. In that regard, Mrs. Thedford is the miraculous exception. But she understands the world she's lived in and survived in now for twenty-five years."

Beasley was thanked and went back to the actors' quarters.

"Well, Cobb, we now have a motive for Merriwether's pathetic attempt at gunrunning: money."

"Least it ain't politics," Cobb rumbled.

"True, though it would be simpler if some crazy Orangeman had broken into the rooms up there looking for the gunrunner, found him already knocked senseless on the floor, stabbed him with Hilliard's sabre to finish the job, and bolted."

"Ogden Frank's an Orangeman, ain't he?"

"But not a rabid one. And why would he risk ruining himself financially with such a messy assassination in his own nest when Merriwether could have been killed more conveniently elsewhere? Or merely turned over to Sir Francis. Besides, no one seems to have been snooping around the guns but us."

"Plus the fact none of them actors saw Frank up there till he was summoned."

"Nor any other Orange lunatic."

Cobb sighed, accidentally sucked in the putrid contents of his pipe-stem, spat furiously, and said, "We been at this all mornin', Major, an' we ain't found much to *ex-culprit* your friend Hilliard. I'm beginnin' to think things'd be a sight easier if it turned out he done it."

MARC AND COBB WERE SITTING IN the taproom with a nervous-looking Ogden Frank, drinking a draught of his best brew, on the house.

"I gotta tell them actors pretty soon if it's okay for them to start gettin' ready for tonight. An' my tapster an' assistant'll be comin' through that door in fifteen minutes to help me open the premises an' get some heat an' light into the theatre. And if I don't let one of the maids up to the actors' rooms soon, questions'll be raised about what's goin' on. An' we can't let that corpse fester an' stink up there much longer."

"You serve a good ale," Cobb remarked affably.

"We must wait for word from the governor," Marc said, "and, if I'm not mistaken, I can hear the martinet tread of Lieutenant Spooner approaching at this moment."

Spooner obliged by pushing open the tavern door, eyeing Frank and Cobb with distaste, and strutting over to their table. He remained standing.

"Is it yes or no?" Marc said.

"It's yes," Spooner hissed.

EVERY PERSON IN THE BUILDING WHO knew something about what had happened in Tessa's room had been summoned to the stage area of the theatre. Here they were seated on stools and a bench hoisted up from the pit, all facing Marc. To his evident relief, Wilkie had been posted beside the bar in the tavern to ensure that no one entered through the door there. Frank had instructed his staff to carry on with the regular opening of the pub, then joined his wife and the others onstage. Spooner stood aloof and rigid in the wings, making it clear to anyone who cared that he was not a party to the insane scheme about to be proposed by Lieutenant Edwards and inexplicably approved by an increasingly unpredictable governor.

It was nearly two o'clock. Cold sandwiches had been delivered to the actors by Madge Frank at twelve-thirty, Mrs.

Thedford had been permitted to keep her luncheon date with Owen Jenkin and, then, in a plan worked out between Marc and Spooner, everyone necessary to the scheme had been brought here. It was Marc himself who had led Mrs. Thedford from the dining-room, then returned quickly to explain to Jenkin that he and Hilliard had been given a special assignment by Sir Francis, and would be absent for the next few days. The fact that both Marc and Rick had worked as security officers for the governor last year mitigated the quartermaster's surprise at this news. Rumours of rebellion had been sweeping through both provinces for the past week or more. Jenkin's ready acceptance of his explanation was also the assurance Marc required that Mrs. Thedford had kept her word and said nothing about Merriwether's death. Marc said good-bye to his dear friend, unhappy to have lied to him, but determined to do his duty by uncovering the would-be rebels and their attempt to arm themselves with Yankee rifles.

"I know you are all wondering why I've brought you here," Marc began. "You've been through hell and its chambers since midnight. You are grieving the death of a colleague. You are puzzled why I have not been content to have Ensign Hilliard charged with murder. Perhaps you are even looking at one another and wondering. And to my great astonishment you are eager to carry on with your theatrical commitments. First of all, let me say that the governor himself has asked me to inform you that he wants you to continue your performances, at least until Wednesday and possibly to completion on Thursday evening."

"You might have told me sooner," Frank said. "I been pullin' my hair out since breakfast." The fact that the only hairs on his head were in his ears did not diminish his dudgeon.

"Sit down an' keep yer trap shut," Cobb said. "Any questions'll come after the lieutenant's done."

"But there are conditions attached," Marc continued, "absolute conditions that must be obeyed to the letter. First, for reasons which have to do with affairs of state and therefore are no concern of yours, Sir Francis Head does not want anyone to learn of Mr. Merriwether's death until Thursday at the earliest. Do not assume that there will be any attempt to protect his assassin: the prime suspect is in custody and I am to submit my report on the investigation at noon tomorrow. The killer will be charged and hanged. Secondly, you are to be confined to your quarters as you have been today, in particular because we cannot take a chance that any stray remark you might make in the tavern or dining-room or elsewhere might give away the secret we are endeavouring to maintain. In a short while, after I have examined the murder scene, Mr. Merriwether's body will be taken out to Mr. Frank's ice-house and kept frozen there until Thursday, when it will be released to the company."

Marc paused to study those before him. There was genuine puzzlement on the faces of the actors and a stoical veneer over the strain and fatigue, but nothing beyond expected curiosity. Thea was signing the information to Jeremiah beside her. Tessa, oddly, looked less strained than any of the others, much of the innocence still aglow in a face designed for it.

"You wish us to present our programs tonight and tomorrow night?" Mrs. Thedford asked, staring at Marc quite intently, it seemed. "We will be happy to do so, as it will provide some relief from the tension and doubt we are now suffering. We also need the funds that such work will bring us."

"Does this mean I must play housekeeper for another two days?" Madge Frank demanded, aghast.

"I'm afraid so, Mrs. Frank, for two reasons: Mr. Merriwether's absence is sure to be noticed and Tessa's room is covered with dried blood. The carpet will have to be removed and burned. But I'm sure the actors will co-operate by doing their own tidying up. They have a bathroom up there and a water-closet. It's mainly their meals we're talking about."

"But Thea hasn't got a room up there, she's been stayin' with us," Frank said on behalf of his wife.

"Mr. Armstrong can move in with Mr. Beasley, and Miss Clarkson can have his room. I want to keep the murder room and Merriwether's empty for the time being. Tessa can bunk in with Mrs. Thedford."

"Now, see here—" Armstrong protested.

"Button yer lip!" Cobb said.

"I ain't emptyin' no chamber pots!" Madge cried.

"What'll I tell my housemaids?" Frank said.

"Tell 'em actors are finicky an' *temper-mental*," Cobb suggested.

"That should do it." Marc smiled.

"There's still a problem, though," Mrs. Thedford said.

"I know," Marc said. "You are due to perform excerpts from Shakespeare tonight, a playbill in which Mr. Merriwether was heavily committed. And tomorrow night you are to repeat the farce, where, again, Mr. Merriwether is not only a principal player but the entire company is required to make it work."

Mrs. Thedford beamed a smile at Marc that discomfited him more than he let on: "You seem intimately acquainted with the ways of the stage."

"I have done some amateur acting years ago in London," Marc said, "and I hung about the wings and back rooms of the summer playhouses and, once or twice, Drury Lane."

"You will know, then, that we are capable, at short notice, of rearranging our playbill."

"I was counting on that, ma'am." Mrs. Thedford made a moue at the word *ma'am,* but Marc continued. "If you could come up with that potpourri or oleo you mentioned earlier, we'll spread the word that Mr. Merriwether is ill and incommunicado and delay the Shakespeare till tomorrow night, then—"

"But I have patrons to think of!" Frank cried, almost rolling off his stool. "I've put notices in the papers an' tacked up handbills everywhere."

"And I'm sorry for that," Marc said. "And I'm sorry you've got a murdered actor upstairs. But you have little choice. I am relaying here the explicit orders of the governor. If you refuse to co-operate, which is your right, then the Bowery Company will be sequestered elsewhere as material witnesses to a crime, and your brand-new theatre will be darkened, leaving your patrons free to speculate on your reliability as an impresario."

"You bastard!" Mrs. Frank exclaimed on behalf of her husband, who winced a smile at her and patted her hand. She jerked it away.

"We'll do whatever Sir Francis requires," Frank said.

"On Wednesday, then," Marc said, leaning forward, "and this is crucial, the Shakespeare program must go ahead in some fashion."

There was a perplexed pause. "We can most assuredly put together a program of short scenes from Shakespeare using the five remaining members of the company," Mrs. Thedford said, "but they will not have the power that—"

"But you miss my point," Marc said, savouring the drama of the moment. "Sir Francis, for reasons of security that I am not at liberty to reveal, wishes the public not merely to believe that Mr. Merriwether is alive but to observe him in action on Wednesday evening."

"Do you intend to bring Old Hamlet's ghost on stage with us?" Dawson Armstrong snorted.

"Not at all. Jason Merriwether will, to all those in the audience, be performing as usual. But the body inside the costume and the face under the makeup will be mine."

TWELVE

Marc himself supervised the surreptitious removal of Merriwether's corpse. He emptied the trunk in the actor's room of its costumes and, leaving the rifles secure beneath the false bottom, dragged it into the hall. There Jeremiah and Cobb were waiting with the body wrapped tightly in a canvas sheet supplied by Ogden Frank. They squeezed the near-six-foot figure into the five-foot trunk in as dignified a manner as possible, shut the lid, and then locked it with the key Marc had used Monday night.

Wilkie was called up from below to help Cobb and Jeremiah lug it downstairs and through the tavern. Fortunately, while blissfully uncurious and lacking entirely in ambition, Wilkie was as loyal as a spaniel. He simply did as he was bid, happy to be relieved of the tedium of sentry duty. The barroom was crowded, but the regulars, having witnessed the comings and goings of such trunks since Saturday, paid them little heed. Then, with Marc keeping watch, the trunk was slipped into the small ice-barn behind the stables. Blocks of ice were freed from the straw and chopped up, and the pieces packed around the corpse. Poor Merriwether would keep until Thursday. The ice-house was then padlocked.

Marc and Cobb repaired to the dining-room, where they sought out a quiet table in one corner, ordered a flagon of ale and some cold meat with cheese, and reviewed the events of the day.

"Well, Major, you left them *thisbe-ans* without a word to spout, that's fer sure."

"Do you think I convinced them that I can pull this off?"

"Dunno. But they ain't got a lot of choice, have they?"

"Thanks for the vote of confidence."

Marc had done his best to persuade Mrs. Thedford and the others that, at five foot eleven inches, Merriwether was a man to be noticed; indeed, he had been noticed during the troupe's social activities on the weekend. But Marc was just as tall, with a similar build: muscular without being heavyset and very wide across the shoulders. Their colouring was roughly the same except for Merriwether's dark eyes, but then Marc would be seen, even by those who might have dined with the tragedian on Sunday, only as a costumed figure up on a distant stage under flickering candles and above the glare of footlights, bearded and bewigged. He would have to make a conscious effort at lowering his voice to the basso range, but the declamatory style of delivery and exaggerated gesturing currently in vogue would assist in the deception. And Tuesday's announced "illness" would be used as an excuse to forestall impromptu requests for backstage visits. It was Mrs. Thedford herself who suggested that the absence of company members from the environs of the theatre be attributed to the news of a death in her family. Her fellow actors would naturally go into mourning in deference to her sorrow.

It had been at this juncture that the only serious question regarding Marc's scheme had been raised by Lieutenant Spooner from the wings. Could Mr. Edwards actually act and, if so, could he memorize and sufficiently rehearse his lines and cues well enough to deceive the playgoers of Toronto? To that, Marc had replied: "I'll know the answer at dinner-hour tomorrow." And before he had left to oversee the removal of the body, Mrs. Thedford said she would put together the pages of script he would have to learn by rehearsal time at one o'clock the next afternoon. In the meantime, the actors, surprisingly animated, set about preparing something to entertain the sophisticates of the colony later in the evening.

"I'll be upstairs while the rehearsal is in progress, having a close look at Tessa's room and doing a thorough search of the other rooms. Though any evidence there will likely have been hidden or destroyed," Marc admitted to Cobb.

"Well, they couldn't've taken it very far. Wilkie's kept them cooped up there tighter'n a maiden's purse, an' he tracked Madame Thedford all the way to the dining-room when she went to meet Major Jenkin."

"There are stoves in each room for burning whatever might need to be."

"You could grovel through the ashes."

"If grovelling will help Rick, I'll do it," Marc said, and Cobb, to be polite, chuckled.

AFTER ASSURING HIMSELF THAT THERE WAS no microscopic trail of blood along the hall carpet—a trail that would have led him to the killer's room—Marc went to Tessa's door. The wax plug, replaced by Cobb after he had removed the body, had not been dislodged or tampered with. The room was as they had left it last night, minus Merriwether's remains.

The beige carpet had acted like a blotter, recording each spill of blood in blurred but indelible outline. The position of the body, on its back with legs splayed, was thus limned except for the head area. There a ghoulish brown ripple indicated where the skull had been smashed and bled thickly. The slash in the carpet where Rick's sword had stuck in the wood below was clearly visible, surrounded by a dark crimson parabola.

What interested Marc much more, however, were the smudges between the feet of the corpse and the settee about eight feet away near the window overlooking Colborne Street.

According to the corroborated testimony of Beasley, Rick was standing over the corpse, holding the sword in his hands. Presumably, his jacket, breeches, and boots had been sprayed with blood from the victim's still-pumping heart, and in order for it to have got all over Rick's hands and the haft of his sword, he would have had either to bend down and immerse himself in it or to rub it all over himself in some sort of ritual triumph. Neither act befitted the man he knew as Rick Hilliard.

But the smudges between corpse and settee, indicative of footprints, however indistinct, were very curious indeed. They had been made by a boot, though the size and nature could not be determined. Without question, however, they went in only one direction: from the settee to the corpse. Only toe-prints were unambiguously visible and he could find none of them pointing the other way, though there were, to be sure, enough random smudges here and there to make any firm conclusion problematic. Beasley and the police had regrettably contaminated the scene while the blood was still fresh. Still, if Rick had done the deed, he would have had to rise from the settee at Tessa's cry, knock the villain down, and skewer him—after which he would have been more or less bloodied, especially around the boots. Then, presumably, he had staggered to the settee, where there were blood-smears on the edge of the seat. The killer had sat down: two fully outlined boot-prints and a palm-print attested to that. Why? To savour his murderous act? Weather the aftershock? Suffer remorse? Whatever the reason, this pause could have lasted mere seconds because when Beasley arrived—say, two minutes after Tessa's cry—Rick was already back over the body and was still there when Mrs. Thedford and Jeremiah appeared on the scene.

Looking now at these toe-prints, one must conclude that Rick had staggered backwards after being bloodied, then staggered forward again, leaving more prints in the same direction. Possible, Marc thought, but not probable. There just didn't seem to be enough prints to satisfy this interpretation. And as far as he could make out, the backward staggering depicted here did not resemble the way any man would actually have done it: the print-pattern was simply too regular. Moreover, Rick had told him that the first thing he remembered upon waking was noticing blood on his tunic. If that were true, and Marc believed it was, then Rick would have struck and stabbed Merriwether while unconscious and with no memory of either act. Besides which, Rick's jacket had seemed to Marc, when he had examined it closely last night, to be too free of splashes and splatter. The smeared patterns were inconsistent with spouting blood. What that portended he could not guess. All he knew was that, despite the contrary eyewitness testimony, there was reason to doubt that Rick Hilliard had committed murder.

Until he could come up with a more plausible alternative, however, he recognized that he had little chance of convincing the governor or the magistrates of Rick's innocence.

MARC NOW BEGAN TO SEARCH THE other rooms. He opened
each actor's trunk, finding no more false bottoms, went
through the pockets, sleeves, and cuffs of every costume, and
sifted through any ash left in a stove. Merriwether, Armstrong,
and Beasley had obviously not lit fires yesterday evening, so
that only a residual ash remained from fires earlier on the
weekend. And nothing was to be found there beyond the ash
itself. Mrs. Thedford, however, had put on a small fire in her
parlour room, and as Marc rummaged about he did find several
charred bits of what appeared to be linen paper or the cloth
cover of a book. At the moment, though, he could find nothing sinister in the discovery. Mrs. Thedford would have many
papers, playbills, script-pamphlets, cue cards, and the like as
part of her business. What he was searching for specifically
was the container for the laudanum that had been poured into
Tessa's sherry decanter, even if it had been shattered into shards.
Chances were it was somewhere on this floor. He even opened
Mrs. Thedford's perfume bottles and sniffed, precipitating several sneezes but no clue. He picked up a candlestick and shoved
a forefinger up the hollow stem of it. No vial there.

Discouraged, Marc went back out into the hall. He put
himself in Merriwether's shoes for a moment: he waits till the
others have gone down for supper or later perhaps when they've
headed for their cramped dressing-rooms to put on makeup.

Then he slips across to Tessa's room, vial in hand, pours the contents into the decanter, and slips out again. He can't very well leave the vial there, and he would not be foolish enough to hide it in his own room lest something go awry with his plan. But where else? Maybe he had taken it down to the theatre with him; Marc would have to search the dressing-rooms at least.

It was then that he noticed the ornamental spittoon sitting near Armstrong's door. It was not used as a spittoon up here, but its brass filigree, when polished, would gleam handsomely. Gingerly, Marc pressed his right hand into the narrow opening and down into the wider body of the piece. He struck sand. Frank had probably filled it with sand to act as ballast. Wriggling two fingers, Marc managed to delve down far enough to strike something harder than sand. Seconds later he drew out a glass apothecary bottle, its stopper in place. He turned it upside down and there, on the bottom, in very tiny type, he read: *Michaels.* Ezra Michaels operated a chemist's shop near the corner of King and Toronto Streets. And while this empty unlabelled bottle didn't guarantee that the laudanum had come from Michaels, containers often being re-used, it strongly suggested that the narcotic had been purchased somewhere in the capital.

Marc sighed. If only he had found the vial in Merriwether's room. It could have been placed out here by anyone—including Rick. However, if it had been purchased at Michaels, there would likely be a record of the sale and perhaps even a physical description of the buyer. Old Michaels, he knew, boasted that

he never forgot a face. He would put Cobb onto this immediately. Remembering a pencil sketch of the actor, out of costume, on Merriwether's desk, Marc returned to retrieve it. He
would have Cobb take it to Michaels and, if necessary, to every
apothecary and quack homeopath in the city. He might not be
able to prove Rick was innocent of murder, but he'd be damned
if he'd let the young man go to the gallows as a rapist.

WHEN MARC CAME DOWN TO RELIEVE Cobb and send him off
to make the rounds of the chemists, the rehearsal for the impromptu evening ahead was in full swing. Marc took up a stool
and sat unobtrusively in the wings to watch. He had little fear
that any one of the five actors would suddenly decide to sprint
to the double-doors at the front of the theatre, fling back the
bar, and make a run for it down Colborne Street.

On the stage in front of him, illumined only by a single,
half-lit chandelier, stood Dawson Armstrong in top hat and
tails, surrounded by the three women in old-fashioned bonnets and Beasley, with a carter's cap on his head. They were in
the midst of a dramatized reading of Cowper's "The Diverting
History of John Gilpin." Armstrong, as the hapless Gilpin,
who cannot control the horse he's borrowed to ride with his
wife and family to their seaside holiday spot, was miming to
perfection the struggle and strain of the runaway, even while
he narrated the tale. The chorus around him added the comic
commentary of his wife and various bystanders. The whole

thing was highly professional and very funny. Certainly, in a town where runaway horses and wagons were not infrequent, this piece should go over well tonight. Marc himself was impressed by the intensity of concentration that these five managed after the trials of the past fifteen hours, but only Jeremiah had noticed his arrival, offering a brief smile of welcome. When "John Gilpin" came to its risible conclusion, Marc announced his presence by clapping out his approval.

Mrs. Thedford turned, caught his eye, and said with amusement, "I hope those watching this evening are so easily entertained." Then, addressing the others, she said, "Dawson, I think you didn't come in quite soon enough at 'The dinner waits, and we are tired.' Your response here should draw the biggest laugh of the piece, so we don't want to mistime it."

They re-did the middle section of the poem, agreed among themselves that it was improved if not perfect, then Mrs. Thedford said, "Tessa and I will now do 'Lenore.'" Jeremiah stepped smartly forward with several bits of costume for the next number. Tessa, pale but remarkably composed, shook out her blond curls, draped a gossamer wrap over her bare shoulders, and sank to the floor in a lifeless pose. Mrs. Thedford donned a black lace shawl that covered her head and shoulders. Staring sorrowfully at the still, beautiful form at her feet, she began to recite one of the most haunting laments Marc had ever heard. Who the poet was he had no idea, but the grief of the speaker for the dead Lenore was agonizingly real:

See! On yon drear and rigid bier low lies thy love, Lenore,
Come! Let the burial rite be read—the funeral song be
sung!—
An anthem for the queenliest dead that ever died so
young—
A dirge for her doubly dead in that she died so young.
By you—by yours, the evil eye—by yours, the slander-
ous tongue
That did to death the innocence that died, and died so
young.

Then, partway through, the sobbing diminuendos of a violin
joined the grieved speaker, and Marc tore his gaze from the
heartwrenching scene of woman and girl to glance over and
see Clarence Beasley with the instrument under his chin. Tears
welled up in the woman's eyes as the poem neared its mournful
conclusion:

The life upon her yellow hair but not within her eyes—
The life still there, upon her hair—the death upon her
eyes.

Marc felt the surge of his own emotion catch in his throat, and
realized he had been thinking of Uncle Jabez and the sister lost
to him forever. Just as Mrs. Thedford recited the final phrase,
she sank to her knees with the grace of a swan settling over her

eggs while Tessa simultaneously rose through the gauze of her garment till she was almost sitting up. Freeze. Tableau. Music fades. Finis.

No one moved. For a full minute all thoughts drifted inward. The ghost of Jason Merriwether was palpable.

"Well, it's time to liven things up a little," Armstrong said in a voice clear, strong, and uncontaminated by drink. He signed something towards Jeremiah, and the black man grinned and went over to the far wings. In the shadows there was a pile of what Marc had taken to be scenery-flats covered by a piece of sailcloth. Jeremiah whipped this cover away to reveal, not a stack of flats, but a gleaming pianoforte, which he began to push out onto the stage. Well, Marc thought, no wonder Ogden Frank had scratched himself bald worrying about the future of his investment. But who would play the instrument?

It was Dawson Armstrong who sat down before it on a stool and struck a thundering introductory chord. "Ready, ladies?"

The three women came down to the footlights. With Tessa between Mrs. Thedford and Thea Clarkson, they linked arms. Then, to Armstrong's zestful accompaniment, they entertained Marc, enthralled him really, for the next twenty minutes with a series of trios, duets, and naughty ditties from *The Beggar's Opera,* mixing male and female roles willy-nilly. Mrs. Thedford sang in the rich alto range, throaty and vibrant; Tessa's note was descant, tremulously sweet. Thea's voice was contralto, haunted and rippled with the shadow of longing and regret. The latter concluded this set with a solo, an aria in Italian about the heroine's sorrow at the loss of her lover. That was all that Marc could decipher, but there was little need for lyrics here: Thea's voice, her posture, and the sonority of the song itself were sufficient. How she contrived to complete it in such circumstance Marc did not know, but he hoped that somehow the effort was cathartic. When she finished, the women curtseyed and the four men applauded.

Without warning or ado, Armstrong now banged out a single cacophonous chord. Beasley and the women retreated to a bench upstage. Then Jeremiah Jefferson, barefoot and stripped to the waist, leapt into stage-centre. From the pianoforte there now came a steady, rhythmic beat from the lowest keys only, a cadence somewhat like the panic of a heartbeat but not quite, for there was the thump of bravery and bravado in it and an intimation of the erotic.

Under the chandelier's flickering cast, Jeremiah's skin glistened as the muscles beneath tightened and released in response to the primal obbligato of the music. His eyes were closed and his whole face upturned as if anticipating a benediction of rain. But it was the legs and bare feet that fascinated. Their dance was so intricate, so alien, so intrinsically staccato that it was impossible to tell whether it was animated by the piano's beat or was simply a coincidental and parallel harmony. As the rhythm-thrums progressed in intensity and dissonance, Jeremiah's feet became a gray blur, sweat shimmered and shook free, both eyes were wide open and gazed sightless before the music stopped in mid-beat and his body froze as if it were abruptly bronzed.

"Wonderful, wonderful," Mrs. Thedford said to him as all the tension in him was instantly relaxed and he became Jeremiah Jefferson, escaped slave, once again. She signed her pleasure as well, and he smiled his acceptance of her approval.

"But how can he hear the music?" Marc said to Beasley, who was nearest him. "He's deaf."

"Oh," Beasley said, "he can feel the vibrations, especially if the notes are low."

"I've never seen or heard anything like that."

"Then you've never spent any time in the United States," Beasley said.

Mrs. Thedford came over to Marc and handed him a sheaf of papers. "We're all through here now, Mr. Edwards. We're going up to rest before supper and the show at eighty-thirty. I've put together, in sequence, the scripts for tomorrow with your parts marked."

"With all this ahead of me, I won't have time to attend the performance this evening, so I am glad I was able to sit in on your rehearsal."

"We look forward to your being part of it tomorrow." Again, she kept her gaze steadily upon him. He could feel in it an intense curiosity and something much more ambivalent and inaccessible. It unnerved him.

"Cobb will look after you when I leave shortly," he stammered.

"I find that immensely comforting," she said with an enigmatic smile.

When the actors had withdrawn, Marc sat on the vacant stage waiting for Cobb and staring out at the vast space where a hundred or more spectators would be scrutinizing his every twitch and stutter when he made his debut as Jason Merriwether. But his overriding concern at this moment was not the distinct possibility of stage-fright or being prematurely unmasked but, rather, a simple question: How could any one of the people he had just observed in the fullness of their generous talent have committed a brutal murder? And if not one of them, then who?

COBB ARRIVED HALF AN HOUR LATER.

"Did you get to Michaels?" Marc asked at once.

"Good day to you, too," Cobb said, staring at the pianoforte. "We gonna have some song an' dance?"

"Yes. And since I will be at Mrs. Standish's boarding-house memorizing a dozen pages of script tonight, you'll have the pleasure of humming along with it here this evening. You might want to bring Mrs. Cobb—I'm sure I can arrange for a box seat."

"I'll have her get the family gems outta storage."

"What did you find out at the chemist's?"

"Several vials of laudanum were bought there last Saturd'y afternoon by people Michaels didn't know."

"Did you show Ezra the sketch of Merriwether?"

"Yup. But Merriwether wasn't one of 'em."

"Damn. Did you get a look at any of the buyers' names?"

"I did. An' one of them was very familiar. Hang on to yer hat, Major: it was Thea Clarkson."

"My God." Marc had not been prepared for that information.

"Want me to haul her down here? Yer idea that she might've been teamed up with somebody to do the cheater in seems *applause-able* now, don't it?"

"Yes. But I'm going to wait until morning before confronting her. I can't take any chance on disturbing the equanimity of the troupe before the performance tonight. And I'm even reluctant to do so in the morning: this ruse we're attempting must not be compromised."

Cobb sighed. "I think you're more afraid of a rebellion in this province than Sir Francis Swell-Head himself."

"Well, at least it looks now as if we'll be able to demonstrate that Rick didn't drug Tessa in order to have his way with her. What possible connection could there be between Rick and Thea Clarkson?"

"I'm sure that knowin' the world don't consider him a despoiler of virgins will give the lad a lot of comfort as the noose tightens 'round his gullet."

Marc ignored the remark. "It's still possible that Merriwether bought his own laudanum."

"Possible. Michaels ain't the only chemist in town, just the richest."

"It would be so helpful if I could make a direct link between the drugged sherry and Merriwether. Keep looking, will you?"

"In my spare time, ya mean?"

"Whenever you can. Please."

"You headed to yer old boarding-house, then?"

"Yes. Have Wilkie return to guard duty, then go home to your good wife for a few hours."

"She'll be thrilled."

MARC HAD LIVED AT WIDOW STANDISH's boarding-house for the six exciting months he had worked at Government House in the service of Sir Francis Head. He had been happily mothered by Mrs. Standish and coddled by her live-in maid-servant, Maisie. He knew he would be welcomed there without question or comment. Moreover, he would have a quiet place to learn his lines and begin to think about the report on the murder he was to present to the governor at noon.

Right now he wanted very much to walk all the way up to Government House on Simcoe Street and visit Rick. But he had so little in the way of good news, he felt he would most likely leave Rick more anxious and depressed than he already was. At least Cobb had got a message to him that Tessa was fine and concerned about him. But Marc would certainly demand to see him before completing his report. If Spooner had not requested a written statement from Rick, then he would get one himself, though he knew Rick well enough to realize that his initial account would be unchanged. However, some small detail overlooked might well prove to be the missing piece to the puzzle. To this point his own investigation had done little but suggest that only three people were in that room when Tessa's cry started a chain-reaction of events and that, short of a massive conspiracy, the window of opportunity for anyone else to have committed the crime and escape undetected was about two minutes.

Since he had to pass Aunt Catherine's shop on his way westward to Peter Street, Marc decided to stop in and say hello. He felt a stab of guilt as he walked through the alley that led to the back door and the stairs up to her apartment. Not only was the wedding set for a week from Sunday in Cobourg, but Aunt Catherine and Beth were now plotting the fine details and, at the very least, he was expected to show some interest and give nominal approval. Daily letters could now be expected. He should have been free to participate fully in the exchange and, further, should have been allowed the luxury of leisure hours to dream, anticipate, and indulge his fondest fantasies.

Beth had insisted they not worry in advance over insurmountable obstacles or impossible decisions. Thus they had not yet worked out where they would set up house other than that Beth would remain with Aunt Catherine and entertain conjugal visits whenever Marc's normally insignificant duties let him loose from the garrison. Only when "things settled down," in Aunt Catherine's polite phrase, would they turn their attention to the question of whether Beth would move into officers' quarters with him or whether they would rent or buy a house he could only occupy intermittently. And the spectre of his being transferred to the Caribbean or India or Van Diemen's Land was not acknowledged at any level.

Hearing a footstep on the back stairs, Aunt Catherine bustled in from the shop. "Oh, it's you, Marc! I was expecting George back."

Marc was quite happy to miss the sullen George Revere.

"Come on upstairs, I've got news from Beth."

Marc wanted to ask "good or bad?" but dutifully followed Beth's aunt up to her parlour, where she fetched a freshly opened letter from the mantel. She smiled broadly, then looked a mite sheepish.

"Beth has ordered me to confess to a little conniving behind your back."

"For my own good, I assume?"

"I couldn't put it any better. But since you've done nothing but dither about arrangements for a honeymoon—using that god-awful army of yours as an excuse—we've gone ahead and done it ourselves."

"A month in New York or London?"

Aunt Catherine laughed, quite at ease now and more certain than ever that her niece had found a man to match her own spirit and particular humours. "Three days and four nights at Sword's Hotel on Front Street—the bill to be sent to me."

Marc was touched. "That is more than kind," he said.

"Well, it isn't Paris, but at least you won't spend your honeymoon being interrupted by the silly chatter of seamstresses and the loud complaints of over-indulged dowagers looking for the perfect hat!"

"May I see Beth's letter?"

"Certainly. And you'll see there that you and your bride are booked on the mail packet out of Cobourg that'll get you to Toronto before supper time. Now I've got to get back to the shop. Can you stay for a meal?"

"I've got a lot of work that can't wait. Sorry."

"No need to be. Drop in tomorrow if you can." With that she headed down the stairs. "Ah, George," he heard her say, "just take those things right through to the girls."

Marc read eagerly through Beth's letter, written several days after her last one but, not surprisingly given the state of the mail service, nearly overlapping it. He was searching for the slightest negative remark, but the only one that even remotely qualified was a reference to Thomas Goodall's depression over the low commodity prices tempered, Beth assured him, by the healthy progress of Baby Mary and the decision that they had just taken to store their grain and wait for better prices in the spring. According to Beth, the cash they had received from the army as a result of Marc's visit in March and Owen Jenkin's generosity had made the decision possible. Hence, the chances of Thomas, Winnifred, and child pulling up stakes and rushing off to the edge of the earth beyond the Mississippi had been temporarily forestalled. All the other news was upbeat, some of it bordering on the naughty, the letter ending thus: "Auntie, stop reading here. Darling, I long to be in your arms, anywhere but most especially in bed. I count the days and the hours therein. Be well. Your loving wife-to-be, Beth."

Marc found himself trembling. It was actually going to happen. And that knowledge immediately gave him the strength he knew he would need to face the morrow.

THIRTEEN

When Mrs. Standish and Maisie ceased fussing over him, Marc retired to his former room and opened the package of scripts that Mrs. Thedford had given him to study. All three of his scene-sequences were with Mrs. Thedford, which simplified any rehearsal required, and left the rest of the cast and their contributions more or less intact. First up were the two excerpts from *Macbeth* wherein Lady Macbeth tries to drive her waffling mate towards the assassination of King Duncan, followed by the murder scene and its aftermath. These scenes had not been rehearsed yesterday but were obviously ones that Mrs. Thedford and Merriwether had performed often. Next up was a series of excerpts from *Antony and Cleopatra,* cleverly selected, edited, and sequenced to trace the tempestuous affair from its inception to final farewells, concluding with Cleopatra's suicide at stage-centre. Lastly, there was the closet-scene in *Hamlet* where Hamlet beards and upbraids his mother.

Marc was puzzled by this selection because Merriwether was famous for his role as King Claudius, not the younger Hamlet, usually played by Beasley. Hamlet's role here had been clearly assigned to Marc, but as far as he could tell from the program notes scribbled hastily by Mrs. Thedford, in the other scenes from the play surrounding this one, Beasley would take his customary role and Armstrong would do Claudius. Besides being an unusual and potentially confusing arrangement, it seemed to Marc to be exceedingly risky since, as Hamlet, he would be beardless and made up to look like the young man he actually was. The odds of someone in the audience recognizing him or guessing that this Hamlet was not the forty-five-year-old Merriwether were surely increased. But he had little choice. His morning would be taken up with interviewing Thea about the laudanum, writing a report for Sir Francis, and talking to Rick before handing it in. So he sat himself down and began to commit the Bard's iambics to memory.

AT TEN O'CLOCK THE NEXT MORNING, with his report sketched out and under his arm, Marc slipped past Ogden Frank into the empty taproom. He opened the door to the theatre, startled Wilkie awake, and asked him to bring Thea Clarkson down to the hotel dining-room. Moments later, Thea, Wilkie, and Cobb arrived simultaneously. Wilkie scuttled back to his sentry post. Marc mouthed the word *laudanum* at Cobb, who shook his head slowly. Marc then turned to Thea, who looked very nervous, wondering no doubt what new calamity was about to strike. He got right to the point. "We have discovered, Miss Clarkson, that you purchased a quantity of laudanum from Ezra Michaels's shop on King Street last Saturday afternoon."

Thea went white, then red. She stared at the table and said nothing.

"As you know, Tessa Guildersleeve and Ensign Hilliard were drugged with laudanum. The empty bottle, which is un-questionably the one you purchased, was found in the hall up-stairs near Tessa's room. We know you couldn't have committed the murder yourself, but as the supplier of the drug, you must be considered—"

"I had nothing to do with that!" she cried. "Nothing! Why are you doing this to me?" She laid her head in her arms and wept wearily.

"All we need to know," Marc said soothingly, "is whether you have any plausible explanation for why you purchased lau-danum last Saturday."

Thea's tears slowed and stopped. Summoning her strength, she raised her head and faced her tormentors. "I bought the laudanum in order to kill myself."

"I don't understand," Marc said lamely.

"I'm carrying Jason's child, and the bastard refused to

marry me. He wasn't even man enough to admit it was his." Her voice was thin, but very cold.

"But you couldn't go through with it."

"I would've," she said. "But when I got back here, I found I'd lost the stuff somewhere. You can believe me or not. I don't give a damn anymore."

"Oh, I believe you," Marc said. Cobb could only look at him in astonishment.

WHEN THEA HAD BEEN PUT INTO the solicitous care of Madge Frank, where she was to remain for the time being, Cobb lit up his pipe and said to Marc, "You sure she didn't just happen to drop that *loud-numb* near somebody who didn't like Merriwether any more'n her?"

"What I think is that Thea Clarkson is much more likely to harm herself than anyone else. What we know for certain, though, is that we still have a vial of laudanum unaccounted for."

"She could've dropped it anywheres between here an' Michaels's place."

Marc sighed. "And there's still no way to link it to Merriwether himself. By the by, did you and Mrs. Cobb enjoy the performance last night?"

"Yes, we did, though I kept thinkin' I was gonna fall outta that apple-box an' land on somebody I oughtn't to! But them

Yankees can sure sing an' dance! I figured Missus Cobb's foot-tappin' would wake the dead at Lundy's Lane!"

"Well, I want you up there again this evening, and Dora, too, if she so wishes. I want you as my eyes and ears in the theatre proper. I'll assign Wilkie to watch the dressing-room area."

"Even if we manage to fool the traitors inta believin' you're Merriwether, how're you gonna know where an' when they'll get a message to you about a *round-a-view*?"

"That's the Achilles' heel of my plan, I'm afraid. But the rebels or whoever they are know the guns are here in Toronto, and they believe for now that Merriwether is alive and waiting for the second message: they'll deliver it all right. I've just got to be alert enough to recognize it when it comes."

"You gonna take that report up to the governor?"

"Yes, but I'm going to see Rick first. There has to be some detail he's forgotten: I've got to try and help him recall it."

"I better come with ya."

They slipped out the back entrance to Frank's quarters into the alley there.

"You don't haveta come to supper, ya know," Cobb said. "You got more'n enough on yer plate as it is."

"I wouldn't miss it for the world."

SET BACK FROM KING STREET AMONG the autumn vermilion and gold of maple trees and with its cozy gables, its homely chimney-pots and rambling verandahs, Government House looked more like the estate of a country squire dozing in the Dorset sun than it did the seat of power and nerve-centre of a troubled British colony. The duty-corporal recognized Marc and led him and Cobb into the foyer.

"Where are they keeping Hilliard?" Marc asked.

"In the old pantry at the back, sir," the corporal replied, then added in a lower voice, "but it ain't locked."

"Good. Cobb, would you mind waiting here with the corporal? When I'm finished with Rick, I'd like you to accompany me when I present this report to the governor. Your corroboration will be helpful."

"I c'n manage the 'helpful' part," Cobb said, and the corporal smiled.

It was now about eleven o'clock. Before leaving the theatre, Marc had gone upstairs with Cobb and reviewed with each of the actors a written summary of the testimony they had made to him during the interviews on Tuesday morning. He then had each sign the document, with Cobb as witness. Marc knew he wasn't a surrogate justice of the peace, but he needed the semblance of notarized legality if he were to lay out for Sir Francis the apparent scenario of the murder and then point out the anomalies, such as they were. (Thea had been resting and so was excused, but since Cobb had been present during both interviews with her, Marc was not concerned.) He had hoped to have linked Merriwether to the laudanum, but that was now a lost cause. Though the villain most likely had found or purloined it from his distraught mistress, there was no proof of this. Marc realized also that, distracted as he was by the gun-running business and the deteriorating situation in Quebec, Sir Francis would not give Rick Hilliard's case his usual close attention. Rick would simply have to help himself.

"And where do you think you're going?" Lieutenant Spooner had popped out of his office next to the governor's and sprung to a quivering halt in front of Marc.

"I have a report to deliver to Sir Francis, after which we have details to work out regarding this evening."

"Well, then, I will be happy to accept your report on behalf of the governor."

"I must hand it to Sir Francis in person, Lieutenant. There are additional explanations and comments that are necessary to his full understanding of the situation."

"Be that as it may, Lieutenant, you will not be able to see the governor today. He's gone down to the Legislature for emergency meetings with the Executive and the Legislative Council. You have no choice but to give the report to me. Moreover, I have been placed in charge of tonight's operation."

Marc was not prepared for this. While he knew Sir Francis had never forgiven him for what he took to be a personal betrayal, he also knew that the governor liked to be informed directly of matters that concerned him and would, despite everything, be willing to accept Marc's word in regard to statements of fact and reasoned judgements. "All right, then," he said graciously, suppressing his rising anxiety, "I'll give it to you just as soon as I have interviewed Ensign Hilliard. His testimony was given while he was in a state of exhaustion and not yet recovered from having been drugged. It would be unfair to him, and improper of me, not to have him corroborate my notes."

"Oh, I don't think anything as elaborate as that will be necessary," Spooner said with a smug smile.

"Are you refusing me access to him?"

"No, you may see him anytime you like." The smirk oozed and widened. "And you may put any gloss you wish upon the ensign's actions; it won't matter a fig."

Marc felt a sudden alarm. "What in hell do you mean, sir?"

Spooner, who had been teetering heel to toe with hands locked behind his back for balance, now brought the latter into view. In his right hand he held an official-looking document. "I have here an affidavit, duly signed and notarized just minutes ago before Magistrate Thorpe."

"An affidavit signed by whom?"

"By your Ensign Hilliard, of course. Who else?"

"You interviewed him without my permission? Sir Francis put me in charge of the investigation, not you."

"I didn't say boo to him. I didn't need to. He called me in and asked for a magistrate."

"That's not possible." But, of course, it was.

"It seems our young swain was materially moved after his visit with that little trollop from the theatre."

Marc heard Cobb gasp behind him. "Tessa?" he asked, dumbfounded.

"She came flying in here a short while ago, wide-eyed and demanding to see the man who had tried to save her from a fate worse than . . . whatever. What could I do? My heart is not made of stone. I let her have a few minutes alone with him. Then I had her escorted back to the theatre: you must have passed her en route." Spooner was enjoying himself immensely.

"You had no authority to do so!"

"Perhaps not, but I doubt very much if Sir Francis will quarrel with the result of my decision."

Marc knew Hilliard well and was not surprised when Spooner delivered the coup de grâce. "He signed a confession. It's all over."

Marc's furious glare rocked Spooner back on his heels, but he gave no further ground. "I still want to see him." Marc struggled to control the anger building in him: this was no time to lose his composure.

"If you attempt in any way to have Hilliard withdraw his sworn statement or otherwise obstruct the course of justice, sir, I'll have you court-martialled."

"Are you questioning my honour, sir?"

Spooner took a step back, the flush of triumph fading from his face: images of a foggy meadow at dawn, pistols poised, and "seconds" holding their breath flitted before him. "Go in there and do as you like, then. It won't matter. He's finished. And then present yourself in my office—without your henchman. We have more important business to discuss."

• • •

IF MARC HAD EXPECTED TO FIND his friend haggard and anxious after his ordeal, he was soon disappointed. Rick was sitting on a stool in the windowless room reading what appeared to be a novel by the light of a single candle. When Marc entered, Rick looked up and grinned a welcome that might have been meant for the happy arrival of a delinquent brother. "Marc, I'm so glad you've come. The most wonderful thing has just happened, and I need to tell it to the world!" He was beaming. The lines and pouches deposited on his face from two sleepless nights and endless hours of unceasing worry had been drawn into the service of a smile that, however transitory, was nonetheless genuine.

"What in Christ's name have you done?" Marc said before he could stop himself.

"I told you she was an angel, didn't I? Did you see her leaving?"

"You've as good as written your signature on a gibbet," Marc said, still boiling, "and I've been working my balls into a sweat over you for the last thirty-six hours."

Rick looked wounded, but rallied instantly with another ingratiating and infuriating smile. "But I killed him to save her, don't you see?" The smile turned beatific.

"Are you telling me that you now have remembered smashing Merriwether on the skull and driving your sword through his chest while he lay stunned and helpless on his back?"

"I have no memory of doing either. But I must have, mustn't I?"

"Then, for the love of God, tell me what you *do* remember."

"I've put it all down in the affidavit."

"Humour me." Marc's emotions were oscillating between anger and fear, and he fought to keep his mind clear and focussed on the task ahead.

"As I told you Monday night in the tavern, I fell asleep on the settee with my flies open. When I woke up, I felt something sticky all over me, like blood."

"You couldn't see it?"

"Not till I stood up in the moonlight."

"Beasley swore he saw some light coming from the doorway."

"Well, I think the little candle on Tessa's night-table was still lit, but I was staring straight ahead at what I had done."

So much for that discrepancy. "But how do you *know* you did it if you have no recollection of it? Could you stab someone so forcefully and have no inkling that you'd done it?"

"Ah, but I'd been drugged, Marc. I was confused. Some part of my brain must have seen that blackguard on top of my darling and brought me strength enough to smash him on the head with my sword-butt and then—this is what I wrote in the affidavit—I must've seen what he'd done to her and gone a bit crazy. But I was under the influence of the opiate, you see, and my motive was the purest one that any gentleman could have had."

Looking into the guileless and callow face of his young friend, Marc recognized that Rick was assuming he would be released eventually because of the laudanum and the chivalric impulse behind the homicidal deed. "Neither of those defenses will stand up for one minute in a court. You must face the truth, Rick. I know: I've studied the law. And unless you recant and withdraw your confession immediately, using Tessa's visit to explain your quixotic behaviour, your affidavit alone will propel you straight into the hangman's noose."

Rick peered up at Marc, suddenly serious. "I don't wish to die, unless it's in battle. But other than that kind of noble death, to die defending the honour of an innocent is surely a close second." Rick's eyes lit up again, pulling the sagging flesh of his face with them. "And you weren't here, Marc, you didn't see her, you didn't hear her. She got down on her knees and thanked me from the bottom of her heart. She said I would live there forever. She wept for me—oh, they were the most beautiful tears of love and gratitude! And when she left, she gave me her favourite book to read and cherish. Look at the inscription. Is it not the most moving poetry you've ever read?" Rick held out the book and quoted from the inscribed flyleaf: "To my darling hero, Rick Hilliard; yours forever, Tessa."

Marc noticed the title on the spine: *Ivanhoe* by Sir Walter Scott. He wasn't surprised. He needed something sharp, cruel even, to shock Hilliard—the normally intelligent and ambitious ensign—back to reality. "You realize, Rick, that Spooner has suggested to Sir Francis that it was you who drugged Tessa for your own nefarious purpose and then savagely murdered Merriwether when he intervened? And so far, I have not been able to find evidence to wholly refute the charge. You will be hanged as a rapist and a killer, not as a hero out of the pages of Scott or Malory."

Rick took this in. "The corporal told me about Spooner's theory. But Sir Francis knows me: he'll never believe a story like that. And with my confession, why would he bother anyway?"

"Because Merriwether is an American citizen. It just might suit Sir Francis's political interests at present to have the American made the victim."

"But he painted them all as Antichrists during the election!"

"That was then. Right now the governor may be more concerned to keep the U.S. government from financing the local rebels he sees under every bush." Marc was improvising this argument as he presented it, but he had to do something, even if it was underhanded.

"I'll take my chances on that score. Besides, I have Tessa's judgement here in writing, and I'll take the sight of her clutching my knees and weeping for me to my grave."

While Tessa herself will be on the steamer for Detroit tomorrow afternoon, Marc thought, but knew better than to try to tarnish the saint's halo in the eyes of the idolater. Instead, he turned and left without another word. Spooner was right. It was finished.

MARC ASKED COBB TO RETURN TO the theatre and make sure that Tessa was there. Wilkie was due for a tongue-lashing, but there was little point in chastising the girl or her warder: the damage had been done, and Hilliard was, after all, the author of his own fate.

Marc then spent one of the most difficult half-hours he could remember in the service of his country. He and Spooner had to establish the ground rules for their attempt to ensnare the rebels in quest of Yankee rifles. Spooner began by admitting that he had surreptitiously placed a watch on the storage-shed and ice-house. While Marc was annoyed that such a move might already have alerted the rebels to the presence of the military and thus spooked them, he grudgingly accepted the necessity of ensuring that the guns were not simply carted off. Spooner wanted to surround the theatre with troops and have mounted officers nearby, but Marc convinced him to have both groups at least a block away and well hidden. An agent secreted in the loft of the livery stable, with Frank's help, would be able to observe both sheds, the rear entrance to Frank's quarters, and the alley beside the tavern. A second agent could be hidden in a market-stall directly across the road with a view of the tavern-entrance and of Colborne Street in front of the theatre.

If and when contact had been made, word would be relayed by Cobb or Wilkie to Spooner, who would be in the audience and remain in the pit after the play was over. Because they did not know when or how the contact would be made, much had to be left to chance. If there was no time for Marc to consult or relay details, a small group of mounted officers was to follow Marc to any rendezvous, maintaining a safe distance, since the rebels would be very wary of being caught or betrayed. Marc would be unarmed—to Spooner's horror—because he was certain to be searched and wanted nothing to frighten off the plotters. He stressed, with only moderate success, that his principal task was to try to identify them, not capture them. They could be rounded up easily, but only if the ruse was complete and undetected. Spooner provided Marc with a canvas tote-bag for the two rifles—to be secretly marked—which he was planning to take as bait. The exchange of even one dollar for the sample would constitute high treason. The two men nodded agreement, and Marc left for the theatre, determined to get at least one thing right before the day ended.

As both he and Cobb had been doing all day, Marc slipped into Frank's place through the back door because Marc's exceptional height and distinctive tunic made him an easily recalled figure, as did Cobb's uniform and eccentric profile. If the rebels were keeping an eye on the theatre and hotel, then the frequent arrivals and departures of officers would have raised more than suspicion. Of course, if the rebels had engaged one or more of Frank's stable boys to act as scouts, then the jig was up anyway. He would only know for sure sometime this evening when "Jason Merriwether" hit the boards with his inimitable presence and panache.

FOURTEEN

The rehearsal went much more smoothly than Marc had anticipated. Mrs. Thedford had arranged that only those actually involved in the scenes shared by her and Marc be present: that meant Dawson Armstrong, who delivered the famous "barge" speech describing Cleopatra, cleverly placed at the beginning of the sequence, and Thea Clarkson, who played Charmian, the great queen's confidante, in the death-by-asp scene at the end. For most of the two hours they spent together, Marc and Annemarie Thedford were alone on the Regency stage. The other scenes in the program, well rehearsed on Monday afternoon, had been reviewed earlier for any changes necessitated by the star's absence and the cast was then sent upstairs to rest.

They'd begun with *Antony and Cleopatra*. As Cleopatra, Mrs. Thedford seated herself upon a low stool near the unlit footlights. Antony was to stand off to her left and gaze soulfully at her as Enobarbus (Armstrong) introduced the Egyptian queen to him and to the audience. Armstrong had barely begun when Marc felt a chill run up his spine. Without costume or makeup, Mrs. Thedford had transformed herself into the figure described by the Bard's poetry. Moreover, it seemed to Marc that many of the phrases described Mrs. Thedford herself.

> I saw her once
> Hop forty paces through the public street,
> And having lost her breath, she spoke, and panted,
> That she did make defect perfection
> And, breathless, pour forth breath . . .
>
> Age cannot wither nor custom stale
> Her infinite variety: other women cloy
> The appetites they feed, but she makes hungry
> Where she most satisfies . . .

As Armstrong finished, Cleopatra gave a flick of her right hand and Enobarbus withdrew. Marc heard him clumping offstage towards his room upstairs. Then Cleopatra spoke her opening lines:

> If it be love indeed, tell me how much . . .

Antony, besotted with her lethal beauty, found himself replying:

There's beggary in the love that can be reckoned . . .

The scene unfolded, speech and counter-speech, as the ageing lovers bantered and probed, swore fidelity and recanted. The lines which last night had been words on a page and vague phrasings in the head now came readily to Marc's tongue, and he felt the emotion behind the rhetoric when he declaimed:

Let Rome in Tiber melt and the wide arch
Of the rangèd empire fall! Here is my space,
Kingdoms are clay . . .
                    The nobleness of life
Is to do thus.

Yes, he was thinking—even as he flinched under Cleopatra's scornful, teasing ripostes—there is truth here: kingdoms *are* clay, and love is . . .

"I am amazed," Mrs. Thedford was saying, "and it takes much to amaze a woman of my years and experience. You did that as well or better than Jason, who always made too much of himself as Antony to be a credulous dupe of the queen's charms." There was a catch in her voice and Marc realized that the mention of Merriwether's name had unexpectedly upset her.

"He was a fine actor," Marc said. "He will be missed."

"Yes, he will."

"And I feel like a fraud and a cad pretending to be him, but what we're doing tonight is an urgent matter of the province's security. I would not be part of such a scheme if it were not so."

"No wonder you can play Antony with such ease." She smiled, her composure regained. "Let's work through the rest of these scenes, then I'll have Thea come down for my grand exit."

The next two scenes went more haltingly because they involved a range of suddenly shifting emotions as the conflict of sensual love and moral duty, personal commitment and public politics, the power of love and the love of power played itself out. Cleopatra's death-scene, with Thea's assistance, was a moving and grandiose bit of theatre, and only an actress of deep character and subtle sensibility, like Annemarie Thedford, could rescue it from mere melodrama. With period costumes and stronger lighting, it would bring the audience to its knees.

"Now, let's see if you can switch to Macbeth," she said when Thea had left. "I've seen few actors under thirty-five years of age who can do the part justice. However, in the three scenes we're doing together, Lady Macbeth is the dominant force—goading, wheedling, and bolstering her weak-willed husband, who, nonetheless, is an impressive military man."

"What do you suggest? I've got the lines down and I've seen the play at Covent Garden in London, so I can visualize this part of the play leading up to the murder and the moments just after it."

"Well, perhaps you could think of me as a mother figure. Lady Macbeth is often played as an older, haglike virago—bossing you about and taunting you over your lack of courage and questioning your manhood when *you* believe you're a grown-up boy who can think for himself. That should give you the tenor of these scenes and put some vigour into the lines."

This stratagem took less practice than either of them imagined, for so quick and cutting were Lady Macbeth's barbs, so mocking and sardonic her tone, and so convincing the fury in her face that Marc found himself reacting viscerally. Macbeth's pathetic and ineffectual replies popped out with the requisite cowardice firmly attached. It was only the speed of the exchanges and their pacing that prompted repeated run-throughs. Marc found it very difficult to re-establish his role during such repetitions, but Mrs. Thedford, to his wonderment, was able to recapture the intensity of a dialogue even when it was restarted in the middle. He soon acknowledged to himself that, in the *Macbeth* sequence at least, Mrs. Thedford would have to carry the audience: his amateurism would be on full display. Fortunately, the concluding piece of the *Macbeth* sequence was to be Lady Macbeth's hand-washing scene with Thea as the gentlewoman and Beasley as the doctor, which had been rehearsed to perfection earlier. She would be cheered to the echo.

By the end of the *Macbeth* rehearsal Marc felt drained. The post-murder scene, with its multiple references to blood and seas being incarnadined, stirred up images of the carnage in Tessa's room and a soldier's sword steeped in gore. Mrs.

Thedford seemed to be capable of charging her lines and gestures with legitimate passion and then simply withdrawing to whatever constituted her own personality with its separate virtues and feelings. But then, of course, here was a woman something less than fifty years of age who had succeeded in a man's world against insuperable odds. Extraordinary emotional strength, self-confidence, and perseverance, in addition to intelligence and talent, would have been necessary. To own and manage a theatre and theatrical troupe would require the ability to motivate and supervise people who were inherently competitive, envious, and insecure, to navigate the shoals of financing and legal contracts, and to weather the inevitable economic setbacks and personal betrayals that were the thespian's lot. Undoubtedly, it was such strength of character that had carried her through the crises of the past two days. If she had wept or lost her nerve or entertained despair, she had done so in private and alone.

"Now, then, Marc, let's do the *Hamlet*. It should be child's play after Antony and Macbeth."

"But why not let Clarence play Hamlet in this scene as well as the others?"

"In order to keep our audience happy and unquestioning, I felt we needed to find a third piece for you, but Beatrice and Benedick would have been impossible for us because it's all tempo and tone, and our complete *Hamlet* sequence is too long and involves too much blocking. So I just picked out this edited version of the bedchamber scene between Hamlet and Gertrude—one we could rehearse alone."

So they proceeded as before. The lines and speeches came easily, as Mrs. Thedford had foreseen, in part because Hamlet was closer in age and temperament to Marc and in part because Marc had been compelled to memorize copious swatches of the text during his home-tutoring period with Dr. Crabbe. But he found it much harder to be on the attacking side than the receiving end, as he had been in *Macbeth,* much harder to be shaming his mother with lines like.

> Nay, but to live
> In the rank sweat of an enseamèd bed,
> Stewed in corruption, honeying and making love
> Over the nasty sty!

and to watch in horror as the proud and confident Mrs. Thedford reduced herself to a cringing, mortified creature, defenseless against her son's moral tirade. With the ghost's appearance edited out, the scene wound down with the queen utterly abashed and Marc having to mouth epithets that caused his gorge to rise, but apparently made young Hamlet feel purged and righteous:

> by no means . . .
> Let the bloat king tempt you again to bed,

Pinch wanton on your cheek, call you his mouse,
And let him for a pair of reechy kisses
Or paddling in your neck with his damned fingers,
Make you ravel all this matter out . . .

When Mrs. Thedford had concluded the piece with "I have no life to breathe / What thou hast said to me," she took a deep breath, reached over, and caressed Marc's wrist. It was a simple gesture, wistful almost. But it struck Marc like a jolt. He felt himself physically aroused—attracted and intimidated at the same time. There seemed to be something mysterious and taboo in her appeal that left his feelings in turmoil.

"Are you all right?" she asked, her concern now taking over. "I've pushed you too hard, I believe. I've forgotten that this ordeal has had a personal meaning for you as well as us."

"I haven't slept well, but I'll be fine."

"Your friend, Mr. Hilliard, stands in the shadow of the gallows?"

"I'm afraid he does. And there is nothing I can do to help. He has confessed."

Marc could see his own pain mirrored in her eyes, and some of his confusion. "Was it Tessa's visit?"

Marc nodded. "He is under the illusion that he has killed for love, even though he has no recollection of doing the deed."

"That sounds Shakespearean, doesn't it?" she said lightly. Then her face became grave. "But I *am* sorry that Tessa escaped us this morning. She went out through the tavern. She's still a child in many ways, but she has done Mr. Hilliard a great wrong."

"And he has wronged himself also," Marc said. He smiled with some effort and said sincerely, "Anyway, I would like to thank you for helping us with this enterprise tonight. I may not get a chance to do so again."

"Oh?"

"You are free to make arrangements to leave tomorrow, if everything works out as we expect this evening. Unless you want to stay and complete your schedule."

"Tempting as that is, I think it best for the others if we get on to Detroit as soon as possible. I'll give you an address in Buffalo where you can ship the body, if that is all right. Jason has an elderly aunt there, his only relative."

"I'm sure the governor will approve that."

"And Major Jenkin tells me you are to be married soon."

"Yes. A week this Sunday."

"Lucky young woman," she said. She paused and went on: "This . . . enterprise tonight, will it put you in danger?"

"Not if my acting skills hold up."

Mrs. Thedford smiled. "They'll do just fine." It seemed for a moment that she might take him in her arms and . . . what? But she didn't, and for that Marc was grateful beyond measure. If she had, he had no idea what he might have done or what irrevocable train of events he might have set in motion.

"Break a leg," she said.

IT WAS FIVE O'CLOCK WHEN HE left Merriwether's room, where he had been mentally rehearsing his roles, and started walking towards the Cobb residence. Using the key that Ogden Frank had given him, Marc left the theatre by exiting through the door that led directly into the owner's quarters (thus avoiding the tavern altogether) and then out the rear door into the alley. Frank, with his hand-wringing now more anticipatory than despairing, had even supplied him with a key to the outside door so that he could slip in and out by this means whenever he wished.

On the bed in Merriwether's room Marc had laid out a suit of the dead actor's clothes from cap to boots. If he were called out to a rendezvous tonight after the performance, then he would have to go in Merriwether's guise, not his own. But for now he was just another soldier strolling east along King Street towards the "old town," where Cobb lived.

Marc felt somewhat guilty that he had not visited the constable before now. Despite the differences in background, life experience, and class, Marc had developed a comfortable rapport with Cobb, without either of them having to resort to pretense or false formality, or move an inch away from who they were. Marc respected Cobb's native cunning and hoped Cobb's admiration of his intelligence was not misplaced. He soon found the clapboard cottage on Parliament Street just above Front. He was delighted to find a neat little house freshly painted or whitewashed and, around it on three sides, the vestiges of the summer's vigorous vegetable garden. Bean-hills, withered tomato plants on stakes, yellowed cucumber vines—all attested to care and diligence. He almost tripped over a fat pumpkin-squash beside the stone path that meandered up to the front door.

"Kickin' 'em won't make them ripen any quicker!" Cobb called from the doorway.

"A bit like us, then?"

Cobb chortled. "Glad ya could make it, Major. I figure a solid meal and a restful pipe or two should set us both up fer the ruckus later on."

"I needed to get away from that place—and Government House. Thanks for inviting me."

Cobb led Marc inside, where he found himself in a cozy parlour with cushioned chairs, a throw rug, a stone fireplace, and a deal table set for supper. The remains of a log in the hearth radiated a welcoming warmth.

"It may be 'umble but 'tis h'our h'own," Cobb said in his execrable imitation of a Cockney accent.

"It's very comfortable. Your missus must be a conscientious homemaker."

Cobb looked decidedly uncomfortable at this compliment. "Most times, I'd agree with ya, Major. But not today."

"Is Dora ill?"

"Healthy as a horse," Cobb snorted, as if this state were somehow sinful. "Healthy as two horses!"

"What's wrong, then?"

"She ain't here, that's what."

"Oh," Marc said, confident that Cobb would get to the point sooner or later.

"Off on one of her calls—again."

"I don't quite understand."

"She's a midwife," Cobb said in a tone that was both boastful and accusatory. "An' the women of this town arrange to have their *off-springers* at the most *inconvening* time they can think up!"

"I didn't know that," Marc said, casting about for an appropriate place to park himself. "But surely you are proud of her: she plays a most important role in the community."

Cobb looked as if one cheek or the other would soon burst. "But *she* was the one that went an' invited you!"

Marc just laughed, and sat himself down in one of the two cushioned chairs. "You're worried about a breach of manners? Well, don't be. Besides, I smell something delectable cooking in the other room."

"Well, as long as you're not upset, then I guess I can't be, can I?" Cobb smiled, sat down opposite Marc, and offered him his tobacco pouch. "I just figured the English *gentle-tree* was a stickler for good manners."

Marc took the pouch, packed his pipe, and soon both men were smoking with meditative satisfaction. The aroma of some kind of meat stew grew more enticing.

"You didn't get the lad to change his story, then?"

"No. And now it's too late. We can't keep the troupe here any longer when there's a confessed murderer already in custody. I've talked Spooner into waiting until the morning before taking Rick down to your chief and the magistrate. Thankfully, Sir Francis has been incommunicado all day and Spooner, I suspect, is afraid to have Rick charged without the governor's explicit approval."

"You still think one of them actors did it?"

"That seems less and less likely. But one of them knows more than he's saying."

"Shall I bring in the supper, Dad?"

Marc turned to see a girl of nine or ten years standing under the curtained archway between the parlour and the kitchen. Marc blinked and stared. She was beautiful: tall and willowy with long brown hair, large brown eyes, and a freckled grin. How she had contrived to be born from the union of Horatio and Dora Cobb was a mystery, Marc thought, one of those miracles of generation that keep humans humble and awe-struck.

"This here's Delia," Cobb said proudly. "My first-born. Say hello to the officer, girl."

Delia performed a brief, under-rehearsed curtsey, blushed, grinned, and said, "How d'ya do, sir?"

"Now that you've gone an' *inter-ruptured* us, ya might as well bring the other one in fer viewin'," Cobb rumbled with mock annoyance.

"Fabian wants to see the soldier," Delia said, and rolled her eyes.

Fabian was duly ushered in so that he and Marc could carry out a mutual inspection. The boy was a masculine copy of his sister: bright-eyed, handsome, and shy without being self-effacing.

"And what do you want to be when you grow up?" Marc asked him.

"A grenadier," said Fabian smartly.

"And you?" Marc said to Delia.

"A grenadier's wife," she said promptly.

"I warned you kids not to start yer teasin' ways 'round our guest," Cobb said. "Now get out there an' bring in the food."

Brother and sister exchanged grins, bowed theatrically, and pranced out of the room.

Amused, Marc said, "You disapprove of grenadiers on principle?"

"They do that just to *aggra-grate* me, Major. They're both smart as a whip on a bare bum! The common school up the street ain't seen nothin' like 'em since it opened."

"And you don't need your sums and Greek declensions to be an officer in Queen Victoria's glorious army?"

Cobb gave an invigorating pull on his pipe. "I wouldna thought so," he said.

$\bullet \quad \bullet \quad \bullet$

Supper consisted of a tasty venison stew, replete with vegetables from the garden and cellar—turnips, parsnips, potatoes, onions, carrots—and crowned with dumplings. On the side there was bread baked earlier in the day and butter from the market. An apple pie capped off the feast. The children served the meal, mimicking and perhaps mocking their notion of what waiting on high table entailed, but they ate quietly on their own out in the kitchen.

When he had finished his pie, Marc said, "I'm still puzzled about how that bottle of laudanum got from Thea's possession into the spittoon where Merriwether or the killer left it. If Rick is to hang, then the least I can do for him is to prevent his being thought a rapist."

"Well, Major, if that silly actress was befuddled enough to try an' do herself in with *loud-numb*—I figure she'd've needed two or three bottles fer the job—then heaven knows what she might've—"

"What actress're you talkin' about, Mr. Cobb?"

The two men swung around to face Dora Cobb, who now filled the lower portion of the curtained archway. Her round cheeks glowed red from an exertion she had not yet fully recovered from.

"You wasn't supposed to hear that, Missus Cobb."

"Well, Mr. Cobb, I could stuff me thumbs in me ears, but it wouldn't wipe away the words. Now, tell me, what actress an' what laudanum?"

"Now, you know, Missus Cobb, we agreed to keep our oars outta each other's canoe—"

"Or else you'd've known I had one of them actresses here in the house last Saturd'y."

Dora Cobb demanded to be fed and watered before she would elaborate on a remark that had elicited gasps from her husband and guest. So they waited patiently until she wiped the gravy from her lips with a delicate pinky, gave Cobb a reproachful look, and started in on her tale.

"This Dorothea person comes knockin' at my back door about two o'clock in the afternoon. She looks like Death's daughter, so I ask her in. Even before she starts talkin', I recognize the symptoms, so I ain't surprised when she tells me she's pregnant."

"We already know that," Cobb said.

"An' that's all you'll be knowin', Mr. Cobb, if you have the impudence to butt in one more time."

Cobb flushed, but decided not to risk retaliation.

"Please, go on," Marc said soothingly, but he, too, found his heart beating with anticipation.

"'Well,' says I, 'it'll be a few months down the road before ya need my services.' At that, she busts out cryin'. An' pretty soon I get the whole sad story. Seems this actor fella got her in the fambly way an' then, havin' had his fun—like most men—he tells her to bugger off. Seein' her life is now ruined, she decides to do away with herself an' the unborn child, so she goes to old Ezra fer some 'poison.' When she gets outta the shop, she changes her mind—goes back in and asks Ezra's wife if she knows of a midwife in town. That brings her here. What she wants now, of course, is to do in the bairn but not herself, an' she reckoned I'd know how to go about it—fer a fee."

"Missus Cobb don't have nothin' to do with that sort o' sin!" Cobb said. "Do ya, sweet?"

Dora acknowledged his defense of her integrity with a dip of her chins, and went on. "I told her just that, an' she sets inta bawlin' somethin' terrible. I was glad the kids was out. Anyways, I set her down an' let her talk and talk. An' by the time she left, she was feelin' a whole lot better. I told her that men often reacted that way at first, but if she gave him a little time an' space an' was real patient, he'd probably come around. 'Course, that was a wad of malarkey, but I didn't want the woman's suicide on my hands."

"You obviously did well for her," Marc said. "She is suffering, but I believe she'll be all right." He didn't think it prudent to mention the brutal death of the child's father.

"I know, luv. Me an' Mr. Cobb saw her last night: she was warblin' like a robin after a good rain."

"Missus Cobb's the one fer curin' any ailment that's female," Cobb boasted.

"Just to make sure, though," Dora said, "I did sneak that bottle outta her pocket before she left."

"WELL, MAJOR, WE NOW KNOW THERE was two vials of that stuff," Cobb said as he fingered the bottle of laudanum that Dora had taken from Thea. The children had gone out to play, and Dora was getting herself "prettied up" for the theatre later on.

"And the only person with any motive for drugging Tessa's sherry is Merriwether. I figure he put it there in the afternoon and hid the bottle in the spittoon when he came out of Tessa's room, expecting to dispose of it permanently at a more auspicious time. But, damn it, Cobb, that vial had Michaels's name on it, just like this one. I'm convinced that Merriwether bought the drug here in Toronto, on Saturday or perhaps Monday morning."

"But I showed that picture of Merriwether's head in every place that might peddle the stuff."

"And you saw the names on Michaels's ledger that neither he nor his staff nor you recognized?"

"I did. Besides Thea Clarkson, there was only three of 'em, mind you, 'cause we was only lookin' at Saturd'y an' Monday, right?"

"That's right."

"And I even took them names along with the picture inta the dives where my snitches hang about."

"You have the list of names Michaels gave you?"

"Right here, Major." Cobb got up, went over to his

greatcoat on a nearby chair, rummaged through one of the deep pockets, and fished out a crumpled piece of paper. He handed it skeptically to Marc, who scanned its contents:

Chas. Meredith

Martin Acorn

Claude Kingsley

"What is it, Major?"

"Merriwether was at Michaels, all right. In disguise."

"How do ya figure that?" Cobb was amazed, as a child is before a magician.

"Claude Kingsley is King Claudius—Merriwether's little joke."

"But Ezra never forgets a face."

"True, but he didn't see the face in the sketch you showed him. He saw the one on the playbill: Claudius with his black wig, bushy eyebrows, and beard. I'll bet Merriwether even hunched over to lessen the effect of his height." Marc looked at Cobb. "You did mention his height, didn't you?"

Cobb took offense. "I said he was a big bugger about so high, but I didn't think I needed to go on an' on about the body parts when Michaels had a picture of the fella's mug starin' up at him!"

"It's still two hours till the show starts at eight-thirty," Marc said. "That should give you time to fetch that portrait of Claudius from Merriwether's dressing-room and show it to Ezra. But I have absolutely no doubt that we've traced the drug to the villain who violated Tessa."

"I can do that, Major. Dora'll be some time gettin' herself harnessed up."

"Don't you see what this means, Cobb? We have incontrovertible proof that Rick Hilliard is not a rapist."

Cobb grimaced. "That oughta make his mama feel a whole lot better."

FIFTEEN

The third evening of performances by the distinguished Bowery Touring Company began much as the first two had. Carriages ferrying the self-proclaimed gentry from their august domiciles to the distinction of a theatre-box with padded seat and unobstructed view started to arrive shortly after eight o'clock. By eight-fifteen there was a crush of tardier arrivals along the north side of Colborne Street and, on the south side, a similar crush of gawkers offering gratuitous comment. Under the false façade of the balcony, Ogden Frank, rotund and obsequious, greeted friend and stranger alike and passed them along to Madge, who checked their bona fides with steely-eyed precision.

The air of normality was deliberate. Marc was certain that

those seeking to make contact with the gunrunning tragedian would be scrutinizing the situation from within and without. Spooner's scouts and spies had, so far, kept a discreet distance. By 8:25 the box seats, the gallery, and the pit were full. The Regency was abuzz with anticipation. An evening of the Bard's best comic and tragic bits performed by seasoned actors from New York City was an experience not to be missed in colonial Toronto, one you might wish to tell your grandchildren about, should they be so polite as to listen. For the next two hours or so, the rumours of rebellion and rumblings of discontent could be forgotten.

Marc was with his fellow actors in the dressing-room area to the left of the stage. On a rack next to his mirror hung the two costumes he would need after his initial role as Hamlet: Antony's imperial Roman togs and Macbeth's royal robes, the latter complete with wig, chin-beard, and ersatz eyebrows. Thea Clarkson graciously assisted him with his makeup for Hamlet. There was no wig or full beard, but his own sandy hair and eyebrows were powdered to look as blond as a Viking's, and a small goatee of similar hue depended from his chin. He hoped that these changes and the costume would be enough to deceive whoever might be watching for reasons unconnected with the stage. At least he would be tested early on. And if his cover were blown, his assumption was that the rebels would merely vanish, smarting but unlikely to risk exposure by ex-acting any revenge. Just how the contact would be made was still anyone's guess, as Merriwether was supposed to know its nature and Marc did not. Nevertheless, he felt he had to try to anticipate it. His intuition told him that the most obvious opportunity for receiving instructions for a rendezvous would be during that fifteen-minute period after the performance ended when well-wishers pushed onto the stage to meet the stars and press gifts upon them. One such gift could easily contain the clandestine message. But just in case a surreptitious entry to the dressing rooms was attempted, Marc had Wilkie placed where he could keep an eye on them as well as upon the door that led to the Franks' quarters. On the other side of the stage, Chief Constable Sturges stood guard over the tavern-entrance and the stairway to the upper rooms.

Marc checked his Hamlet image in the watery mirror, then joined the others in the wings.

"No need to be nervous, Marc," Mrs. Thedford said, touching him on the forearm. "I can't imagine you requiring a prompt, but if you do, watch my lips." She leaned across and gave him a phantom peck on the cheek, exposing, as she did so, the upper-halves of her unmotherly breasts. Then she was sweeping onto the stage as the first scene from the play got under way to welcoming applause.

From his position in the wings, Marc could see the boxes on the far wall of the theatre. Dora and Horatio Cobb, along with Owen Jenkin, were in the one most distant, which afforded the constable a wide view of the pit, the gallery, and the other boxes. On the opposite side, Marc knew, Lieutenant Spooner and his guests occupied a middle box. There was nothing any of them could do now but allow the drama to unfold.

Dawson Armstrong delivered Claudius's soliloquy at prayer with such spit and verve that the audience brought him back for two bows. Marc cooled his heels and trembled in the wings. Mrs. Thedford, as Gertrude, stood beside him again, but she was fully in role now and said nothing. He could hear her taking deep, rhythmic breaths. Then it was their turn and Marc, feeling as if he were stepping into the cauldron of battle for the first time, walked with knees aquiver into a blaze of light. When he turned to the audience to deliver his opening lines, the words, mercifully, came out. The hundred pairs of eyes appraising him in his nakedness—for so he felt—were, with equal mercy, invisible, drowned in the sea of black set up by the footlights.

HAM: How now, what's the matter?

GERT: Hamlet, thou hast thy father much offended.

HAM: Mother, you have my father much offended.

The quality and pitch of their long rehearsal yesterday was instantly rekindled, and Marc soon forgot the audience, himself, and why he was doing this. He was the Prince of Denmark excoriating his faithless mother. The applause, as their scene ended, came more as a shock than an expectation, so engrossed was he in Hamlet's angst. On the other hand, Gertrude dissolved immediately and Mrs. Thedford took her formal, practised curtsies as a matter of right, while tugging him into his hesitant bows. Then, as they were leaving the stage, the adrenaline of praise struck: he felt as if he might float down the steps to his dressing-room.

"Well done," Mrs. Thedford said. "You were to the manner born."

"I've still got Antony and Macbeth to negotiate," Marc said with a modesty he didn't actually feel. "Oh, here's your looking-glass: I know what it means to you."

During the *Hamlet* scene, when Hamlet holds the hand-mirror up to his mother and her sins, Mrs. Thedford had insisted that they use the one she kept in her room upstairs, "for good luck," she had said. He was happy now to return the treasure intact.

"Solid work, young man," Armstrong said, and meant it.

Apparently Marc had passed more than one test out there on the boards.

MARC HAD NO MORE SCENES UNTIL after the interval, but he did return to his dressing-room to change into Antony's toga and sandals. Although unbearded, Antony sported a close-cropped black wig and charcoal eyebrows with artfully darkened skin, effectively camouflaging Marc's fair complexion and light brown hair. As he waited anxiously for the interval to begin, he could hear laughter and spontaneous applause as the scenes from *Twelfth Night* completed the first half of the evening. Wilkie came over to report that no one had tried to enter the premises under his watch. Minutes later, the other actors hurried past to their individual cubicles to rest and prepare for the second half.

Meanwhile, Ogden Frank and his assistants made sure no spectator got backstage from the pit through the doors to the left or right, but they did not discourage the relaying of messages and bonbons under the auspices of Madge Frank. Tessa, whose performance of Ophelia had brought audible sobs from the viewers, received a box of sweets and a proposal of marriage. Thea Clarkson as Cordelia was rewarded with a bouquet of chrysanthemums, and Mrs. Thedford with an array of cards and billets-doux. There were no messages for either Hamlet. At one point before they resumed, Cobb managed to catch Marc's eye from his position near the refreshment stall, and shook his head slowly. Perhaps no contact would be made, either because the rebels had simply got cold feet or they had begun to suspect subterfuge and betrayal.

While Marc flubbed a line or two as Antony, as he had predicted, Mrs. Thedford's Cleopatra was so sensual, sardonic, and touching, with quicksilver shifts in mood and tempo, that few in the audience cared what kind of Antony provoked such a complex woman into being, so long as he had. Mother and whore, wanton lover and calculating bitch, goddess and little lost girl—she played them all within a single body with a singular voice. When she rose from her death-scene to accept the approbation raining down upon her, Antony, long dead and forgotten nearby, remained where he was.

Marc returned to his dressing-room to change into his Macbeth costume, but sensed something amiss as soon as he stepped inside. It took him several seconds to realize that there was an extra costume on the rack beside the other two. He reached into one of the pockets of the tunic and, unsurprised, drew out a plain envelope. Inside was the note he had been expecting, printed by hand in block capitals:

IMMEDIATELY AFTER THE PERFORMANCE, GO TO EAST MARKET STREET, NORTH END. MOUNT THE HORSE THERE. RIDE EAST ALONG KING TO SCADDINGS BRIDGE. TWO MILES UP THE KINGSTON ROAD YOU WILL BE MET. BRING SAMPLE. DO NOT ALLOW YOURSELF TO BE FOLLOWED. YOU WILL BE WATCHED ALL THE WAY. DESTROY THIS NOTE.

So, this was it. His ruse had worked. Now if he could only remember his lines as Macbeth, all might yet be well. Then, with a guilty start, he remembered that he had not thought of Rick Hilliard once in the past two hours. But there was just too much to do here and now. He went down to find Wilkie. Someone had delivered this costume and was, most likely, part of the conspiracy.

"I found an extra costume in my cubicle," Marc said to Wilkie.

"No mystery there, sir. I put it there myself," Wilkie offered cheerfully.

"And who delivered it to you?"

"Oh . . . I see. It was the same fella that's been here a coupla times before, bringin' costumes from some repair shop in town."

Marc froze.

"They usually let him come in through the tavern, but seein' as the play was goin' on and all, the barkeep took him through Frank's place and in this here door. But I didn't let him get more'n a foot inside here. I told him to halt, an' said I'd be the one to deliver anythin' that needed deliverin'."

"Medium height and build?" Marc said, dreading the response. "Sort of baby-faced and fair-skinned? Big smile?"

"That's the fella all right," Wilkie said, nodding his large head. "You seen him too, have ya?"

Unfortunately he had: it was George Revere, bringing another mended costume from Aunt Catherine's shop, except that this one contained a message which could send all who had handled it to the gallows. Marc sat back on the bottom step below the wings. He could hardly breathe. Incurious as ever, Wilkie drifted back to his post. Surely it was Revere, recent arrival from the United States and boisterous republican, and not Aunt Catherine, who was involved. Even so, Beth's aunt was herself a recent immigrant from New England and, Marc grimly concluded, might well be tarred with the kind of broad brush he had seen wielded by members of the establishment here. Was there no end to the entanglement of politics and his personal life? Perhaps Revere himself was innocent, a dupe of treasonous types around him.

Marc had little time to rationalize further, for Clarence Beasley touched him on the shoulder and said, "Lay on, Macbeth."

THE *MACBETH* SEQUENCE DID NOT GO well. Marc felt sorry for Lady Macbeth, who did her best to carry the scenes beyond his missed cues and omitted lines, including one entire speech, in addition to his pathetic attempt to deploy volume and basso profundity to compensate for his lack of timing and passion. Fortunately this sequence was first up after the interval, giving the audience plenty of time to forget it in favour of what followed. The public knowledge of Merriwether's indisposition (that, alas, had begun to affect the great man's performance) would have made his fans more sympathetic than critical. In any event, it concluded with Lady Macbeth's sleepwalking scene, and as Mrs. Thedford had nicely arranged, thunderous applause greeted her effort.

Marc went straight back to his dressing-room. There were still thirty minutes remaining in the show. He needed to think about what lay ahead the moment it ended. It appeared that the rebels had taken every precaution. Under the moonlight, the Kingston Road would be visible for its entire length, while the forest on either side remained impenetrably black: if anyone tried to follow Marc—a lone, moonlit horseman on an empty road—they could be observed easily by those standing watch in the woods. Moreover, any such followers would easily be seen if they attempted to cross the Don River via the only bridge, while a midnight fording by inexperienced, mounted infantry officers was too hazardous to contemplate. He had little doubt that the horse waiting in the shadows of the market would be on its own, tethered loosely, and untraceable. If he were met some two miles or so east of the bridge, he would be spirited away to a predetermined rendezvous so quickly that any loyalist who managed to trail after him would have no chance of finding him. Thus, he would be on his own, having to convince the rebels of his authenticity, effect an exchange of sample guns and initial payment, and, presumably, arrange a drop-point for the rest of the rifles. Somewhere along the lake-shore, he speculated, where three trunks of costumes destined for New York City would inexplicably go missing.

As he waited out the agonizingly slow minutes left in the evening's performance, Marc tried not to think too much about his dismal failure to help Rick Hilliard, who was certainly not guilty of murder, only of misguided chivalry. Cobb had earlier confirmed Marc's theory about Merriwether's purchase of laudanum, but he now felt much as Cobb did about such a minuscule triumph of detection. He also tried not to think of the consequences of having to arrest George Revere for sedition, with his wedding into the family a mere ten days away.

The loudest roar of the night told him that the show was over. Within minutes the stage-area would be overrun by enthusiasts eager to touch the garments of the great. He walked quickly through the shadows at the rear of the stage to the far side, past a startled chief constable, and up the stairs to Merriwether's bedroom. There he stripped off his Macbeth robes, but left the wig, eyebrows, and beard in place. He got into Merriwether's street clothes and boots, and then removed the two rifles and the ammunition from the trunk. Earlier in the afternoon he had marked the stock of each rifle, using an awl to drill a tiny hole, filling it with a single drop of ink, and rubbing the surface smooth again. He tucked them into the canvas bag Spooner had supplied, wedged open the window overlooking the alley below, and dropped the bag into some bushes. He waited, breath indrawn, for thirty seconds, but the noise had attracted no attention. Then he went back downstairs. Cobb was waiting for him, with Sturges.

"Jesus!" Sturges cried. "Fer a second there I thought you was Merriwether!"

Marc drew them up to the landing, where, by the glow of Sturges's lantern, they read the rebels' note.

"Spooner's out there tryin' to look casual, but nearer to a conniption fit," Sturges said with some satisfaction. "Should I take this note to him?"

"What do you make of it?" Marc asked Cobb.

"Damned clever, I'd say. But I do know exactly where they're gonna take you."

"Two miles up the Kingston Road is scarcely a precise co-ordinate," Marc protested.

"But it's where there's a path of sorts through the bush towards the lake, used by trappers an' hunters mostly. It's an old Mississauga Indian trail with a bunch of deer-runs off of it, a perfect maze if ya don't know the terrain."

"Perfect for them, disastrous for us."

"Maybe so, but there's a log hut at the end of the path—been there a donkey's age—about a quarter of a mile from the lake."

"Which gives them more than one means of escape."

"Still, if Spooner knows what he's doin', he might be able to catch one of 'em comin' outta the bush onto the highway or makin' a run fer it by boat."

"You're right, Cobb, but only if he stays at least half an hour behind me. Our only chance is to catch them *after* I do the deal, whatever it is, and not before or during it. There's no mention of guns in either note, and no way to prove one of the rebels actually wrote them. They could claim they thought they were buying Yankee whiskey or cigars."

"I see yer point, Major. Want us to tell Spooner all this?"

"Yes, please do," Marc said, and gave the note to Cobb.

"He'll wanta know where the note was found," Sturges said.

"Later," Marc said.

"Here he comes now!" Cobb said.

Marc threw Merriwether's cape over his shoulders and disappeared into the tavern, leaving the policemen to face the onrushing Spooner.

• • •

THE MOON WAS IN FULL PHASE and the Kingston Road, mostly dried mud and vestigial logs at this time of year, stretched out before him. Marc had retrieved the gun bag from the alley, manoeuvred undetected through the market to its northeast corner, found a horse tethered there, mounted, and rode in splendid isolation towards Scaddings Bridge. Once on the other side of the Don, he looked back, but no one was trailing him. That eyes were watching him intently from several hidden eyries, he had no doubt. He also felt exposed without his sword and pistol. But he knew he must remain Jason Merriwether throughout the meeting ahead and after. There would be no heroic attempt to make a citizen's arrest: he planned to carry on as if he were indeed a Yankee gunrunner, then walk or ride away, leaving the arrest or any follow-up gambits to Spooner and the governor. He would do his bit, then withdraw and try his damnedest to marry Beth Smallman before the sky fell.

"Stop right there, Merriwether."

Marc did as he was bid by the deep voice from somewhere to his right.

"Now get off the horse an' lead him over here."

Marc walked the horse into the shadows, and waited. Two men suddenly appeared in front of him. They were farmers by the look of their overalls and boots, but each wore a battered top hat from which a chequered kerchief dropped down over the face.

"Merriwether?"

"I am he," Marc said, trying out his New York twang. "I've brought the sample with me. Do you have the money?"

"It ain't that simple. Follow us. You can leave the horse and ride it back as far as the bridge, providin' everything's on the up-and-up." The one who spoke was very nervous, and struggled to keep his voice, deep as it was, from skidding upward.

"Whatever you say," Marc replied with deliberate nonchalance. "If you people're buyin', I'm sellin'." He tethered the horse to a tree and unslung the canvas bag.

They walked in silence. Marc could not actually see the path they were using, but his two companions moved along without hesitation or impediment. Soon they were confronted by a blunt shadow blocking the way.

"We're here."

Marc ducked low and followed the men inside. The hut was windowless, floorless, and, except for the glimmer from a candle-stub on a stump-table, nearly dark. The two who had led Marc here sat down beside a third man, his face also hidden behind a kerchief. Marc squatted down on a log across from them. Between them on the stump lay a saddlebag.

The third man spoke first. "This shouldn't take long. We need to see the quality of yer merchandise. Then we'll show you the colour of our money. If both are satisfactory, I'll hand you written instructions about how and where to drop off the remainder of the goods an' pick up your full payment."

"The price has gone up ten percent," Marc said.

After a tense pause, the third man said, "It's fifty per rifle or no deal."

Marc smiled. "No harm in tryin' a little Yankee horse-tradin', now, is there? Fifty it is." Marc sighed with some relief: he felt he needed to know what price had originally been agreed upon when he came to count out the cash in the saddlebag.

"Let's see the goods, then," said the one who had spoken to him beside the highway. The other man who had accompanied him had said nothing as yet, and appeared to be very jittery, jerking his head from side to side at the least tick of sound.

Marc pulled one of the French Modèles out of the canvas casing into the dim light. While the jittery one held the candle uncertainly in his hand, the other two rotated the weapon over it as if they were roasting a piglet on a spit. One of them gave a low whistle of approval.

"An' you got ammunition an' twelve more in addition to these two?"

"Yessiree. But first I need to see the silver." This was it: once the exchange had been made, the treasonous act would be palpable and irreversible. If any one of these three were caught with the marked rifles, they would be fodder for the executioner.

"It's all there: U.S. silver coins. You may need a mule to carry it."

Marc reached for the saddlebag.

"Lemme see the other gun first."

"Whatever you say. The customer's always right." Marc hoped he wasn't putting it on too thick. He reached for the canvas bag. As he did so, he saw the spokesman for the rebels reach into his cloak and begin to pull out an envelope: the drop-off instructions. We're almost there, Marc thought with the tiniest flush of triumph.

At that moment, all four of them froze at the sound of a clatter just outside the hut. A second later, a fourth man dressed like the others stumbled inside and cried out breathlessly, "They're comin' through the bush from the lakeshore! Soldiers! A whole pack of 'em!"

"What the hell is goin' on here?" demanded Deep Voice.

Marc stood up. "Nobody followed me! Some bastard's tattled on us."

"The deal's off, Yankee!" shouted the one in charge. "You're damn lucky I don't shoot you on the spot." He snatched the saddlebag up in both hands and barked at the others, "Leave the guns. When they find them here and then pick up this arsehole wanderin' around lost in the bush, they'll know who to hang!"

With that, they scrambled for the door and the safety of the woods. They could never be caught once they had a running start. But the jittery one did not immediately follow. He got up as if to go, but suddenly swivelled towards Marc, who had stood his ground. In a quivering, two-handed grip, the man held a cocked pistol. Marc felt its muzzle like an ice-pick under his chin. For an interminable half-minute, it trembled there: Marc could feel the man's indecision. He didn't know why, but he closed his eyes. His life, incomplete as it was, did not flash before him.

Then something prompted him to open them again. The pistol was being lowered, inch by agonizing inch. The candle-light from the table was reflected in the barrel and, then, unexpectedly it illuminated the back of the gunman's left hand, an all-too-familiar hand that bore a throbbing, thick scar. Then the hand, the pistol, and the gunman were gone. There was much commotion in the bush, then all was quiet. Ten minutes later, Marc heard the mad crashing of infantrymen as they staggered into trees and pitfalls.

Marc smashed both fists on the stump-table, furious at Spooner's blundering intervention, but also gob-smacked by what had just been revealed to him. Thomas Goodall, in his desperation, had thrown in with the would-be insurgents. And that scar on his left hand was the result of no accident: Thomas had no doubt been injured at the donnybrook with the Orangemen the previous spring near Crawford's Corners. At this very moment he would be skedaddling back home to lay his disappointed body beside that of Winnifred Hatch, and both of them no more than five yards from the woman he was destined to marry. He tried to move, but couldn't. He was numb. His heart kept pumping, but his brain had given up.

He had no idea how long it was before Lieutenant Spooner

careened into the hut, burred and nettled and otherwise beaten about by the Canadian bush. Without ceremony, he teetered in front of Marc and shouted in a furious squeak, "Can you identify any of them?"

There was the slightest pause before Marc heard himself say, "They were all masked."

"Damn it! Did they take the rifles?"

Marc pointed at the marked samples.

"Damn it! Did they give you money?"

Marc shook his head.

"Damn it! Damn it! Damn it!"

Marc brushed by him out into the shadows.

"And just where do you think you're going, Lieutenant?"

Marc did not reply. He found the path and strode steadily back towards the Kingston Road. Several shots rang out: the soldiers shooting at one another, no doubt. He found the horse where he had left it. He mounted and galloped away towards the city. Spooner could clean up the mess he had made. The operation was a total failure. None of the rebels had been caught or identified. And none ever would be.

SIXTEEN

Marc's first thought was to keep on riding right through the city to the fort, where he could stable the rebels' horse (stolen surely) overnight and then find himself a warm, safe bed, preferably a long way from the arrogance of authority and the desperation of those without it. In refusing to name Thomas Goodall, he recognized that he had crossed a line, had committed an act that could not be undone. But what precisely that was he did not at this moment care to know: something other than his mind was now directing him willy-nilly where it wished. So be it.

Thus it was that he did not question the horse when it swung down West Market Lane and stopped outside the entrance to Frank's Hotel. The upper windows of the rooms above the tavern and those above the theatre were all dark except one: the parlour room of Mrs. Thedford's suite. Something was nagging at him, a vague feeling that he had seen or heard something whose significance he had overlooked. He nudged the horse back into the alley that led to the hotel stables. With the motions of a sleepwalker he found an empty stall, unsaddled the beast, threw a blanket over it, and then, stepping over a comatose stable boy, made his way through the dark to the back door of the Franks' quarters. Using Frank's key, Marc eased the door open and felt his way along the hallway that eventually brought him to the theatre entrance. The stage area was pitch black, except where a single shaft of moonlight sliced through one of the upper windows and across the pit. There was no tragedian to take a bow in its mellow beam. Marc crossed the stage, pausing to take in an echo of applause, and tiptoed up the stairs to the hallway above. Jeremiah Jefferson was fast asleep with the storage-room door ajar.

Marc headed for Merriwether's room, where he had left his own boots, tunic, and accoutrements, but halted outside the door with the wedge of light under it. Perhaps Mrs. Thedford was sitting just beyond it at the little davenport-table that served as her desk, working on the company's books or revising the playbill for Detroit or completing the travel arrangements that her murdered colleague would have handled. He felt she was someone he could talk to about matters too painful and complex to be uttered to oneself. He raised his hand to give a one-finger tap on the door, but as his palm brushed it on the way up, it swung silently open. The room was fully lit, but empty. Surely she had not gone to bed in the other room and left half a dozen candles blazing here? But, then, perhaps she had merely gone into that room to fetch something and, overcome by physical and emotional fatigue, had put her head on the pillow and fallen into a deep sleep. He decided he would just take a quick peek inside, then snuff the candles and leave quietly.

He was almost at the bedroom doorway when he heard the sound: a giggle—muted, smothered perhaps, but clearly a giggle. The hair rose on the back of his neck. He listened intently, but did not move. There was a rustling, as of starched sheets. Then a sigh that had no sadness in it. He should have wheeled and bolted, but he didn't. Like a moth to the flame, he was drawn into that doorway and a sight that first mystified and then seared him.

No candle lit the scene on the bed, but the last of the moonlight bathed it visible and shimmeringly surreal. At first blush, it was a silken knot of tawny limbs, intertwined and serpentine. Then a flash of toe, a whipped wisp of hair, a bulb of surprised flesh confirmed the human form—or forms. The willful moans of surrender, the muzzled grunts of pleasure-pain, the yip at forbidden touch would have conjured in any viewer's imagination the lustful conjunction of male and female in the oldest act. But what Marc saw, and his mind at first rejected, was the sexual entanglement of woman and woman: Tessa Guildersleeve and Annemarie Thedford.

They were far too engrossed to notice Marc's shadow fall across the bed, then retreat. Marc did not realize until he had backed across the outer room and sat down on the settee there that he had neglected to take a breath. He was sure they would now hear him gasping, but the moans and sighs continued apace, slowing and receding gradually as the minutes ticked by. Mrs. Thedford's voice became distinguishable: a sequence of soothing sounds above the grateful mewling of the girl. Marc sat stunned. Yet despite the almost visceral revulsion he felt, the tenderness and consolation in the sounds from that room were undeniably those of love's afterglow—not the satiate wheezes of lust's exhaustion. That Annemarie Thedford loved Tessa Guildersleeve was unashamedly revealed.

His mind began to work again. He found himself staring across the room at the commode where Mrs. Thedford kept the only gifts her father had bequeathed her. In a flash, he realized what he had overlooked the day before, and he knew what instrument had stunned Merriwether and made the horrific stabbing possible. Before him was a plausible motive for what he had known all along was a murder committed in the white heat of rage and recrimination. He did not know entirely how the crime had been orchestrated, but he knew for certain who had committed it.

"Ah, Marc. I thought that was you in the doorway. I'm glad you decided to wait."

Mrs. Thedford was standing across from him, her nakedness swathed in a satin robe, and she was smiling a welcome at him, as if he had arrived a bit early for tea and had happily made himself at home.

"Where are the silver candlesticks, the ones you claimed were so dear to you?"

"I was sure you'd notice sooner or later; nothing much gets past you," she said, and it sounded for all the world like a compliment.

"There was one here when I searched the room yesterday. If I hadn't been so obsessed with finding the laudanum, I would have realized it then."

"Ah, so it was you who'd been in here. You didn't quite place the hand-mirror or the candlestick back where I always leave them."

"You hid the other one, didn't you?"

She smiled warmly. "Silly of me, wasn't it? I should have tucked them both out of sight." There was no bitterness in this remark: it was a plain statement.

"You have no idea how much I've admired you . . ." Marc said, his voice nearly breaking.

"And I, you," she said, pulling a padded chair over beside the settee and sitting down to face him. "And now you've come to accuse me of murdering Jason, and I can see the pain it is causing you."

"I don't know how you did it, but I know it was you," Marc said softly, looking away, afraid of what might next be said or done.

"Don't be so disconsolate, Marc. Of course I did it. And

I was positive it would be you who would find me out." She was gazing upon him with admiration and a plaintive sort of fondness.

"You admit it, then?"

"I do. And now I'd like you to wipe that disappointment off your handsome face and relax, have a glass of sherry with me—sans laudanum—and we'll discuss everything."

All Marc could think of replying to this unexpected invitation was, "What about Tessa?"

Mrs. Thedford laughed. "The minute I've finished making love to her, she starts snoring like a hedgehog."

THEY WERE SITTING VERY CLOSE TOGETHER, almost knee to knee, sipping sherry like two old friends after a long absence. Mrs. Thedford did not take her eyes off Marc, even as she tipped her sherry glass to her lips. Her seeming unconcern and aplomb were as unnerving as they were incredible.

"I suggest that you go first, Marc. Tell me all you think you know." She sat back, smiling encouragement. Marc collected his thoughts.

"I believe you heard Tessa cry out when she was attacked by Merriwether, and thinking logically that it was Rick Hilliard behaving abominably, you grabbed a candlestick and ran down the hall into Tessa's room. There you discovered Merriwether in his nightshirt on top of a helpless Tessa who, already drugged and disoriented, had mercifully passed out. You did what any responsive person would have done: you struck Merriwether on the back of the skull with the only weapon you had, the candlestick. He reared up, still conscious for an instant, spun around, then collapsed on the carpet, faceup and legs splayed, but still breathing. Enraged by his actions—after all, he had just violated in the most reprehensible manner possible a young woman who was not merely your ward but your . . . paramour—you decided to finish him off. This was a decision taken in a fury, totally irrational and utterly unlike anything you had ever done or thought to do."

"You are very generous." She seemed amused by this quaint narrative.

"You could have struck him again with the candlestick, but I suspect the fact that he was facing you may have caused you to hesitate. It was then that you spotted Rick slumped unconscious on the settee. There was only one candle lit beside Tessa's bed, and in your fear for Tessa you had not seen him. He had foolishly strapped on his sabre to impress Tessa. You pulled it from its scabbard, gripped it with both hands, steeled yourself, and plunged it into Merriwether's chest. Then, the deed done, you were suddenly horrified at what you'd done. Tessa was unconscious and breathing regularly. You had to place the blame elsewhere if you were to survive and help her through this crisis. Somehow you smeared blood all over poor Hilliard, picked up your candlestick, and ran. I'm certain that the weapon is still in this building and can be found.

"But, of course, Tessa's cry had been heard by both

Armstrong and Beasley, something you hadn't had time to consider. Fortunately, Armstrong was too drunk or hungover to respond. His door was ajar, so he must have seen you, in the weak light from Tessa's room or his own. The bloody candlestick was in your grip. Beasley claims it was no more than two minutes between the time he heard Tessa cry and his arrival there, so he, too, must have seen you in the dark hall. How you contrived to have them lie for you and do it so consistently I can only guess. But it was midmorning Tuesday before I began my questioning. You had ample time before that to intimidate and coach your colleagues, who are after all your underlings and dependents."

"And you believe me capable of that sort of bullying hypocrisy?" She looked genuinely hurt at being accused of this latter, more venial, transgression.

"Not at first and that was my mistake. I thought from the beginning that this was a crime of passion—I could not get the image of that steel stake through Merriwether's body out of my mind. But having watched you rehearse on Monday, having worked with you alone here yesterday afternoon, and performed next to you last evening, no, I could not believe you capable of organizing and manipulating such a conspiracy."

"Thank you. Because, you see, I did nothing of the sort."

"But Beasley and Armstrong must have seen you. There wasn't time for you to hear the cry, realize its significance, pick up the candlestick, stumble into Tessa's room, strike Merriwether down, discover Hilliard, draw his sword, stab

Merriwether, decide to set up the young lothario as the murderer, find something to dip into Merriwether's spouting blood, smear Rick's jacket, breeches, hands, and boots, pick up the dropped candlestick, and flee back to your room. All of this in two minutes? No."

"The reason you believed their testimony was because all of them were telling the truth. What they say they saw is what they did see." She said this proudly, and still there was a twinkle of amusement in her steady gaze.

"It is not possible."

"Well, let me tell you what *was* possible and what *did* happen. More sherry?"

Marc shook his head. Mrs. Thedford leaned forward again, allowing the top of her robe to slip open several inches. She didn't appear to notice, however, for she had suddenly become quite serious, narrowing her gaze and appearing to visualize the actions as she narrated them.

"I knew I would lose Tessa someday. Men were increasingly attracted to her, and I could see her trying out various responses to their overtures. She never stopped loving me, never left my bed except when it was imprudent not to. I'm sure you're worldly enough to realize that our love is considered by most to be unnatural."

"But you were also her mentor," Marc protested. "She must have been terribly confused. And as the older adult, you bore full responsibility for the . . . the situation."

"Again, you are right, and wise beyond your years. But,

you see, I, too, was confused. Tessa was not the first woman I had loved, and I knew when she came to me that I should not approach her on those terms. She needed a mother." Her eyes looked away. "All children do." She covered her momentary distress by refilling her sherry glass from the decanter beside her on the floor.

"You lost your own mother when you were very young?"

"I never knew her. Still, I missed her. Odd, isn't it?"

"Not at all," Marc said, having known such a feeling himself.

"Ultimately, we became . . . involved, and though I tried several times to end it, Tess wouldn't hear of it and I was miserable at the thought. We convinced ourselves it was right."

"Surely you were risking everything, the company, the—"

"Perhaps. But I was determined that Tessa not become entangled with any other members of the troupe. So when I saw Jason pursuing her, I read him the riot act. And for a while everything was fine, until Tessa—"

"Started showing an interest in him."

"Yes. You saw for yourself, though, on Monday afternoon how she used the attraction to get back at me because I refused to favour her over Thea in the distribution of parts. She is too young to understand the difference between personal and artistic decisions. Besides which, Thea has been a loyal member of the company and a good friend since joining it."

"You planned to help her through her pregnancy?"

The smile returned briefly. "My, you *are* good at this

detecting business. Thea came to me after Jason's death. If only she'd come sooner."

"You might have got them safely married?"

"Something like that."

"It must have been you who talked her out of killing herself after his death."

"I certainly tried. Anyway, when I saw Tessa and Ensign Hilliard hitting it off so well, I was not only not concerned, I was actually pleased. I was sure he would take her in the way of a man—she was shamelessly testing her seduction techniques on him—and that she would then have some better notion about that sort of love, with the certainty that we would be on our way to Detroit by week's end and any emotional connection would be broken permanently."

"You were willing to let Tessa make a choice? Was that not dangerous for you? You might have lost her affection for good."

"That is true, and I thought I was strong enough to carry it off. I even pictured myself as noble and self-sacrificing, a mother letting the child choose the world over her." Her face clouded over. "But, alas, I was not that brave. When Tessa and Hilliard went into her room, I assumed the worst, and braced for it. I went to my bedroom, where I could not possibly be privy to any of the goings-on through the wall. I even put my infamous earplugs in. But not for long. Soon I found myself standing, naked and fearful, right over there with my ear pressed to the wallpaper. I could hear their giggling and the clink of glasses. Then nothing for a long time. I became alarmed. Before I could make up my mind what to do—perhaps get dressed and try a discreet rap on their door—I heard Tessa's cry. It wasn't a scream. It was a sharp yelp of surprise and physical pain. That's all. But I knew what it meant." At last she looked away, abashed.

Marc understood at last how the crime had been accomplished. "There were two cries, weren't there? The first one heard only by you."

She swung her head around to face him, the glorious ropes of her sandy hair swinging sensuously in the variable light. She was smiling through a scrim of tears. "Ah, you are far too young to be so clever. You must come from exceptional stock."

Marc was flattered, unaccountably, but pressed on. "That's how you and you alone were able to get down to that room, kill Merriwether, entrap Hilliard, and get back here."

"That's right. Of course, I had no conception of what was actually going on in there, you understand. I was out of my mind with jealousy and anger at Tessa and at my own foolish weakness: I simply ran out into the hall without a stitch on, the candlestick in my hand. I just assumed that it was the soldier on top of her. Then I was shocked to see the candlestick suddenly smeared with blood and hair, even more to see Jason on the floor, staring up and dazed, his eyes slowly closing. I had hit him a savage blow, but had no memory of it.

"It must have taken me a minute or so to comprehend what I had done. Then the rage took hold, pure and unstoppable. The violator was not young Hilliard, whose amorous pawings I could understand, but Jason Merriwether, a man to whom I had given a second life. I put my trust in him, was about to make him a partner in the Bowery Theatre. And I had specifically warned him away from Tessa. You can't imagine how betrayed I felt. In that moment, I hated all men, monsters who had done nothing but betray me all my adult life. I saw the gleam on the sword, I don't think I even knew it was Hilliard's, but I pulled it out, walked over to Jason, and plunged it through the son-of-a-bitch's heart."

The recollection of that grotesque act had brought sweat to her brow and a tremble to her lip. In a quieter tone she continued. "The blood began spouting everywhere, and I instinctively jumped aside. Some splattered me, but I was naked, so no harm done. I went over to check on Tessa, but I was shaking so hard by then I could not properly detect her pulse. She began breathing regularly with that little-girl snore I know so well. I was sure now that she was all right, and had seen nothing. I took a large handkerchief of hers and dipped it in Jason's blood and smeared it on Hilliard—it took several trips to soak his uniform. And I knew, as you said, how it would go when the two of them were discovered. Then I came back here, unseen." *

"That explains why I could find no evidence of blood being splattered on Rick's tunic: you smeared it with a cloth. And there was a set of boot-prints approaching the body because Rick never did stagger back to the settee. You or Jason must have knocked the ashtray onto the floor after he was struck. But you still had a bloody handkerchief and a candlestick to dispose of."

"Yes. I had put on a little fire in the stove earlier, so I started it up and burned the hanky."

"I found traces of it in the ash in your grate yesterday."

"Did you?"

"But the candlestick would be harder to hide. Why didn't you just wipe it clean?"

"I intended to. It took a few minutes for the fire to get going, and I also realized that I needed to wash myself thoroughly—I had some blood on my hands and arms. So I did that, praying that neither Hilliard nor Tessa would wake up too soon, and praying also that it would be Hilliard first so Tessa might be spared the scene in that room. I was more anxious about that than making sure I wasn't caught. I had just dried myself and slipped into a nightgown when I heard Tessa scream loud enough to wake the dead. My heart turned to ice. But the die was cast. I grabbed the candlestick, ran into my bedroom, threw myself down, jammed the candlestick under the blanket, stuffed in my earplugs, and tried to calm myself. It seemed like an eternity before Clarence and Jeremiah came rushing in to fetch me. And the rest you know."

Yes. Rick waking when Tessa screamed, not at the gory sight of Merriwether on the floor, but rather at her handsome young soldier, apparently mortally wounded on the settee. For her, it had been the nightmarish image of a stabbed and dying lover: she didn't yet know that one of her nightmare cries had been real and had sealed Rick Hilliard's fate.

"Tessa didn't see Merriwether," Marc said. "She saw only Rick. Being drugged, she has no recollection of the rape except for the initial jab of pain. She doesn't even know she screamed aloud that second time. And now the blood on Rick has become a hero's badge of devotion."

"Tessa has come through this ordeal better than any of us. I have committed murder, killed a man I once admired and respected. I can never forgive myself for that. Nor will any rationalization justify it or mitigate the remorse I feel. What's more, and just as bad, I have allowed an innocent, even noble, young man to be falsely accused. But I have suffered much before this, and gone on. I hope I have the strength to do so this time."

Marc's head jerked back as if struck. He had assumed that this voluntary and detailed confession had been done as a form of expiation prior to her surrendering to the authorities. But she had just informed him that she expected to carry on with her life, chastened perhaps but unpunished.

"Mrs. Thedford," he began in what he hoped was a severe tone, "you are aware that I admire you and that I abhor the violence done upon Tessa by Merriwether. But I represent the lieutenant-governor and the Crown in this matter, and I have no choice but to do my duty. I intend to wait while you get dressed, then escort you to Government House. There you will be incarcerated, and I will wake up my friend, free him from the fantasy he has been living, and return him to the world."

She smiled. There was true warmth in it. Then she frowned. "You must believe me when I tell you I am truly sorry for what I've put your friend through. I regretted what I had done the moment I saw him again in that room, dazed and self-accusing. But there was no turning back. And I knew it would only be a question of a day or two before he was exonerated. But then, when I learned he was your friend, I felt dreadful."

"You're telling me that you intended to confess all along? And yet you expect to get on a steamer tomorrow and sail off for Detroit?"

"Yes. That is what I have just done, confessed my guilt. And, yes, at noon tomorrow, my company and I will be bound for Detroit." She seemed amused, though there was an edge of solemnness in her gaze as well.

"Then you don't know me very well."

"On the contrary, I know more about you than you can imagine."

"That's as absurd as your thinking I won't take you to the governor."

"You will not do so, not because of what I've said or may do, but because of who I am."

"You're Annemarie Thedford."

"Am I?"

"That may be a stage name, I realize, but what does it matter to me if you have another?"

"A great deal, I hope."

She leaned over and laid a hand on his knee. "My real

name is a variant which I adopted many years ago—after I left England. Look at me. I am tall and fair and blue-eyed."

Annemarie Thedford. A name from the past flashed before him. But it was impossible. That person was long dead. Dead before he had been born. Yet, just as she whispered the words to him—as if speaking them too loudly might annihilate what they named—he said them silently to himself.

"Mary Ann Edwards."

She gazed steadfastly at him, waiting for the shock to pass and the implications to sink in. Finally, he was able to say, "You are my aunt Mary."

"Not quite," she said. "I am your mother."

SEVENTEEN

When Marc had recovered enough to find breath and voice, he heard himself say, "But that's not possible. Mary is dead, I've seen her grave. And my parents were Thomas and Margaret Evans. They are also dead."

Mary Ann Edwards took Marc's hands in hers in a grip that was both tender and firm. "I'm sorry that I could find no gentler way to convey such news to you. But I was as stunned and bewildered by it as you are now."

"But how? When?" Marc stammered as the chilling implications of her claim began to take hold.

"'How' is a very long story. 'When' was yesterday at luncheon."

"When you met Major Jenkin."

"Yes. Such a dear man. I took an immediate liking to him. He loves to reminisce, so I encouraged him to tell me about the wars in Europe. Well, he kept mentioning his best friend Frederick. To be polite, I asked a question or two about this Frederick."

"And you discovered his name was Edwards."

"Yes. My brother, whom I last saw leaving for Europe in 1805 or '06."

"But surely you were not surprised to hear his name mentioned by Jenkin?"

"When I first met you on Monday, I noticed your name, of course, but Edwards is a common enough surname in southern England. It occurred to me that you might be a distant cousin—your height and colouring were right—but that was all. I was more concerned with your bearing and intelligence. But when I realized that Owen knew Frederick well, I began to pester him with questions about the family, about my nephews in France, and he eventually got around to Jabez and the estate in Kent. Then I was certain. It was both strange and exciting to hear about my brothers after twenty-seven years of pretending they didn't exist."

Marc began, vaguely, to sense where the story was heading. "And at some point, my name was mentioned."

"Yes." She gave his fingers a squeeze. Part of him wanted to tear away from her grip and this scourging narrative, but another part admitted that he must know the truth, whatever the cost. "Owen, dear soul, was going on about how wonderful Jabez was—it was all I could do to hold my tongue—and how he'd adopted a five-year-old lad whose parents had died and, he said, this was all the more admirable because the boy's father was a mere gamekeeper and the mother a tenant-farmer's daughter. He must have thought me mad, the look I had on my face, when I demanded to know their names. It took him a minute or two, and I thought I might faint waiting, but he finally said Thomas and Margaret Evans. And then I knew for certain. I let him babble on—oh, how grateful I was for his garrulousness. But the child who was ripped from my breast, who I never would have abandoned for the world, was alive, was thriving, and close enough to touch."

She released his hands, as if perhaps she had said enough to hold him there while she wept quietly and composed herself.

"But I stood over your grave-marker in the garden by the big house, and wished you had lived that I might have an aunt . . . and a kind of mother."

"Bless you for that."

"Uncle Jabez thought you were dead. He grieved over you for years. I was forbidden to speak your name because it hurt him so much."

A series of expressions passed across Mary Ann Edwards's face in quick succession: contempt, anger, sorrow, regret, resignation. She took a deep breath, pulled the lapels of her robe tightly together, and said in a low, sad voice: "I thought I had worked out all my anger towards Jabez—after all, it's been twenty-seven years—but you never do, not when the betrayal is so great."

"Uncle Jabez betrayed you?"

"Yes. But you'll need to know the story from the beginning to understand what happened, if you are to forgive him. I cannot, but you must."

Marc realized that she was as exhausted as he was, but the adrenaline was running strong in both, and he sat back, bracing himself for the secrets that were about to be revealed into a new day's glare.

"When I was almost eighteen, Jabez decided I should go up to London to Madame Rénaud's finishing school, after which I would 'come out' and be matched with a suitable husband. I was a tomboy around the estate, I fought against the plan, but when I was forcibly removed to the great metropolis, I soon discovered I liked it very much. Not the ladies' school, of course—Madame Rénaud was about as French as Yorkshire pudding—but the nearby theatres. I sneaked off every chance I got to one or another of the summer playhouses. During vacations I stayed with an elderly cousin who didn't keep close tabs on me, so I was soon landing bit parts and getting to know many of the actors. Eventually I met your father."

Marc waited, fearing the worst.

"Don't worry so: he wasn't a syphilitic pimp. He was a tall, handsome young man of twenty-five, the youngest son of a country squire who had once been a renowned barrister in the city. His name was Solomon Hargreave. He was a talented actor, but his father disapproved of his chosen profession, cut off his allowance, and impounded his grandfather's legacy. Solomon thought me talented as well as beautiful, and before long I simply abandoned the school and moved in with him. He was very much in love with me. I was still young and na-ively romantic. I was surprised and confused when I was told I was pregnant."

"You did not marry?"

"No. It didn't seem to matter, though Solomon was willing, I believe. We were quite happy as we were but, of course, when Jabez learned I had abandoned school, he came up to London in a perfect fury. We had a great row, but he left, saying he would be back. I was very frightened, but managed to hide my pregnancy from him. Solomon was off on a trip up north with a touring company, so I moved to a cheap flat where Jabez couldn't find me. Solomon was due back in a few weeks, but Jabez discovered me first by bribing someone at the theatre. I went into labour two months early."

"So I was—"

"A bastard, yes. But a beautiful, blue-eyed babe, nonethe-less, wee and shrivelled and underweight at seven months, but kicking and screaming for the teat. I must say that Jabez's concern for my health and that of the baby was genuine and took immediate precedence. He sent for Margaret Evans from the estate, and had her nurse me and take care of you. But when Solomon arrived a few days later, everything changed. After Jabez took a couple of swings at him, he calmed down and settled on a quick wedding. Solomon was, after all, a gentleman, if also a blackguard in his eyes. But I was defiant. I wanted to be an actress, to make a life for myself on the stage. I told Jabez that we would marry when we were ready to and that I would raise my son backstage. Actresses were then, and still are, regarded as no better than whores. But looking back on that moment now, I believe I suspected even at that youthful age that I preferred women to men: something was urging me to resist marriage."

"Yet you became Mrs. Thedford?"

She smiled wryly, but continued her tale. "I did not understand how determined and how cruel my eldest brother could be. When Solomon had gone off to the theatre, Jabez exploded in a fury of curses and recrimination. So towering was his anger that I feared for my life. But it was my baby's life he was after." Her expression darkened at the memory, as lines of bitterness twisted at her mouth.

"Surely not. Uncle Jabez was—"

"Kind and considerate, yes. As he had been to me. But ever since our mother's death when I was myself a baby and our father's death a few years later, Jabez saw himself as responsible for me, for my upbringing, my education, even my morals."

"What happened?"

"Jabez left in a huff. But two days later, after a long nap—I was still weak and not fully recovered from the birth—I awoke to find Jabez standing over me, and Margaret Evans and my unnamed son gone. 'The bastard has been taken to an orphanage,' Jabez said in the coldest voice I'd ever heard in a man. Then he handed me a large sum of money—in cash—and announced that I was no longer an Edwards, and was to have no contact with him or Frederick or anyone else we knew: I was, in his words, 'dead to the family and to the world.' He left before I could think of a reply. I have not seen him since."

"Then how did I get to the estate?" Marc asked after a long moment. He was sure he knew the answer. Even so, Jabez's heartless abandonment and shunning of his own sister was a devastating truth, whatever the mitigating circumstances might have been. Marc had literally been stolen from his mother.

"I only learned the bare details of that much later. You see, when Solomon returned to find the child gone, I thought he would fly into a rage of his own and confront Jabez, demand the return of his son, and scour the alleys and byways of London until you were found."

"But he didn't."

"No. He was, in his way, attached to the notion of a child, but he had only seen you for a short while, squalling for food and attention, and he soothed me by saying it was all for the best, we were destitute, we both wanted to have careers in the theatre, we were young, we would have legitimate children of our own, and so on."

"And he won you over?" Marc said.

"You must believe this if nothing else, Marc: I did not

abandon you. As soon I could walk, I went to every orphanage in central London in search of you. I was frantic, but you were nowhere to be found."

Their eyes locked. "Yes, I believe you," Marc said, "because I've watched you with Tessa, Thea, and the others. You do not let go easily."

"Soon we started to spend Jabez's blood-money. I felt that without Solomon to back me up, I could not go down to the estate and demand you back. As an unmarried English-woman, I had no legal right to my own child: you were Solomon's or Jabez's to fight over. So when Solomon suggested we flee to America to start over again, I said yes. And we did. And except for the child I left behind, I have had no regrets about that."

"But you still thought I had been left with an orphanage?"

"Yes. Solomon and I arrived in New York late in 1810, and having some capital, we managed to do well. I blossomed as an actress, soon outshining him. We lived together as man and wife, but my proclivity for female company and compan-ionship was becoming blatant and undeniable. We quarrelled often. Finally, he decided to return home. His father had died, and he hoped his oldest brother would give him a second chance. I stayed and prospered.

"Then about a year later Solomon sent a letter, the only one he ever wrote to me, saying that he had made a search for our son, and after much effort had located a woman who admitted being the wet-nurse for you at a rented house overseen by Margaret Evans and sponsored by Jabez Edwards. At some point, they had taken you back to Kent and represented you as the child of Thomas and Margaret Evans, who had no child of their own. Solomon didn't know, nor did I, that they had christened you Marcus. But at least I knew you had survived and were being raised by good people on the family estate. That's the last I heard about you—until yesterday. I had no idea that Jabez had adopted you and given you our name. I wanted to dash into the theatre and embrace you till I dropped. But I could not do so. You were investigating a murder I committed."

Neither said anything for a full minute.

"But you 'prospered,' as you say. You became Mrs. Annemarie Thedford."

"That's another long story, but yes, I did. I moved to Philadelphia, where the theatre business was booming. I re-invented myself in a country that encourages a fresh start and admires it when it works. I invented a Mr. Thedford, alas deceased, presented my hard-won capital as an inheritance, played the merry widow, fell in and out of love many times, and finally moved back to New York as that 'widow from Philadelphia,' eventually buying into the Bowery."

"And helped reclaim one or two others like yourself along the way."

"Yes. Including poor Jason."

Marc felt suddenly drained and utterly exhausted. The candles were low and flickering. "What do we do now?" he asked, seeing no way forward. "Either my best friend hangs for murder . . . or my mother does."

"Ensign Hilliard will be freed tomorrow, one hour after our steamer departs."

"But how?"

"You do not think I would have left your friend to pay for my crime? I sat down after our rehearsal yesterday—when I got to spend two hours alone with my son—"

"You deliberately arranged for those scenes, didn't you? Including my playing Hamlet to your Gertrude?"

She smiled. "I knew those hours and our brief moments together on the stage last night would be all that would be allowed me. But listen: I have prepared a detailed confession for the police." She got up, went over to the davenport, and picked an envelope out of the papers there. Marc's mind lingered for a moment in the past.

"That hand-mirror, the one I held up to Gertrude's face, it came from home, didn't it?"

"Yes, as did these brushes and the candlesticks. They were left to me by my father, part of a matched set given to my parents as a wedding gift. All three of their children have pieces of the set."

"I remember seeing that design now, on Uncle Jabez's hairbrushes in his room."

She gently but resolutely brought him back to the present. "This letter of confession is unsealed and undated."

She removed one of two sheets and gave it to Marc. "Can we trust Constable Cobb?"

"Of course." Marc scanned the letter and the signature at the bottom.

"Then bring him with you to the wharf at noon tomorrow. We depart for Detroit then on the *Michigan*. I'll date the letter today, and seal it. I'll ask Cobb to take it directly to his chief. I'll make sure to leave a few papers in here with my handwriting and signature on them. By the time the magistrates have perused the letter and determined its authenticity, I'll be in the United States."

"But they still might not believe you. Barclay Spooner is determined to see Rick hanged."

"On this second page I tell the police exactly where they can find the candlestick. You mustn't see this page: I don't want you compromised. When they find the candlestick, they'll discover Jason's blood and hair still on it. I decided to leave it as it was when I devised this plan. And Owen Jenkin was in this room on Monday afternoon and evening: he can verify that the candlestick was one of the pair he saw here."

"And with the explanation of the two screams laid out in this letter, the sworn testimony of the others makes perfect sense."

"Nor am I underestimating the persuasive powers of my son."

There was nothing left to do now but hold each other.

Neither would let go. From the other room, Tessa let out a contented snore. Marc did not shudder.

THE MID-OCTOBER DAY WAS BRIGHT WITH sunshine in a high, cloudless sky whose deep blue mirrored the unrippled surface of Lake Ontario. On such a day as this, it was hard to imagine the province could be anything but prosperous and peaceful. The weather had made the harvesting of crops seem almost a leisure activity, and an improved harvest it had been throughout the broad countryside. And here on Queen's Wharf at the foot of John Street, Lieutenant Edwards stood bare-headed in the plaintive breeze and bade good-bye to Mary Ann Edwards. Beasley, Armstrong, Jefferson, and Tessa and Thea had already boarded the *Michigan,* and were leaning against the rail, waving or otherwise acknowledging the farewell plaudits of the several dozen fans who had come to see the Bowery players off. An hour earlier, Jefferson and three bulky draymen had muscled a number of steamer-trunks aboard—four of them inexplicably lighter than they had been upon arrival. Constable Cobb stood a few yards away, impassively observing Marc and Mrs. Thedford.

"Will I ever see you again?"

"Only if you come to New York."

"But you will write?"

"Yes. But you must promise to send me long and loving letters about the wondrous woman you are going to marry, and tell me everything about each child as it arrives. I must know that you are happy."

"I will. I'll bombard you with paper and ink."

"And you must promise me one other thing."

"Uncle Jabez?"

"Yes. He must never know about me, or that I have found you. The dead ought to remain dead."

"But not always, surely?"

"Not always," she conceded. "I cannot forgive Jabez, but I can't hate him either now that I see what he's helped you become. It is better for him and you to go on as you have been. I couldn't bear to be the cause of any unhappiness between the two of you. I have more than enough on my conscience already, and I'm afraid I've severely compromised yours."

The steamer blew two peremptory blasts of its brand-new whistle.

"It's time," she said, drawing the sealed envelope out of her reticule.

Marc waved Cobb over. The constable had been given the bare outline of what was to take place, but in order to spare him any improper involvement in the business, he had been told that the letter contained evidence pertinent to the investigation, and it was only in these specific circumstances that it would be passed along. Cobb took the envelope—sealed and addressed to the chief constable—without a word, but his glance at Marc said: I know there's something odd going on here, but it's your affair.

"I'll get this to Sarge right away," Cobb said, and left.

Marc took his mother's gloved hand and kissed it.

"You make me feel like a lady."

"You *are* a lady."

MARC HAD ALMOST MISSED THE *MICHIGAN*'s departure. He had fallen into a fitful sleep at Mrs. Standish's and had continued to wrestle with the various demons in his nightmares until almost eleven o'clock. When he returned to the Regency's guest quarters, all the doors were open and the rooms empty. Merriwether's trunk and clothes were gone. The Bowery Touring Company had departed. A few minutes later, he found Ogden Frank in the tavern, counting the take from last night's performance.

"That Spooner fella was here at daybreak with a squad of goons, rippin' open trunks an' haulin' away guns. He was mad keen to find you, but I told him I hadn't seen hide nor hair of you."

Marc thanked him, went to the stable to check on the horse (Spooner had got it also), then sent a stable boy with an urgent message to Cobb at the police station just up the street. Looking dishevelled and very unmilitary, he started to walk west towards John Street at the other end of town, but got less than a block away down Colborne when a familiar female voice hailed him. He turned to find Aunt Catherine running towards him at a most undignified gait. She seemed in worse shape than he was: her coat and bonnet were askew, her hair unpinned, her eyes red with weeping.

"My God, Auntie, what in the world's happened?" His only thought was of Beth.

"It's George," she said. "He's gone."

"Gone?"

"When he didn't come in for breakfast, I went to his room, and he wasn't there. His bed hadn't been slept in. He's packed up all his belongings and vanished in the middle of the night!"

Marc was not surprised, but could not say so to Aunt Catherine. At least her deep anxiety confirmed for Marc that she herself had not been involved.

"What'll I do, Marc? I'm beside myself. I feel responsible for the boy."

"First of all, he's a young man, not a child. And, secondly, I have some reason to believe that he may have been mixed up in some dubious, possibly illegal, political activities."

"Oh, no, he couldn't be!" she protested, but he could see her conviction on this point was not strong.

"I'm positive he's safely over the border by now, Auntie. Most likely he'll write and let you know within the week."

"He's in no danger, then?"

"None that I know of, at least not imminently. I suspect he's fled more out of prudence than alarm."

"Oh, Marc, I'm so relieved."

Not as much as I am, Marc thought.

"I do hope this doesn't upset our plans for the wedding."

Marc gave her a peck on the cheek. "Nothing can upset those plans."

Two hours after the *Michigan* had departed, Magistrate Thorpe and the police had taken note of Mrs. Thedford's unexpected confession, discussed the case with Marc, and sent Wilkie off to find the candlestick sewn into the mattress where she had said it would be. A writ for the formal release of Ensign Roderick Hilliard was issued, and Marc having declined the privilege, Cobb begged to be the one to serve it on the governor's staff—hopefully in the presence of Lieutenant Barclay Spooner.

"I figured you'd be dyin' to waltz in there an' strut out with Hilliard on your arm," Cobb said as he and Marc headed west on King Street towards Government House.

"I did, too. But suddenly I found it didn't matter. Don't mistake me, I'm delighted Rick is being freed. He's gone through hell. But he also helped put himself there."

"That blond thing, ya mean?"

"Yes. And I suppose you ought to give this billet-doux from Tessa to him, though I considered tossing it in the lake." He gave Cobb a pink, perfumed envelope.

Cobb accepted it with two fingers, sniffed it in disgust, and dropped it into the maw of his overcoat. "You gonna walk all the way back to the garrison?"

"Yes, I am. I've got a mountain of thinking to do." They

were nearly at Simcoe Street. "I want to thank you, Cobb. I couldn't have survived the past three days without you."

"I'm awful sorry about the lady. I know you liked her a lot."

"You're very observant."

"Maybe so. But I never once thought she could be a murderer."

MARC DID HAVE MUCH TO THINK about as he left the city and walked pensively along the road that wound its way towards Fort York. He had a life-history to rewrite in his dreams and in those waking moments when the hours of the days could not be numbed by action. The simple, honest couple, whose deaths he had mourned and whose lives he had honoured as only an orphaned child can, were now something less than father and mother. The yeoman's blood he had felt sturdying his veins was diluted blue-blood after all: he was an Edwards and a Hargreave with a birth-father he might never set eyes upon, with faceless cousins somewhere sharing his genes but not his life. He was also a bastard, conceived—in society's pitiless eye—in sin and born irredeemably out of wedlock.

But he had a mother who had delivered him gladly into her world, fought for his freedom and her own, had been abominably used and declared dead, before resurrecting herself alone in a brave new land. Yet the man she had every reason to hate was the man he himself loved more than any other. True, Uncle

Jabez had not abandoned him outright, but until his adoptive parents died unexpectedly, he had been content to watch him grow up as another's son. Could such behaviour be forgiven? Could it outweigh the happy years he had spent, after the age of five, as the "lord" of the estate, coddled and fussed over and supported through life until he became a man? He did not know.

And there were other matters pressing in upon and disturbing the conscience of the man he had supposed himself to be. He was still wearing the Queen's colours and he had not yet heard himself recanting his oath of allegiance. But in the space of a few hours he had contrived to let a killer escape to safety in the United States, had lied to a fellow officer when asked if he could identify any of the would-be insurgents out there in the bush, and had failed to inform his superiors about a young man acting as the messenger between the rebels and the gun-runners. He was also deliberately avoiding the governor's aide-de-camp and his attempts to debrief the man who knew the most about the whole sordid business.

What was most surprising to him, however, given the number of times he had tumbled these quandaries in the cauldron of his mind, was that he seemed to be caring less and less that there were no answers, no pat resolution, no reconciliation of any kind. What he invariably ended up with, regardless of any particular configuration of the problem, was a single-word conclusion: Beth. Of course she did not provide an unambiguous answer to any of these ethical dilemmas: she merely rendered the questions irrelevant.

By the time he walked through the gates and aimed himself at the officers' quarters, he could think only that he had survived the past three days. He was alive and Beth was alive. In nine days they would be married. Then, perhaps, like his more famous Roman namesake, he would be able to stand up and shout, "This is my space, kingdoms are clay!"

Corporal Bregman hailed him. "Welcome back, sir. You've come just in time."

"In time for what?"

"I'm not sure, sir, but Colonel Margison has called a meeting of all his officers for three o'clock And he asked me specifically to have you go to him the minute you arrived back."

"Thank you, Corporal," Marc sighed. It was conceivable that Spooner had sent someone out here looking for him, armed with a list of complaints about his behaviour and deportment as an officer. It was the last thing he wished to talk about, but he had no choice.

Major Jenkin was standing beside the colonel when Marc entered the office, both looking grave. He steeled himself for a serious dressing-down.

"I'll come right to the point, Lieutenant," Colonel Margison said. "I'll be informing the other officers in fifteen minutes but, as you have made plans of a personal nature for next week, the major here and I thought it would be kinder to tell you now—as friends as well as fellow officers."

"Tell me what, sir?"

"Governor Head has ordered every regular soldier, officers

and men alike, out of the province and into Quebec. Insurrection there is imminent."

"But that's suicidal! We've got a countryside full of rebels right here!"

"It seems that Sir Francis considers himself invulnerable."

"Our orders are to leave immediately," Jenkin said. "This afternoon."

"But I have a wedding to—"

"It'll have to be postponed, I'm afraid," the colonel said.

"You'll have time to write Beth before we embark at five o'clock for Kingston," Jenkin said. "Our company is to be the advance unit. You can drop it off at Cobourg when we stop for supplies."

This is it, Marc thought, incredulous. What I have wished for since my first day at Sandhurst: to stride into battle to preserve the honour and integrity of crown and country. And Beth, bless her, had given him leave to do his duty.

Why, then, was it all ashes in his mouth?

EPILOGUE

Saturday, October 21, 1837

Dearest Marc:

I received your brief note the day after your ship left Cobourg on October 13. By then we had already heard the disquieting news. I have waited a few days before writing back in order to marshal my thoughts and, in view of what has been happening here, offer you what comfort I can. First of all, you have nothing to apologize to me for. Our wedding, which we had every hope would take place tomorrow, has merely been postponed, not our love. I am twenty-five years old, and I have lived long enough in this world to know that we are not wholly responsible for what happens to us. Nor, I'm beginning to realize, is God. We are responsible only for what we feel and how we act upon what we feel, insofar as we are allowed to in a land simmering with hate and aggrieved hearts. I have come to know many of the ideals you hold and how bravely you try to act upon them. Those are the things I love in you. So, please do not be sorry that the mad governor has sent you off to fight in a war you did not make.

You may find it strange to hear me speak like this. I am finding it strange myself. But we are living in difficult and treacherous times. Forgive me if I burden you with matters close to home when you are—I shiver at the thought—bracing yourself for battle, but you must know that Thomas and Winnifred are in some serious trouble, possibly even in danger. I was shocked to discover that Thomas has not been off doing his road duty at all, but still attending radical meetings in the township and consorting with people who are talking and acting as if a farmers' revolt is inevitable. That is, an armed insurrection. I do not know whether Winnifred knew or, if she did, whether she approved: she says little and broods much. But last week, Thomas came home quite shaken, and swearing that he was finished with politics for good. I overheard him telling Winnifred that he had almost shot some American fellow before he came to his senses and he fled. But now the poor man is terrified that one of his cohorts will betray him. Several of them— you remember Azel Stebbins, don't you?—have been hauled in by the magistrates for questioning about subversive activities, and he fears one of them will rat on him to save his own skin. He and Winn are talking again about going west across the

Mississippi to the Iowa Territory. But their grain is unsold, they are too proud to ask me for money, and Erastus would not lend them a farthing to abandon him and their home. Then, three days ago, we heard that a gang of Orangemen ambushed and beat up a dozen young men near Perry's Corners, claiming they were "drilling"—with hoes and forks for guns! To top it all off, Aunt Catherine writes that her relative, George Revere, has run off to the States without explanation and that, this week, the windows on our shop were smashed by vandals.

Enough. I will write only happy news from now on. The thought of what you may have to do there, if there is a war, fills me with dread, but am I unforgivably selfish for thinking mainly of your safety, or your coming through such horrors whole and still able to smile at me? Believe this, my darling: I will be waiting for you when you come back. I live for your return. What I ask of you is equally simple: survive. Please.

All my love,
Beth

TELL THE WORLD
THIS BOOK WAS

Good	Bad	So-so

S. Fi !

JH